CARSON'S GARAGE

KD Storm

First published by
Books by Storm

Edited by Theresa La Russa

ISBN: 978-1-7331389-0-1

Love is the sweetest of dreams
and the worst of nightmares.
Author Unknown

1

Darkness engulfed the entire neighborhood, except the corner of an old brick apartment building illuminated by the flickering of a light. Sparky, the pup, walked with caution. He didn't see danger but sensed it all around him. He heard a low growl just as he passed underneath the light on the corner of the building, he heard growling. It came from behind. Sparky stopped in his tracks. He turned his head. A slender, gray dog stood towering over him. It was larger than the biggest dog he'd ever seen. It didn't look as if it was going to attack. The dog didn't even look like he was the one who growled. Sparky was confused. He was deathly afraid of the dog, but didn't see any signs of peril coming from him. Sparky was stuck. He couldn't move. Sparky's legs were glued to the ground. He pulled and kicked to no avail, losing his balance and falling over sideways.

Sparky jolted out of his round mattress onto the cold tile floor. He looked around and saw dozens of people walking and pointing at other cages. Everyone was here to adopt a dog. Sparky's location was in the center of the shelter. His room was the prettiest and most attractive, intentionally designed to get attention. However, most parents turned their kids away from him. As a pup, he was already the size of a full grown dog. Sparky saw a boy who just entered. The boy hadn't set his eyes on any dog yet. Sparky desperately tried to get the boy's attention. The golden black pup's tongue dangled from its mouth as it stood on its hind legs, hopping around the room surrounded by plexiglass. His attempts to attract attention were exhausting, given his size and weight. Nonetheless, he kept his sights and focus on one prospective owner, Tommy, a teenage boy. And once Tommy's gaze landed on the pup, he couldn't look away either.

"Sparky," a young voice called out. "His name is Sparky," Katie, the teenage volunteer told Tommy.

Tommy turned to her, "I want this one. I want him," he pointed at the bouncing pup.

She was taken back at the way Tommy spoke, as if he were a child. Tommy was tall and slender wearing a clean white t-shirt and old jeans. His shoes were covered in scuff marks, and the sole on his right shoe flapped when he walked. Tommy's blonde arm hair blended well with his yellowish tinted skin. The hair on his head, on the other hand, stood out like a sore thumb. Uncombed dirty red hair fell to his shoulders, which looked like it hadn't been washed in some time. His mother, Ann Carson, justified her son's look as a new trend.

"Boys these days. I guess that's the new style. You can't get away with that in my day, no siree. You wouldn't catch a girl looking at a boy who looked like that, ha Tommy?"

Tommy didn't know what she was talking about. All he knew was he wanted that dog.

Ann was of average stature and size. Her calves revealed themselves through her flowery dress with every stride. Ann loved dresses. She dyed her black hair red and wore freckles on her face.

"Have I seen you in English class?" Katie asked Tommy.

Tommy looked like a deer in headlights. He didn't reply, sending the volunteer back a step. She felt awkward, again.

"Never mind," she said.

Katie has been trying to push for Sparky's adoption since he came into the shelter over two months ago. Most families were turned off by the size of the pup. It's been a drain on the shelter's limited resources to feed Sparky. He's larger than most full grown dogs, yet, only a few months old.

Katie moved in on Tommy. She whispered, "Make sure you talk to your mother and convince her." She stepped aside, removing her 90-pound anorexic body out of Tommy's line of sight to his mother.

"Mom. Mom. Mom!" he yelled.

"What the hell, Tommy?" she yelled back. "Can't you see I'm talking to this worker?"

The worker talking to Ann lost her train of thought, distracted by Ann's reaction to Tommy. Tommy didn't lose his enthusiasm.

"I want this one, mom. I want this one. I'm in love with this one," he pointed.

Tommy placed his hands against the glass. Sparky pressed his large body against the same area. The oversized pup sat on his hind legs, tongue sticking out, and watched Tommy. Tommy sat on the floor looking and talking to his new friend. He crossed his legs and watched Sparky watching him. They stared at each other, desiring each other's companionship. Sparky let out a gentle bark. The worker approached Tommy while resuming the conversation with Ann. She knelt down beside Tommy.

"He's a German Shepherd."

"What's a German Shepherd?"

"It's a type of dog. It's the kind police use to help them find criminals."

"I don't want to find criminals. I just want this dog."

"I know," the worker laughed. She looked up at Ann.

Ann whispered, "He's kinda slow."

"Oh," the worker said, turning back to Tommy. "He wants you too. Look at him, he's staring at you. You guys make a perfect pair."

"I know," Tommy sighed, "But, I don't know if my mom will let me. I really want this doggy."

"What's your name?" the worker asked.

"Tommy."

"Tommy, you're a grown young man. If you ask your mom, like the young man you are, I'm sure she will get him for you."

"What do you mean, like a young man?"

The worker got off her knees. They started hurting, but not nearly as much as her head hurt from Tommy's child-like dialogue. She turned to Ann and said, "I think Tommy has a request."

Ann smiled at the worker.

Tommy was still confused by the young man talk. All he wanted was a pup, the big pup, Sparky.

"I don't know, Tommy. He looks full grown. Don't you want a small puppy who could get used to you from the beginning?

"No, I want this one."

"Oh, Sparky is very young, ma'am. He's only a few months old, not even a year," the worker explained.

"A few months?" Ann asked. "And he's that big?"

"Yes. He's a special pup," the worker smiled and looked at Sparky. "To be honest, the reason why we need a home for him right away is because he eats a lot."

"Psht, I'm sure. You guys should offer free food every month to the family who takes him," Ann laughed.

"I wish we could. We are limited on funds, and with the low donations, we might have to put some dogs down," the worker said in a bereaved tone.

"Put dogs down? That's not good," Ann said.

"No, it's not. But, because of good people like yourselves adopting our dogs, we get to make room for others that come into the shelter."

Ann thought for a second. "How big is he gonna get?"

The worker shrugged her shoulders. "That might be it. Maybe a couple of inches taller and wider, but we think he might have hit his max growth. He's a German Shepherd, and those dogs don't get much bigger than he currently is, even the biggest in the world won't get much bigger than him. I did some research."

Tommy wanted to say something to Ann, but saw the worker looking at him. Tommy felt embarrassed in front of her, so he approached Ann and whispered in her ear.

"I want this dog, mom."

"Yeah," she thought, "And they might put him down."

"What's that mean?"

"Nothing, honey. We'll get him."

Tommy jumped with joy, "I love you mom. Thank you. Finally, you did something good for me."

"Hey, young man. What's that supposed to mean?"

Tommy tapped on the glass where Sparky was, "We're getting you. You're coming home with me."

Ann grabbed her receipt and bag of free goodies that came with the dog. She looked at Tommy. He looked back at her, holding Sparky's leash with a grin from ear to ear.

Ann was about to walk out when the worker said, "There's some information about the dog in the bag. If you have any questions, please call us. There's also a list of veterinarians in your area. I hope you guys are very happy with him."

"Thanks," Ann replied. She took a peek inside the bag before leaving. "Ain't no one reading all that crap."

"Tommy, strap yourself in, and put the dog in the back seat. Make sure he don't get all wild while I'm driving.

"Mom, Sparky can stay by my feet, in the front."

"No he can't, look at how big he is. He won't fit."

"No – look," Tommy shoved Sparky in the passenger seat before trying to squeeze in.

"Tommy, honey. You guys won't fit."

Tommy bumped Sparky into Ann's space as he forced himself in.

"We didn't even leave the parking lot, and you're already causing problems."

"No – I'm not," he struggled.

"The dog is blocking my arm. I can't drive like this."

Tommy exited the car, pulled the seat way back and guided Sparky into the foot rest.

"Look – see, mom?"

Tommy sat on the seat with his legs curled up against him as Sparky towered in front of him. He struggled to reach for the door.

"Quick, honey. I'm gonna miss my show. I knew we should'a came tomorrow."

Tommy reached for the door again, grabbed the handle, and shut it. Tommy's legs grew tired of sitting crouched. He searched for a spot to place his foot on the mat. The dog squealed.

"I'm sorry."

"Damn it, Tommy. Did you just step on its paw?"

"It was an accident." Tommy rubbed Sparky's head, "I'm sorry, boy. It was an accident."

Ann lied on the living room couch and watched The Magician, her favorite show about a magician during the reign of a tyrant king in ancient times. She was watching the climactic moment where the magician and the woman he loved, might finally get together after family interference.

George Carson, Ann's husband and Tommy's father, was a chubby fellow, average in height, wearing dirty jeans and a t-shirt. He sat by the dining table in the kitchen, reading the paperwork that came with the dog. He left his zipper and button to his pants open when he sat. The extra space allowed for comfortable breathing while sitting, and eating. George didn't believe in buying new pants to fit his larger portions. He couldn't afford new clothes and hoped, by some miracle, one day he would fit comfortably into the same pair of jeans.

"Did you read this damn thing?" George yelled.

"What are you yelling at now, George? Can you let me be for a while? I'm trying to unwind."

"No, I can't let you be. Here you are bringing this monster into the house with health issues. We can't afford to feed him."

"Your son wanted it. He wouldn't take his eyes off him."

"This is what happens when you don't read or ask questions."

"Oh, and you love to read, is that right Mr. Genius, who hasn't read a book in his life? And what do you mean health issues?"

Ann was curious to know what George discovered about the dog. Maybe, they could find a reason to return it and get a smaller one without Tommy throwing a fit. However, she didn't want to engage George in a conversation. She regretted asking a question. Whenever they talked to each other it usually turned into a conflict. Conversations involving compliments, or anything positive, were a foregone memory.

"He came from a shelter where all the animals got sick and died. All the animals, except him. He must be sick from whatever disease killed the others. Did you ask them any questions? Or did you decide to take the biggest dog in the whole damn shelter? Do you know he's gonna get bigger? He's already the size of a bear."

Ann knew George had a point. She didn't want to argue, but wanted to ease one of his concerns so he could stop yelling.

"They said he's not gonna get much bigger. And he's got all his shots and stuff, so he shouldn't get sick."

"Wow, and you believe that. He's a puppy, Ann. A God damn pup that could eat me in one swallow."

"Tommy didn't want any other dog except for him."

She lost focus on the show and, suddenly, felt the tide of the conversation changing. "Your son, George. Your son who you would do anything for, including getting him that damn dog. Don't blame me for how you raised your son. You have an issue with the dog, take it back to the pound, I dare you."

Ann got up and stormed out of the living room into her bedroom. George knew he couldn't take the dog back against Tommy's will. He dropped the paperwork into the bag and stared at the kitchen wall. He got up and looked out of the window watching Sparky chase Tommy and then Tommy chase Sparky. George's stomach started grumbling. He ran for the bathroom, looking for something to read on the way; about the only time he would read. He didn't find anything. George threw himself on the toilet and after the first blast of relief, he felt relaxed enough to look around for something to occupy his mind with. He went for the toilet paper.

"Oh, damn it!" George raised his voice for Ann to hear. "How many times do I have to tell you to put the toilet paper on the other way?"

Ann didn't respond. She knew George was looking for another argument after she made her point about Tommy.

"It's harder to reach the damn thing when you have to pull from behind. IT'S HARDER TO REACH!" he yelled.

George unhooked the toilet paper and flipped it around.

"Why do people put it on that way? It's common sense. Keep the pulling point closer to the user."

George flushed the toilet and exited the bathroom. Ann didn't hear the bathroom faucet turn on. She felt sick by his disgusting behaviors. She never understood why or how someone who used to be neat and clean could change to become so messy and careless. Ann left the bedroom and headed for the living room door.

"Where you going now?" George asked.

She turned around. George plopped himself on the couch with the TV remote. She stared at his hands.

"What are you looking at?" he cried. "I dried my hands already."

"You disgust me, George. I have to wipe that remote every time I wanna watch TV."

"WHERE ARE YOU GOING? This is my second time asking."

"Away from you," she opened the door.

Ann walked out and slammed the door behind her.

The Carson's met when Ann was in high school. She lived with her parents outside of Scott City. 150 students attended Scott City High. The school was understaffed and teachers were inconsistently bounced around, teaching whatever subjects were needed in whatever grade levels the need came from. No teacher, except for Mr. Phelps, had a consistent subject to teach. Mr. Phelps was the only English instructor, and he taught ninth graders all the way through to the seniors.

Ann had one friend in high school, Elizabeth Parkinson. Elizabeth was dense and heavy, but not what anyone would consider fat. She was outgoing and social, compared to Ann, but not as much compared to Elizabeth's friend, Catherine. Catherine towered above them in height, and was the elder of the three. Catherine was a repeating senior who didn't take school serious. She took money from her parents, whom she knew they knew, and never said anything to her about her habit. When she was a child, Catherine's parents let their little girl do anything she wanted. They felt that imposing any limits on her in any way would stunt her mental growth and limit her possibilities. Thus, her parents never learned to set limits. They allowed Catherine to steal money from them, and justified it by saying, "Well, we know she's taking it and she's not being sneaky about it, so, that's not really stealing. It's the same as you and I using each other's credit cards. We have a mutual understanding." On more than one occasion, they saw Catherine pulling money out of her father's pant pocket. Catherine saw them as well. Her parents smiled without saying a word. Catherine smiled back and left the house. The reality was, Catherine's parents were afraid to approach her about anything, afraid they might disappoint her and make her want to move out. Her parents were successful Kansas City lawyers. They hoped Catherine would follow in their steps, or strive for something better. As long as she remained at home, her parents maintained hope.

One day, Catherine's parents questioned her about her absences from school. Catherine justified her lack of interest.

"I don't want to be a lawyer like you guys who lie to earn a living."

"Lie? We try our best to bring justice and give people their rights."

"Justice? Rights? You lie and twist words to win a case. School isn't for everyone and it isn't for me. I'll be successful without being made into some robot my teachers or the school system tries to turn me into."

"Who've you been hanging out with, Catherine? Why do you talk like this? We've always given you what you want. Did we do something wrong?" her mother asked.

"No, mom. You guys haven't. You're awesome. I'm just telling you I'm different, and school is not for me. That's all."

Ann walked toward the school entrance when she heard Elizabeth calling her from behind.

"Ann, Ann. Don't go inside."

Ann looked back and saw Elizabeth waving her down.

Ann threw her arms in the air, "What?"

Elizabeth signaled for Ann to come to where she was, under a tree, which was out of sight of the main entrance. Ann went over.

"What is it, Liz?"

"Catherine wants to treat us for breakfast. Hurry up before someone sees us."

"Breakfast? I'm about to go inside and have free breakfast in the cafeteria."

Elizabeth pulled Ann by her arm, "Let's go. It'll be fun."

Ann hesitated.

"Come on," Elizabeth cried.

Ann gave in, and they ran off.

"Where is she?" Ann asked.

"She's waiting for us at the Old Town Café."

"I still don't understand why she would pay for breakfast when it's free in school. Why does she want to spend her money like that?" Ann asked hoping Elizabeth would change the plan.

"Stop asking so many questions. We're ditching school. Besides, she doesn't get free breakfast like you and I. Her parents make too much money."

"She's only gotta pay a couple of dollars."

"OK. Stop being so annoying and just enjoy the day."

Ann stopped. "The whole day? I thought we were just going for breakfast."

Elizabeth grabbed her arm again. "Let's go."

It was warm inside the café. Steam exuded off the grill while eggs and bacon popped and sizzled. Fat juices leaked off the slices of bacon. Catherine watched the grill in action. She couldn't wait for her favorite, sunny side up with extra bacon strips laid across the eggs.

"What do you guys want?" she asked.

"I'll take scrambled eggs with hash brown," Elizabeth said.

"No bacon?" Catherine asked.

"No. I don't like meat in the morning."

"You're crazy. Meat anytime of the day for me, baby, especially bacon. Ann, what do you want?"

"Umm, I guess I'll take a couple of eggs."

"What else do you want with it?"

"Oh, I don't want you to spend too much money. The eggs are fine."

"Honey, it's not my money. Don't worry about it. What else do you want?"

"I suppose I'll take a side of hash browns too."

"No meat?"

"No. I'm like Elizabeth."

"Ann, I'm going to need you to lighten up."

"What do you mean?"

"I mean, if we're gonna ditch school, then damn it we're gonna make it fun. You look all tense and nervous."

"I'm just a little worried. I don't want the school calling my parents, and I don't want one of our parents seeing us."

"No one is going to see us. Our parents eat breakfast at home, and then go to work."

Catherine rubbed Ann's shoulder to get her to relax.

"No one is going to find out. Let's just enjoy this. You can go back to school if you don't feel comfortable after this, but at least enjoy breakfast with us."

Ann took in a deep breath. She hoped they would eat fast so she and Elizabeth could get back to school. What she didn't know was that this day would be a day she would remember forever, and it didn't involve going back to school.

Breakfast turned into a long conversation filled with laughter. The young waiter, encouraged by the owner, checked on the girls to see if they needed anything else. The owner wanted them to vacate their table for other customers, and because they were loud. Their unrestrained laughter filled the café.

"Can I get anything else for you?" the waiter asked.

"No, we're ok," Elizabeth replied.

The waiter waited and looked around. He felt awkward, so he wiped his hands over and over with a cleaning rag.

"Why do you keep wiping your hands," Ann asked.

"Oh, I don't know. I like to be clean, I guess."

He kept looking back toward the kitchen, waiting for instructions. Elizabeth and Ann were distracted by the annoying waiter, but Catherine insisted on carrying on the conversation, and ignoring him.

"Let's go somewhere else," Elizabeth said.

"Why, because we're having a conversation? I'm a paying, repeat customer," Catherine said. "That's not right. I'm gonna stay right here."

The waiter didn't mind. In fact, he enjoyed their presence, especially Ann's.

"Can I get you guys some extra water or something?"

"Yes," Catherine said rudely. "Go on and fetch us some water."

The waiter left. He had an exchange with the owner. A lady came out from behind the counter.

"Young ladies, shouldn't yalz be in school or something?"

Catherine, still frustrated, replied, "No. Why?"

"Well, because it's late in the morning and yalz look young."

"Well, we're seniors and don't have any classes until this afternoon."

"A, ok, whatever. I don't know what's going on, but yalz been here long enough. Yalz have to order something or leave, so we can clean the table and prepare for the next guests."

Catherine looked around. Ann and Elizabeth looked at each other. They wanted to leave.

"There's still plenty of room. Look, there's a table over there, and one over there," Catherine pointed. "Why are you bothering us?"

"Look…"

The owner, who watched and heard the conversation made his way from behind the counter to their table.

"Yal gotta leave or I'll call the cops."

Ann nervously laughed and got up.

"No need to do that, sir. We're leaving now."

Elizabeth got up. Catherine stared at the lady, avoided eye contact with the owner, and didn't want to call his bluff. She finally got up and followed the girls out.

Scott City was a small town. The tallest buildings were two, four-story units situated on each end of Main Street. One building was an apartment complex, and the other was Employment Central. About 90% of Scott City's employed residents, outside of business owners, worked in EC. Legal offices, public assistance agencies, and an insurance company shared the space. Main St. was the pride of Scott City residents. The road spanned a quarter of a mile, decorated with all sorts of shops and eateries. Gift shops, home appliance stores, clothing outlets, cafes, and restaurants attracted many customers. Main St. livened up and was a gathering place for people from far away during the holidays. It was also the only shopping district for miles around. Old Town Café was located by the west end of Main St.

Catherine was still frustrated at having to leave the café because it interrupted their conversation. Ann became distracted with the thought of going back to school, again. Elizabeth had her attention pulled away by something she saw in the distance.

"What are you looking at Liz?" Catherine asked.

Elizabeth appeared nervous. Ditching school was a new thing for her as well. She hoped her first experience would go smooth. Elizabeth heard of kids doing this type of stuff all the time. She overheard classmates making plans to leave in the middle of the day, and saw them at school the next day as if ditching was no big deal. They never got caught, in trouble, or suspended. No one ever found out. She hoped for a similar experience. However, what she saw in the distance shook her core. The tension and nervousness rubbed off on Catherine, the rebel who wasn't bothered by anything.

"What is it, Liz? You're freaking me out."

The object of her focus drew closer. Elizabeth pointed. It was a police car cruising around, looking for trouble to resolve, and getting ready to turn onto Main St.

"Really? Girl, you got eyes like a hawk," Catherine said.

"What do we do now?" Ann asked.

"We gotta get the hell outta here!" Catherine shouted.

Catherine ran off, and the others followed. They came upon an alley and turned into it. A locked fence split the alley in half. Catherine ran full speed slamming into the fence before climbing over. Ann immediately followed, climbing over nearly as quickly as Catherine; Elizabeth struggled. The chain linked fence dug into her fingers and palms. The girls hurried her on.

"Hurry your fat ass up before we get caught!" Catherine yelled.

"Come on, you can do it," Ann encouraged her.

Catherine kept an eye out for the police car. Elizabeth made her way to the top, climbed over, and began to descend when she realized her shirt was caught on the top of the fence.

"Come on, Liz," Catherine said with urgency.

"I'm trying."

Elizabeth's voice was muffled by her shirt stretched across her face. She pulled herself back up, hurting her fingers even more, as she tried to unhook her shirt. She didn't get up high enough to free herself. Her hands were in pain. She wanted to give up and let go. She thought about letting her shirt rip and falling, that it would spare her from the pain and stress she was currently in. Elizabeth continued trying to pull her shirt up over the fence. She took in a deep breath and lowered her head in defeat.

"Climb higher, Liz" Ann called out from underneath her.

"I can't!" Elizabeth cried. "My hands are hurting."

"Then tear your damn shirt off. I'm about to leave!" Catherine yelled.

Elizabeth yanked on her shirt. She heard a tear. She stopped pulling, wanting to make another attempt at unhooking it. Elizabeth liked her shirt. Plus, she couldn't buy another one anytime she wanted. And how was she supposed to explain the tear to her parents? She gave it one more attempt, tippy-toeing on the fence, raising herself an extra inch, and pulled the shirt. She heard another tear. Elizabeth was furious with herself. She pulled it as hard as she could. The shirt tore. Elizabeth lost her balance and grip. She came crashing down on top of Ann. Ann didn't move out of the way in time. Ann broke Elizabeth's fall, sinking into the ground with Elizabeth on top.

"You ok? Are you ok, Ann?" Elizabeth asked.

Her worries shifted from getting caught to Ann's well-being.

"Hurry up and get up. We gotta go," Catherine said.

Ann got up and hobbled along behind Catherine toward the other end of the alley. Elizabeth walked behind Ann to wipe the dirt off Ann's back. Catherine came to a stop just before reaching the other side. She wanted to make sure they didn't rush out into public view, creating unwanted attention.

"What the hell?" Catherine asked.

Her heart stopped beating for a moment. Everything went silent, and her body felt numb. The patrol car approached them. It didn't stay on Main St. like they thought. Catherine froze. Any attempts to run at this point were futile. Elizabeth watched the car as it slowly drove along, passing by right in front of them. She expected it to stop and reverse, but it kept going.

"They didn't see us," Catherine exclaimed.

"Oh my God. Look at me. I'm shaking," Elizabeth said.

"Let's go. The coast is clear," Catherine said.

The adventures of ditching school, eating out, walking the streets of Scott City, and hiding from authorities continued. Catherine and the girls felt emboldened by their first escape. Although they were terrified during the ordeal, the rush of adrenalin became an addiction, particularly for Catherine. A part of her wanted to be seen, so she could experience the thrill of the chase again. Catherine was practically a drop out, hardly attending school. She stayed home, pretending to be sick, although she didn't have to try too hard with her parents who took her at her word. She hung out in Scott City whenever the girls weren't available. She thought about picking up on a part-time job at one of the clothing boutiques she frequented. However, Catherine didn't like being told what to do. Elizabeth cut school with Catherine a couple of times a week, and Ann managed to work up the nerves to ditch school once a week. She looked forward to Old Town Café, the food, and its waiter.

"Let's go to Old Town for lunch," Ann said.

"Seriously?" Elizabeth asked. "We were there just a few hours ago."

"I know, but that was breakfast. It's lunch time."

"Who do you expect to keep paying for your meals?" Catherine laughed.

"I don't know. I'm hungry and I'm sure you guys are too."

Catherine teased, "I know why she wants Old Town."

"Yea, cuz I'm hungry. That's it," Ann tried to end the conversation.

"Hungry for Jorge," Catherine laughed and high-fived Elizabeth.

"Hor-who?

"Yeah, yeah, Ann. His name is Jorge, but they call him George. He's from Mexico."

"Who's he?" Ann pretended not to know who they were talking about.

"The waiter at Old Town that you're hungry for."

He's Mexican?" Ann asked with an authentic distaste in her voice.

"Gosh, Ann. Why do you say it like that?" Elizabeth asked.

"Like what?"

"Like, he's from outer space or something."

Catherine added, "Well, he is an alien," she laughed. "Ann better marry him fast, before they send his ass back to Mexico," Catherine laughed and threw another high-five at Elizabeth.

Elizabeth held her palm up for Catherine, but didn't share in the enthusiasm.

"Whoa, did I offend you?"

"I don't think it's cool. My father's friend's wife was deported a couple of months ago, and now he's alone taking care of two kids, and trying to keep a full-time job."

"Your father's friend's, who?" Catherine laughed again.

Elizabeth wasn't happy.

Catherine tried to change her tone, "Whoa. Yea. That's not right."

"No, it's not."

"Geez, girl. Don't gotta be that sensitive."

"Whatever. Anyway, Ann, you don't deserve a guy like him if that's how you feel."

"No, no. I don't feel no kind of way."

Ann stopped talking in the fear that she might accidentally spill her feelings.

"Yeaaa, you like him, alright," Catherine laughed and high-fived Elizabeth again.

Catherine felt guilty about her prior statements. She grabbed Ann by the hand and set out to Old Town Café.

"Come on, girl, it's my treat."

Ann dragged her feet, "No, no. It's fine. Let's go somewhere else."

Ann wanted to see Jorge, or George, but not with her friends, not after they knew how she felt about him. She didn't want them to embarrass her in front of him. Elizabeth and Catherine laughed their way toward the café. Just a few feet from reaching the door, the girls heard a loud horn in the distance. A freight train passed through town at least once a day. This time, it caught Catherine's attention. She stopped in her tracks.

"What happened?" Elizabeth asked.

"Hey, I have an idea. Follow me. I want to check something out."

They ran toward the west end of Main St and looked out into the open. A freight train was traveling at exceptionally slow speeds.

"Let's take a ride," Catherine grinned.

"A ride? What are you talking about?" Elizabeth asked.

Elizabeth turned to Ann with a look of concern on her face, hoping Ann wouldn't want to go either. Elizabeth didn't want to be the only party pooper.

"I'm talking about hopping on the train and going for a ride," Catherine reiterated.

"I don't understand. How?" Elizabeth asked.

"Jump on the train while it's moving. Look how slow it is. But we gotta go before it's gone."

"Umm, I don't think Ann can go, and honestly, I don't know about me either. We should plan something for next time."

"Liz, the fun is about being spontaneous. No one plans train hopping. Well, at least I don't."

Elizabeth turned to Ann, again. "You can't go, right Ann?"

Ann shrugged her shoulders. The idea sounded like fun, but she was also concerned about getting in trouble.

"How do we get back?" Ann asked.

"These trains come and go all day. We take one to wherever we want, and come back on another. Haven't you seen them?"

"I wanna go. It looks like fun, but, what if it takes too long to come back? I mean, what if the train doesn't come back until late night? We'll get in trouble, and our parents will know for sure we've been ditching school."

Elizabeth stared at Ann, hoping Ann would notice the dismay on her face.

Catherine compromised, "Ok, fine. We'll catch the first train we see going back toward home. How about that?"

Elizabeth jumped in, "Do you know there will be another train coming back this way soon? I mean, it's not like they have a schedule we know about."

"Of course," Catherine said with certainty, but couldn't have been more uncertain. "Come on. We can argue on the train, and jump right back off if we decide we don't wanna go." Catherine headed for the train. "We don't have all day."

Freight cars passed, one after another. Metal rolled on metal creating a squealing sound and causing a rumble in the earth around it. Elizabeth's senses were heightened. She was nervous about this, not because of getting caught, but because of the physical requirements she felt were necessary to hop on and off a train. Flashbacks from the failed fence climb made her lose confidence in this apparently, easy task.

"Ok, here it comes. This is the one we need to catch," Catherine said.

The next few cars had stairs and a landing pad that led up to the door of the car.

"Don't jump on without letting us know first. I have to get ready," Elizabeth said.

"Then get ready. I'm about to get on!" Catherine said. She got into a runner's stance as if she were in a race. "Wait here. Let me check it out first." Catherine ran in the opposite direction from which the train was headed. She wanted to get on and inspect one of the cars before it passed the girls. She hopped on with ease. The sliding metal door had a lock on it. Damn." Catherine jumped off, nearly stumbling to the ground. She regained her balance and hopped back on to catch the next car behind it. Catherine's near fall alarmed Elizabeth. She turned to Ann.

"I don't think we can do this."

"Speak for yourself. I wanna try this."

Catherine pulled herself up to the next car. The door didn't have a lock. She tugged on it, but it didn't open. She pulled harder and harder. The door squealed open. Catherine looked inside. The car was empty. She waved to the girls, "Quickly, get on this one as soon as it approaches."

Elizabeth asked Ann, "Can you let me go first? You're faster than me."

"Sure, just hurry," Ann said with a sense of urgency, afraid the slow train might pick up its speed and leave her behind.

Elizabeth ran and grabbed the railing, holding on tightly. In her mind, that was an accomplishment. Her body relaxed and her legs stopped moving. Before she knew it, Elizabeth was being dragged by the train. Her feet bounced along the tracks. Elizabeth's hair threw itself over her face. The scene looked horrific.

She yelled and screamed, "I can't get on."

Catherine yelled, "Get up. Give me your hand."

"I can't!" Elizabeth cried out.

"Pick up your legs. Just stand."

"I can't. It's dragging me."

Ann caught up to Elizabeth and tried coaching her.

"Liz, it's ok. Stand up and run with the train."

"I said I can't!" she cried.

"Then let go. Just let go."

"I can't. It will drag me under."

"Girl, you're not going under the train. The wheels are far away. You'll fall and roll toward me."

Catherine was frustrated. She always wanted to advise Elizabeth about her weight and getting in shape, but didn't want to hurt her feelings. At this moment, she wanted to tell Elizabeth off. Catherine opened her mouth, but the words didn't come out. A part of her felt bad. Catherine knew she would hurt Elizabeth if she said what was on her mind. Catherine also felt bad for what Elizabeth's been through because of her, the fence, and now this. Catherine was overcome by remorse.

"I'm getting down Liz, as soon as you let go. I'm not leaving you behind. Let go, and I'll get off right after you."

Elizabeth finally let go. She tumbled to the ground and rolled like a rag doll. Ann had to jump over Elizabeth to avoid trampling her.

Catherine jumped off the train, tumbled, and rolled herself back on her feet like a parkour athlete.

"Damn. Getting off was harder than getting on," Catherine said as she made her way to the girls.

Elizabeth sat on the floor, groaning in pain and clutching her lower back. "What happened?" Catherine asked.

"My tailbone hurts."

Catherine looked at the train; the cars were coming to an end. She hoped Elizabeth would get back up, dust the dirt off her clothes, and make another attempt. Elizabeth finally got up. Catherine watched as the cars passed one by one. The end of the train was approaching. She knew they had time, but Elizabeth's facial expression meant there would be no more attempts for today. The end of the train passed them by and grew greater in distance, riding off into the afternoon sky. Elizabeth's clothes were blackened from coal dust that lined the side of the tracks. She had a hard time walking. She was upset at the train hopping venture. She was upset at Catherine for talking them into it. How was she going to explain her soiled clothes to her parents, which only got worse when she tried to tap it off? How was she going to explain her limp? It's bad enough she had to hide the tear in her shirt from the other day.

Catherine managed to persuade the girls to ditching school twice a week. Elizabeth refused to give in any further, and Ann needed Elizabeth's firmness, or she may have succumbed to Catherine's pressure.

Failed attempts at train hopping was a thing of the past. Elizabeth figured out how to get on and off without difficulty. The girls loved and enjoyed their outings together, thus Catherine encouraged the girls to ditch school more often. "We don't know how long we have to live. Let's have fun and live for today. If we waste our time in school, we'll lose our youth. We'll never get these moments back."

They hopped trains east to Dighton, Alamota, and Beeler; and west to Leoti, Selkirk, and Tribune. Catherine suggested longer trips, but Elizabeth and Ann stuck to their boundaries.

Catherine insisted, "Guys, we've seen these places and been there more than once. It's getting boring. Let's travel further away. You guys thought we would get caught, afraid someone would find out and tell on us, but that never happened. Now, you're afraid that someone will find out, that we'll get caught because we are going a little further out. Afraid of nothing, just like before."

"Well, when is this going to stop? I mean, how far is too far? Where is the line drawn?" Elizabeth asked.

"As long as we're back before school ends, we'll be ok. If we happen to be a little late, we can tell our parents we were in the library, studying," Catherine said.

Elizabeth shook her head. She liked the way things were going. She didn't feel the need to travel further, just to see more dry and plain terrain. Ann shared Elizabeth's sentiment. Catherine was outnumbered. The girls weren't going to totally risk school like Catherine did.

Catherine suffered from boredom when the girls weren't around. She forced herself to school when boredom hit hardest. She talked during class, and distracted other girls during breaks from returning to class. Catherine met a senior during lunch break. She was also repeating the 12th grade. Her name was Autumn, and she soon joined the girls on their train hopping ventures. She also accompanied Catherine on extra days when Ann and Elizabeth weren't around.

Elizabeth didn't enjoy Autumn's company. She had a bad feeling about Autumn. Although, Catherine was their leader and formed the group, Autumn quickly gained influence over Catherine. Pretty soon, it was Autumn making their plans without any consideration for what Elizabeth and Ann wanted, and Catherine followed. Shortly after Autumn joined their group, Elizabeth ditched school less often. Ann felt uncomfortable without Elizabeth, and ditched only when she did. Catherine felt that Elizabeth was changing. She confronted Elizabeth outside of the school gates before first period.

"What's gotten into you?" Catherine asked.

"Into me? What's gotten into you?"

Autumn stood behind Catherine, and Ann was beside Elizabeth. Their tones caught the attention of other students in passing, who were slowly making their way through the school gates, watching for a fight.

"Me? You've been a party-pooper since Autumn joined us!" Catherine yelled.

"Party-pooper? What the hell Catherine? You and I were the only ones in the beginning, until you brought her into the picture," Elizabeth looked at Autumn.

Autumn tried to move Catherine aside to confront Elizabeth, but Catherine gave her a light shove to stay back.

"And what's wrong with her? She does everything I want to. She knows how to have fun."

"Everything you want to, it's only about you. I, literally, bust my ass trying to please you. Not anymore. Especially now, since you're not in control anymore. She is, and she's no fun," Elizabeth pointed at Autumn. "Anyway, I'm going to class. Just be careful around her. She's trouble."

"What the hell!" Autumn yelled while shoving Catherine out of the way to get to Elizabeth.

"Leave her alone. Let's get outta here. This place is for kids, as we can clearly see."

Ann walked Elizabeth to her first period class.

"Are you still gonna meet them at Old Town tomorrow?" Ann asked.

"I'm done. I can't hang out with her. Not when she's like that, and not if Autumn is around. I'm gonna get into a fight with her the next time I see her, I know it. But don't let me stop you from joining them. I know you've been enjoying the hangouts."

"I don't feel comfortable if you're not there."

Catherine and Autumn were eating at the café. They weren't talking much, and Catherine didn't eat like she normally did. Autumn noticed Catherine had something on her mind.

"What's the matter, Cathy?"

"Nothing. I'm fine."

"No, you're not. You're not talking, and you're not eating."

"Well, neither are you. Does that mean something's wrong with you?"

"Girl, I'm just trying to help."

"I know, I know. I'm ok though." Catherine combed her hair back to get it out of her face. "It's my stupid friends – so called friends."

Autumn wanted Catherine to forget about her friends. She had something else on her mind that required privacy.

"Hey, I got a surprise for you. I guarantee it'll make you feel better."

Autumn reached into her backpack. Catherine looked on with interest, wondering what guarantee she was about to pull out. Autumn took out a zip lock bag with a few, half blue and half red, capsules.

"These are feel-good pills," Autumn said as she waved the zip lock bag in front of Catherine before quickly shoving them back into her backpack.

"Feel-good?" Catherine asked with concern. "Are those –?"

"No, they aren't." Autumn moved in closer and whispered, "I would never do that. When you take these, it makes you feel as if you can go anywhere and do anything you want, without having to really go. Get it? They're just like virtual reality. Know what I mean?"

"I know virtual reality, and you don't have to take anything. This, on the other hand…"

"Cathy, you don't get it. Just like virtual reality, you're tricking your mind. What difference does it make if it's from pills or something you're watching?"

"They're drugs," Catherine insisted.

"Girl, stop using that word, unless you wanna get us in trouble. They're not! I already told you. It's a form of virtual reality. Instead of using those fancy glasses, you just take a pill. When you take these, you can go anywhere you want, do whatever you want, and all you have to do is think it. It kind of feels like Heaven."

"You been there before?" Catherine laughed.

"You know what I mean. It's the best feeling. You're in charge of everything that goes on, and you don't need your petty friends. This way, we won't get in trouble for going far away or something like that. All we have to do is go to a safe place, like someone's house or somewhere private, take the pills, and voila; magic."

"I don't know."

Autumn knew she already had Catherine hooked. She planted the seed and sat back as the thoughts sprouted in Catherine's head. Autumn crossed her arms, smiled, and watched.

Catherine thought to herself, "What the hell. All I do is preach to others about how short life is, and to have fun. Here I am with someone who is by my side, and has done everything I wanted. What's wrong if I give it a try? I can always stop if it's no fun."

"I'm in."

Autumn's smile went from ear lobe to ear lobe.

"You're on the verge of becoming my best friend, and I guarantee, you won't regret this." She wrapped her arm around Catherine as they left the café.

Jay was a skinny, older, balding male whose house Autumn frequented when she needed privacy. He wore shorts and a wife beater that looked as if it hadn't been changed in a week. Autumn unlocked the door, and walked in with Catherine behind her. Jay rested on the couch while watching television.

"What's up, Autumn? What you got for me?" he asked while staring at Catherine.

"She's not here for that. Just spending some time with me."

"Really?" Jay got upset. "I suppose she's gonna use some of my shit too?"

"Chill. Relax, buddy. It's my stuff, not yours."

"EVERYTHING YOU BRING INTO THIS HOME IS MY STUFF!" he yelled as he bounced off the couch.

Catherine walked back to the door, "I think I'll leave. Maybe next time, Autumn."

Autumn calmly walked over to Jay and whispered something in his ear.

"You better," Jay said. "You better. I'm not a kid, you know. Don't make false promises and think I'll forget. You better," he pointed his finger at her.

"Put your finger back in your hand. I need you to leave, and not get yourself into trouble."

Jay put on his shoes while staring at Catherine. Autumn turned up the radio and turned off the TV. Autumn waved goodbye to Jay, who stood by the door, still staring at Catherine.

"Bye, Jay."

Catherine didn't look back at him. His stare molested her. She felt uncomfortable and wanted to leave, but Jay stood in front of the door. He finally left, and closed the door behind him.

"Lock the door, Catherine."

Catherine locked the door. She turned around and noticed Autumn holding out a pill. Before Catherine could say anything, Autumn said, "Just in case you want one, and I'm too much in my own world to give you one," she smiled. "In the meantime, watch me enjoy myself."

Catherine didn't say anything. She watched Autumn down the pill with a glass of tap water, and relax on the couch with her head tilted back, looking straight up at the ceiling.

"How many times have you done this?" Catherine asked.

"Oh, man. Who's keeping count? Once you start, you never wanna stop. It's the best. Matter of fact, I had one this morning."

"This morning?"

"Yup," Autumn laughed.

"Is that safe?"

"I already told you this stuff's safe. I'm still alive, ain't I?

Autumn looked at Catherine, hoping she was going to take the pill. "It's much more fun when we're both in the same zone."

"Don't worry," Catherine said. "I just wanna watch you for a while."

Autumn rested her head. She began to giggle.

"What are you laughing at?"

"Don't ask me no questions," she laughed. "Nothing will make sense when you're not in my world. Everything will make sense when you take the pill and jump in."

Catherine got up and poured herself a cup of water. She looked at the pill in her hand, and then at Autumn. Catherine set the sweaty capsule on the table. She continued to watch Autumn, waiting to see if something bad would happen. Instead Autumn kept getting happier and happier. Autumn turned to blank television screen, and laughed. She pointed at the TV set and mumbled words that didn't make sense. Catherine wanted to ask, but held her tongue, remembering Autumn was in a different state of mind. Catherine couldn't take it any longer. She wanted to experience the world of fun Autumn was in. She took the pill and followed it down with a gulp of water.

"I'm in," she said excitedly, hoping Autumn would reward her with some kind of recognition.

Autumn threw a thumbs-up in the air while continuing to laugh and giggle. Catherine couldn't hold herself up anymore. She needed to lie down. She rested her head against the opposite side of the couch from Autumn, and stretched her legs beside Autumn's. Autumn turned away from the television and stared at the ceiling. Her laugh faded. Catherine turned to the television set and started giggling.

"I don't even know what's funny," she covered her mouth and laughed.

Catherine felt Autumn's legs stiffen. She turned to Autumn. Her face was pale. Catherine sat up and shook her.

"Autumn?"

Autumn didn't respond. She couldn't breathe. Catherine got up and stood over her. The effect of the pill suddenly vanished. Catherine became worried. She shook Autumn. Autumn's face was drained of any sign of blood, and her eyes looked as if they were going to pop out of its sockets.

Catherine's seriousness quickly turned to laughter, "You look like a damn ghost."

Catherine clutched her stomach from the excessive laughter. She fell on the couch beside Autumn.

"Stop it, Autumn, you're killing me," Catherine laughed.

Autumn grabbed the cushion of the couch and held on tightly. She tried to pull herself up, but couldn't. Paralysis set in. She couldn't speak nor breathe, and her friend was of no help. Autumn started trembling.

A couple of hours passed. Jay came back to the apartment. Both of the girls were sleeping beside each other on the couch. Jay smiled and locked the door. He gently rubbed Catherine's arm. Catherine woke up, but barely had enough energy to open her eyes. She saw Jay standing above her and felt vulnerable. She woke up from a dream to a nightmare. Catherine wanted to get up, but wasn't in full control of her faculties, like a patient awakening from anesthesia. She was too tired to fight the feeling, so she closed her eyes, hoping the nightmare would go away. Jay checked on Autumn. He hoped she would remain asleep while he took advantage of Catherine, but he discovered something else.

"No way! Damn it, what did you guys do?" Jay yelled.

Catherine squinted her eyes. She remembered something had gone wrong. Again, she tried to bring herself to it, but the drug was still active in her system. She stopped trying, hoping Jay would take care of Autumn. Jay slapped Autumn. He became frantic. He looked around the apartment, grabbed some items, stuffed them in a back pack, and ran out of the house. Catherine knew something went horribly wrong. She knew something happened to Autumn. Catherine mustered enough energy to move her hand. It fell on Autumn's leg. She squeezed it.

"Autumn," Catherine said in a faint voice.

She shook Autumn's leg.

"Autumn," Catherine called out a little louder.

She continued shaking her leg.

"Autumn!"

Catherine lifted her head and saw the lifeless body of her friend staring back at her with eyes wide open. A cold chill spread throughout her body. Catherine was scared. She didn't want to look or move. She didn't want to disturb Autumn, afraid she might wake up and seize her for not helping. Tears streamed out of Catherine's eyes. She closed them and tried to go back to sleep, hoping the nightmare would end.

Six months of prison felt like six years. Upon her exit interview, Catherine burst into tears and swore to change her life, never to return to drugs and the legal system.

"I never wanna see the inside of these walls again," Catherine stressed to her counselor.

Catherine's parents decided to start joint family counseling sessions. The meetings took place in their home on a weekly basis. Shortly thereafter, it shifted to bi-monthly, then monthly, and within six months, schedules returned to normal. Old habits and priorities returned. They barely saw Catherine, as busy work schedules resumed, and Catherine didn't stay home. She dropped out of adult school.

Elizabeth realized she needed to keep space between herself and Catherine after learning about her troubles, and Ann didn't want to hang out with Catherine without Elizabeth. Catherine soon found herself with her worst companions, loneliness and boredom. These two acquaintances reintroduced her to the rundown sections of Scott City. She was in pursuit of that feeling; the feeling from that fateful day. Yes, her friend died. However, Autumn had the pills twice in the same day. Catherine didn't have any intention of overdosing. She merely wanted to take the pills whenever she needed.

Catherine scouted Scott City's streets hoping she'd run into Jay, Autumn's former roommate who ran off that day. Some of the locals and business owners assumed Catherine was a self-employee of the enticing kind. The residents whispered whenever she passed by. Mothers pointed to her as an example of what their daughters should not be like, while men made unwelcome advances. People approached her with gestures, offers, and advice.

"Get out of here before I call the cops. You shouldn't be here like this. Go to school. Do something with your life instead of wasting it on the streets," a baker shouted after shooing her off.

"You must be a new one in town. What's your cost?" a passing man whispered.

"Hurry up and get in before someone sees us," another man shouted as he drove by.

Desperate to find the blue and red pills, Catherine finally asked a homeless man.

"Excuse me. I'm wondering if you know where I could find some blue and red pills?"

The man's beard was long and dirty. His clothes were torn and browned from the accumulation of filth. Half of his teeth were missing. He leaned against the back of a thrift store.

"Honey, I'll give you whatever you want, if you can be my friend."

"Can I see them?"

The man reached into his pocket and pulled out a balled-up napkin. He unrolled it and showed her a few pills, white, tan, and brown. They looked like prescription medications.

"No. I'm talking about blue and red capsules."

The man straightened up, reached into another pocket and pulled out dirty blue and red pills. "You mean these?"

Catherine's mouth dropped, "Where'd you get those?"

"Here, take 'em. You can have 'em."

Catherine reached for the pills, but he balled them up in a fist.

"Only if you give me a kiss."

"A kiss?"

"This costs a lot more than a kiss, but that's all I'm asking for."

Catherine reached in, slowly, looking for a clean place on his face to plant the kiss. She couldn't find one and hesitated. The man grabbed her arm, pulled her in, and licked her face.

"Eww, get off me."

"Calm down. Let me get a taste."

"Get off me nasty man. Let go before I yell."

The man let her go. He shook the pills in his hand and said, "Now, don't you go doing that or you'll never lay a hand on these."

"Ok, you got your kiss," she said while wiping the wetness off her face. "Now give me the pills."

The man took a pill from the palm of his hand and gave it to her.

"What about the others?" Catherine asked.

"You can earn those later."

She got up, kicked the sole of his shoe, and walked off.

Ann felt bad for Catherine, and finally let her guard down. They managed to coordinate a late lunch after school at Old Town Café, during Ann and Elizabeth's senior year.

"His name is George, not Jorge," Ann explained.

"Who? What are you talking about?" Catherine asked with a fork full of food in her mouth.

"The waiter. I finally got to know him."

"Oh, that's great. But, why are you telling me his name?"

"Because. You remember? When we came here before, all three of us with Elizabeth, you said his name was Jorge."

"Oh," Catherine said, but didn't remember.

"His Mexican name is Jorge, but his American name is George. His father came to America and tried to make a life before being deported, and was forced to leave him behind."

Catherine became frustrated, "They don't teach you that stuff in school?"

"What?" Ann was confused.

"That America actually means North, Central, and South America. The United States is our country's name."

"Wha?" Ann sounded more confused.

"Mexicans are Americans too, so are Canadians, and so are Guatemalans. Get it?"

"Oh," Ann said as she tried to understand what Catherine explained. "So, what do we call ourselves? United States-ans," she laughed.

"That's why I don't like school. They teach you boring stuff that's not important and leave out important stuff. No wonder we're so far behind the rest of the world."

"Well, Ms. Jailbird, where did you learn that from?"

"In prison. There's nothing to do but read."

"Is that why you keep going back?"

"Shut up, Ann. That's not funny."

"Sorry, I didn't mean that." Ann leaned in, "When is this gonna stop, Catherine?"

"Autumn told me it wasn't a drug. She swore they were just some other type of pills. They're God damned

41

drugs, and I'm hooked. It feels crazy good, but I didn't know, and now I can't stop. I kinda don't want to," Catherine laughed.

"You have to. Forget about jail. What about your health?"

"That's ok. I'm not worried about it."

"What? Look at what happened to Autumn," Ann whispered.

"She overdosed. She took too many that day. Like I said, the feeling's great, and you can't stop."

"I'm sure it doesn't feel good to her anymore, now that she's buried six feet deep," Ann said.

"Yea, I know. I gotta stop, get my life on track. I promise, once this last court crap settles up, I'll be back with my parents, and take advantage of their help to get my life straight. This lifestyle ain't gonna workout forever."

"Wow, I'm so happy to hear that from you," Ann said as she sat back in her chair.

"Yeah, well when you see the results of your actions – gotta call a spade a spade," Catherine said.

Ann struggled in school, and Catherine never changed. Ann used Catherine's death as the excuse to drop out, claiming emotional stress prevented her from being able to carry on. Nonetheless, Catherine's passing was an emotional hit for Ann. She tried to get around to Old Town Café as often as she could, to spend time with George. Like Catherine, Ann often found herself bored and alone, which drove her into an early marriage with George. Ann's parents didn't tolerate the dating scene.

"What are we waiting for?" Ann asked George. "How long are we gonna be together, and hang out in secret?"

"I guess you're right. I'm just worried that we're too young."

George, not wanting to lose Ann and deciding she's the girl of his dreams, agreed.

Catherine didn't get a chance to witness Elizabeth's academic success, or Ann's five-person marriage ceremony. She passed away a couple of months before Elizabeth's graduation. Catherine knew to be cautious about the pill, knew it was an illegal drug, and witnessed first-hand its dangers, but addiction is a bastard and a difficult habit to kick. Her body was found lying face down in a motel room. Several blue and red pills were found in her tiny purse. Ann recalled one of their recent outings, just before Catherine passed away.

"Drinking, drugs, none of that stuff makes any sense to me," Ann said.

"Did you say drinking? You've never drank alcohol before?" Catherine asked.

"Never touched it to my lips."

"Oh my God! You're missing out on life."

Ann leaned in with confidence, looked Catherine in the eyes, and said, "Explain what I'm missing out on." Ann counted off using her fingers, "One, the taste is awful."

"How do you know?"

"Two, there's nothing positive about it. You and Autumn are proof that I can get hooked on something that's bad for me."

"Girl…"

"Three, I might do something while I'm drunk that will cost me for the rest of my life. My God, Cathy, look at what just happened to your friend. That's not a wake-up call for you?"

"Ok, forget about drugs. I'm talking about alcohol."

"Alcohol too! Look at how much violence there is because of it. How much domestic violence is there because of alcohol? I hear stories of people blacking out, throwing up, sick the next day… What's that, numbers four and five? I mean, do I need to go on?"

"I don't know. You're just missing out, that's all I can say."

"Cuz that's all you got to say," Ann laughed.

Elizabeth hadn't seen nor spoken to Catherine since their falling out. On a couple of occasions, Catherine invited Elizabeth, via Ann, to join them for a meal at Old Town Café, but Elizabeth ignored her request. She was too focused on school and didn't want Catherine to distract her. Elizabeth didn't show any emotion when Ann told her of Catherine's death.

"I knew it. That girl was gonna end up like her stupid friend who got her into this mess."

"Aren't you sad?" Ann asked.

"Sad? Why? She did it to herself. She's the one who dropped out of school. She even tried to get us into that crap, 'All about having fun, life being short' she said. Well, she definitely cut her damn life short."

"Liz, why are you talking like that? Our friend just died."

"Listen, Ann," Elizabeth's guilt kicked in. "I don't want to be bothered with this right now. I have to focus." Her lips trembled, and she ran off before getting too emotional.

Both girls attended Catherine's funeral and eulogy. Elizabeth gave a speech in honor of Catherine. This relieved her guilt for their fallout. She gave the same speech on graduation day, in front of hundreds of people, classmates, former classmates, parents, and friends alike. Ann, who didn't graduate, spent part of graduation day by Catherine's gravesite. Ann brought a rose she picked from her neighbor's yard. George gave Ann privacy and leaned against a tree several feet away. He took in the scenery. The graveyard was full of trees. He'd never seen so many trees crowd a single space. A skinny, grey, medium sized dog walked toward Catherine's grave. George watched the stray dog to make sure Ann was safe. The dog approached Ann, but appeared harmless. It stopped a few feet away from the tombstone.

Ann's knees grew tired. She stood and said, "Well, it's time for me to go. I'm glad you were in my life. I'll never forget the fun times we had. I hope you're in peace, and to see you on the other side." She tapped on the tombstone and said, "Take care, girl."

She walked off with George right beside her.

"Did you see the dog?" George asked.

"What dog?"

"There was a dog right next to you, on the other side of her grave, watching you. You didn't see?"

"No."

"Wow, you've got no peripheral vision. What would've happened if he wanted to attack, or if a mugger was right beside you?"

"Take me home. I wanna rest."

George looked back. The dog was gone. He stopped to look for the dog.

"What are you doing?" Ann asked.

"The dog. He just disappeared."

"Take me home, please. I'm tired"

They proceeded to the car. George kept looking back for the dog, but didn't see it anymore.

2

George and Ann were watching television, resting side-by-side on the couch with popcorn and soda. Not long after they relaxed, the front door burst open. Ann was startled. She pulled her feet off the coffee table. Chuck Carson, George's father, headed straight for the kitchen, breathing heavy, and rummaging through the cabinets. The sounds of tools, knives, and other items filled the house. It was early in the afternoon. Carson's Garage, Chuck's auto shop, was still open for business. George wondered who was looking after it, if Chuck was home.

"Chuck?" George asked.

"Yea, boy."

"Do you need help with something?"

"Yea, as a matter of fact, I do. Thanks for asking. Do me a favor, George."

Chuck turned to the living room and saw the couple sitting comfortably side-by-side.

"Hi, Mr. Carson," Ann waved and smiled.

"Hi-ya there, sweetie." Chuck thought for a moment. He didn't want to ruin their time together, but he needed help. "Why don't you guys take a little trip down to the shop, hang out there for a bit, check out the scenery," Chuck tried to sound convincing, "And ah, wait there till I get back. If you see any customers, take very good care of them, and let them know I'll be there shortly. Sound like a plan?"

George looked to Ann. He was exhausted and hoped Ann would come up with a good excuse. She didn't respond in time. George had to answer because he didn't want to give Chuck the impression that they didn't want to help.

"Sure," George stood up. He held out his hand for Ann. She grabbed his hand and they left the house, on their way to the shop.

"I wanted to relax with you," Ann said.

"Believe me. I wanted it more than you, but I can't ignore his request, especially when he needs help."

"You're a good son. I hope our future son is as nice to his parents as you are."

Around the time George and Ann met, Chuck secured an auto shop just off of route 96 outside of Selkirk, and named it Carson's Garage. Chuck, ecstatic about his first business endeavor, purchased a truckload of snacks and automobile accessories. He remodeled the shop with new posters, carpet, countertops, and chairs. Attached to the right side of the waiting area, separated by a door, was the repair garage. Chuck, unlicensed and uncertified, had the ability to repair most automobile issues.

The Carson's home was a small charmer in the center of a few acres of land. There were surrounding properties, one to its southeast, and the other to the west. There were no fence barriers separating the properties. The neighbors were situated approximately a quarter mile away from each other. The front of the Carson's property faced their southeast neighbors. The backyard faced the neighbors to the west. The entrance and exit for the homes came through a road that split three ways to each of the properties. The neighbors hardly interacted with each other, except on the rare times when they happened to enter or exit through the road at the same time.

Chuck made it to the shop in his old beat up clunker just a few minutes after George and Ann arrived. Chuck also had a newer car that he left for Ann and George to use.

He walked into the repair garage with some tools, heading straight for the car he was working on. A couple of people were sitting in the waiting area, looking through some magazines.

"They were already here when we got here. They said they were waiting on you," George said.

"Yea son, they are. I need to fix the brakes on their car, and I need your help." He turned to give George his full attention. "Matter of fact, I think I'm gonna need your help a lot more around here. We need to take care of our customers, make sure they get the best service, you know?"

"Umm, sure," George affirmed.

Chuck got on his knees and examined the brake pad on the customer's car.

"I'll need you here early tomorrow morning."

"I have work tomorrow at Old Town. Working the morning shift."

"After we're done here, why don't you take your friend with you, run down to Old Town, and tell them you can't work there anymore."

"Wait. What?"

Chuck turned to George again.

"I thought we just discussed that. I need help. Here. Business is picking up and – ."

"But, I like working there. I like earning money. I like helping with the bills."

"I know you do. Your help has always been appreciated." Chuck stood up and placed his hand on George's shoulder. "Son, you're getting older and need to start taking on new responsibilities. You're married now. I can pay you with the profits from the shop. You don't have to pay any rent, or bills, or anything. This is the Carson's Garage, not Chuck's Garage. I can't run this shop on my own. I thought I could, but business is picking up. Your help is really needed here. I hope you do the right thing."

Chuck waited for a response from George. George was speechless. Chuck went back to working on the brakes, taking George's silence as acceptance. George stood above his father, watching him make the repair. He was frustrated, but didn't want to argue.

"How can I help, Dad?" he asked unwillingly.

"That's my boy."

Cigarettes and beer were break time habits for father and son. George, now in his late 20's, ran the garage with more enthusiasm than any other job he had. He took on the lead role of managing the garage, working its books, and handling all customer related concerns.

Carson's Garage was situated in the midst of dried, barren, and vast landscape. The end of each horizon was clearly visible with no buildings or structures to interrupt the view. Chuck's shifts ended in the afternoon, while George remained until sundown, catching up on the books, and shutting down the garage. He was eager to get home with a readied appetite, and to see Ann.

Ann was a homemaker. Ann was happy with her life, with George, living with her in-laws, and residing on the large acreage. She slept until rested, had whatever she wanted for breakfast, ate whenever she wanted, willingly took on most household chores, and spent much of her day outside. She enjoyed the views, and took walks to the cliffs just beyond the trees that lined the north side of the properties. She tended to the flock of chickens, fed them, watched them intermingle with one another, gave them names, and sometimes played chase games. It was exercise for her, although their runny stool indicated a stressful experience for them. Just before sundown, Ann came inside to avoid the mosquitoes, and get ready for George. She took a shower, put on some lipstick, and dressed up as if it were a special occasion. George barged through the door, as his usual entrance, hollering, "Lucy. I'm home." Ann ran out from wherever she was and wrapped her arms around him. George swung her around and planted a big kiss on her lips. Christina kept herself in her room during the evenings, and forced Chuck to remain in the room with her, until their son and daughter-in-law had some time to themselves. Ann hoped things would remain this way forever. Every now and then she heard George and Chuck discussing the books from Carson's Garage, and the numbers didn't sound too good. Ann was worried she might have to get a job and help out with the bills, but that day never came.

After supper with the family, Ann excused herself from the table, grabbed George by the hand, and went outside for a walk. They strolled around the yard and looked up at the clear skies, free from city lights. The stars were numerous and bright. On several occasions during their first year of marriage, Ann asked, "Do you think we'll be like this forever?"

"What do you mean, babe?"

"Like this, lovey-dovey and all. Holding hands, hugging, kissing, going out for walks?"

"I suppose. As long as you don't change, and your cooking don't change..."

Ann laughed and punched George on the arm. He turned and kissed her.

"Never. I'll never change," Ann said.

Not long after, Ann gave birth to Tommy Carson. Tommy was premature and a little underweight. Nonetheless, it was the happiest moment of their lives. A new love entered their world; a different kind of love.

George was head over heels. He spent all his time in the nursery with Tommy, and away from Ann. Days passed, and Ann hadn't seen George since giving birth. Ann was emotional. She wanted George by her side. In her heart she was happy for George, that he was so happy to be with their son. But, she missed him and needed him, especially during postpartum. Ann inquired from Christina about George's whereabouts, even though she knew he was in the nursery. Ann hoped Christina would talk to George, since he hadn't set foot in Ann's room since Tommy was taken to the nursery. Instead, Christina talked to Ann.

"Honey, why don't you tell him how you're feeling? Tell him that you need him to be here with you. If you don't tell him, it will be meaningless coming from us," Christina said.

"I would, if he were here. I can't get up and leave this room to find him and tell him."

Ann had high expectations of George. They were inseparable. George and Ann could not wait until they saw each other every day. They loved spending time together. But, where was he now? How could he completely forget about her? She expected him to come to her room, sooner or later, with flowers and kisses. That never happened. Ann left the hospital a week after giving birth. She was completely silent during the drive home. She wanted George to recognize his mistake and make up for it. She waited for him to return things to normal.

"How are you feeling?" George asked.

Ann looked out of the passenger window and didn't respond. George quickly turned his attention to Tommy and had a conversation with him. Every word felt like a needle piercing her ear drum; the overwhelming attention he gave their son while neglecting her.

"Can you be quiet, please? I'm tired. I just wanna go home and rest," she said.

Ann never told George why she gave him the cold shoulder. Every day was another opportunity, as she saw it, for George to apologize for neglecting her, and rekindle their relationship. George never felt bothered by Ann's behavior because he was so engulfed with his new love. Each day the assumption continued, their conversations lessened, and the wedge between them drifted them further apart. George remained oblivious to the growing resentment. He knew things weren't the same with Ann, but didn't feel the magnitude of it, because Tommy filled his emotional voids.

Because of the resentment built against George, Ann had a difficult time bonding with Tommy. She tended to Tommy's cries and needs, but as soon as George entered the room, she finished doing what needed to be done and left Tommy to George. Tommy was a continuous reminder of the reason things changed between them; he became her replacement. Ann made an unconscious effort to torture herself with reminders of her past with George, and despise him for not returning to his former self. Every single day, a new sense of disappointment set in about George. She could not understand and believe how a loving husband could so suddenly neglect his wife at a moment of need. But Ann never raised an eyebrow. She watched the father playing with his son, transferring all of the love that once belonged to her unto him. Ann had thoughts about how to separate Tommy from George so that, at best, he may refocus on her, and at worst, he will be deprived of the happiness in which George deprived her of. However, she quickly put the negative thoughts to an end. Divorcing George and moving away with Tommy would guarantee an end to any hope of improving their relations, which was her primary aim. Should she kill her son?

"Oh my God," Ann shook the thoughts out of her head. "I can't believe I even thought of that," she said to herself.

Ann gave up on the hopes of a revival of their relationship. In order to prevent from drowning in depression, Ann decided to focus on George's imperfections and replace her sadness with resentment and frustration. George's body odor, when he returned from work, became reprehensible.

"Take a shower before you touch the baby," Ann demanded. "You'll make him smell like sweat, and I just cleaned him."

One night, a thought to reinforce her frustration with George occurred to her. Ann realized she was the initiator of nearly everything they did together.

"He never really loved me to begin with," she reasoned. "If it wasn't for me, he would have never done the things he did. We would never have done the things we did. Now, that I don't initiate anymore, we're falling apart. He never loved me. It all makes sense now."

A part of her felt relieved because something made sense; their relationship was only kept afloat because of her. Now that she tested George, she realized he never met her half way. The greatness of their relationship was an illusion that was going to end sooner or later. That's how Ann tried to cope with the pain of losing the pleasant past. Ann fell asleep with feelings of despair mixed with anger.

One night she had a dream. It was about a gray, skinny, medium sized dog. It felt like déjà vu, although she'd never seen the dog before. The dog appeared harmless and friendly, but Ann felt terrorized by the dog's presence. The dog didn't bark, or display signs of aggression, or give chase. The dog simply stood there, looking into nothingness; his gaze piercing through her soul, waiting and watching. Ann screamed. She knew she had to get herself out of the dream. Ann woke up in the middle of the night yelling, while George remained sound asleep.

Despite never visiting the doctor after birth, Tommy grew physically normal, but not so mentally. Ann lost the enthusiasm in raising a happy and healthy child. She left extra care, apart from the boy's basic needs, for George to handle. She didn't bother enrolling him in school, as she didn't care for school herself, and she definitely wasn't about to drive 30 miles round-trip twice a day to take him to and from school. Their home was too far for the school bus. Chuck spent most of his time at the shop, and Christina tried to keep the peace, which is why neither of them intervened in their son's issues.

"Ann, why don't you enroll him in school?" George asked.

"You love him so much, you take him to school," Ann replied.

"What? You're his mother. You don't love him?"

"That's not the point. It's always about you two, you two do everything together, and I don't exist. So, now too, I don't exist. Take him to school yourself. I didn't finish school myself, so you know I don't give a damn about his schooling."

"Ann, he has to go to school. I have to work at the garage with Chuck. I open and close the shop. What's the matter with you?"

"Let Chuck open and close the shop while you take him to and from school."

"Ann," he pointed his finger at her, "If you don't take him to school –."

"What, George? What?" Ann dared.

"He'll be dumb. He won't learn anything. He can't go to college, and he'll never become anything."

"You know what you need to do, George. Leave me outta this. I'm doing the house chores, and then taking care of myself. You do what you gotta do."

A few days later, after closing the shop, George came home and sprang through the doors with excitement.

"Ann. Ann. Guess what?"

"What?" she was disinterested.

"I met a customer and we talked about school. Guess what?"

"What, George? Just tell me."

"She told me that she home-schools her kids."

"What the heck is that?"

"I didn't know either, until she told me. Basically, she stays home and teaches her children from home."

"I don't get it. How is that? What's your point?"

"My point is that if you go to his school and tell them you want to home school him, they'll give you everything you need to teach him at home."

"Teach him at home? You mean full time classes and subjects?"

"Yea, I suppose. They'll give you details at his school."

Ann took in a deep breath and turned away from George to distract herself with a chore.

"George. I don't know if you forgot, but I dropped out of school. School's not my thing, and I'm not bringing it into the house."

"Ann," George stormed to his wife, grabbed her by the arm, and swung her around to face him. "What the heck's gotten into you? I mean, ever since he was born, you haven't been the same."

Ann felt dumbfounded. She was overcome with bewilderment; she was thunderstruck, bamboozled, and speechless. Ann collapsed to the floor and started crying. George didn't know what to make of her reaction. He went out for a walk.

Tommy never saw the inside of a school. He spoke slowly, and his vocabulary and understanding of words were limited. Tommy shrugged his shoulders whenever he didn't understand something, which was often. He was not fond of physical affection, despite George's over affection and attention to him while growing up. He played outside with the chickens, and ran around amidst the trees, which he called "the forest". One day he reached the north end of the trees and made a discovery. Young Tommy found the cliffs. It was a beautiful lining of red and yellow rock mixed with brown earth. Its opening was wide and deep. Tommy approached it with caution. He looked over the cliff with awe. A hawk glided above him. It screeched hoping little Tommy would fall into the canyon. Tommy ran home. He was excited. He needed to share his discovery with mom.

Ann heard that Elizabeth moved back to Kansas, after she left the state for college. Elizabeth became an immigration attorney. Her cases were primarily of Latino immigrants seeking a way to make the United States their permanent residence. Some had their wishes honored, while others were forced to return to their homelands. Elizabeth gained satisfaction from her job, helping people to make their dreams come true.

Shortly after Tommy's ninth birthday, Ann received a knock at the door, while Chuck and George were at the garage. Two police officers were outside; one who stood a few feet away with his hands grabbing his belt.

The officer at the door asked, "Is this the Carson's residents?"

"Yea," Ann replied with hesitancy.

She had flashbacks of Catherine, which was the last time Ann had any encounter with law enforcement. She began to self-incriminate, trying to figure out why the police were at her home. "Ditching school? Train hopping from years back?" she thought.

"Does Christina Carson live here?"

Ann panicked. The police had the right house. But what did they want from Christina? She was away at the grocery store. Ann didn't know if Christina was in trouble, and she didn't want to lead the police to her.

"Ye – yea," she replied.

"And you are?" the officer asked.

Ann's heart rate increased.

"I – I'm her daughter in law."

"Your name?"

"Ann. Ann's my name."

"Ann. Is there anyone else home?"

Ann took a step inside, as if they asked to see inside of her home. No, just myself and my boy. Ain't no one else here besides us."

"That's fine. I wanted to give you my business card ahead of time, so you have it. My name is Officer Mahone. Earlier today, your mother in law, Christina, was in a car accident. Her body was found dead by the side of the road after her car hit a tree and was ejected."

Ann's mouth dropped. She collapsed to the floor while holding on to the door handle.

"Mrs. Carson," the officer tried to help her up before deciding it was best for her to remain on the ground.

She was speechless. Ann stared at the officer's card on the floor beside her. The officer's voice became background noise. After a couple of minutes, she looked up.

"Are you going to be ok?" the officer asked.

Ann was in shock and didn't respond.

"Do you need anything before we leave?"

Ann shook her head.

Chuck was emotionless during the ordeal. To an outsider, he appeared strong and unwavering. However, he was suffering on the inside and his family knew it. Chuck was speechless. He didn't talk unless it was out of necessity. During the burial, however, Chuck couldn't contain himself. His breaths grew deeper for every inch Christina was lowered into the ground. Ann placed her hand on Chuck's arm. She rubbed the sleeve of his jacket to comfort him and let him know he wasn't alone. Chuck's chest expanded and contrasted. A tear drop hovered over the edge of his eye. He tried to keep it in. Chuck was concerned about snapping in front of the people. He imagined pulling the casket out of the grave, taking it home, and spending every minute with Christina's body, holding its hand, rubbing its face, and talking to it until he fell asleep. The mortician lowered a cement slab into the grave. The permanent barrier separating Chuck from Christina was about to be set. The tear drop finally eked out, and like the collapse of a dam, tears poured out uncontrollably. Chuck cried and fell to his knees, banging on the ground with both his hands. George felt tightness in his chest from seeing the anguish his father was in. Ann knelt down beside Chuck and hugged him.

"Why, Christina? Why did you leave me? Why so early?"

"George, there's nothing anyone of us can do to bring her back, but I want you to know this; her soul has left our station and is on the way to her next destination, and we'll all be taking that same journey, soon," the priest said.

Chuck stopped crying and wiped his tears away. The leader thought his words gave Chuck some strength.

He continued, "She can't keep you away that long," he smiled.

Chuck looked upset.

The leader got nervous, but continued, "I just hope those words could offer some kind of comfort during this rough time."

"So, we'll be reunited?" Chuck asked.

"With the will of God," the leader answered.

Chuck wiped away another tear.

"And, what if I don't believe that?"

The leader thought for a moment. "It's a tough and cruel world otherwise. I hope you find it in your heart to believe."

Chuck stood up.

The leader felt uncomfortable, and said one last thing before leaving, "You know how to get a hold of me if you need anything, Chuck. Anything."

Chuck lowered his eyes and gritted his teeth to prevent more tears from streaming out.

Chuck spent his days and nights at the garage. He took over the responsibility of opening and closing the shop. Home was a painful reminder of Christina. It's been two years since Christina's death, and Chuck's been drinking hard, especially at night. During the day, Chuck busied himself with vehicle repairs. A lit cigarette accompanied him round the clock, except when he worked too close to motor oil or anything flammable. However, business was failing. He lost interest in the upkeep of the shop; he lost interest in life. Without the enthusiasm necessary to succeed in the business, Chuck did the bare minimum. He forgot about the Carson's Garage's mission, to be a support for the traveler. Chuck's lack of motivation rubbed off on George, who merely handled the books. Supplies weren't restocked, and the ones that remained didn't sell. In return, fewer and fewer customers came back. Dust settled everywhere, especially since the parking lot was gravel. The counter tops, cash register, snacks, and chairs were all covered with dirt. Drink stains marked some of the chairs. A few locals returned because of their relationship with Chuck, and the prices he offered them. However, Chuck's inability to keep up with advancing technology in the automotive repair industry set him at another disadvantage. It took him three to four times longer to perform common repairs compared to other shops.

Occasional travelers stopped out of necessity. Fortunately for them, their vehicles received immediate attention, for they had nowhere to go and wait. If the job was too demanding or would take too much time, Chuck referred the travelers to other repair shops. Nonetheless, Chuck had enough work to keep himself busy. When there were no vehicles to repair, Chuck turned to his own clunker. He never bothered to correct the clunking sound. The noise reminded him that age was just a number; that a hard working old timer can still get things done.

Dirty dishes conquered the kitchen counters and filled the sink every evening till the morning, when Ann preferred to do the dishes. Chuck came home in the evenings, rummaging through plates and Tupperware, looking for a few morsels. He wanted just enough to keep him from feeling hungry. Chuck inspected the refrigerator when he couldn't find any leftovers. He looked for bread and anything he could spread across it, washing it down with cheap beer while resting on the couch to whatever television program was on. He fell asleep to the TV each night. One late evening, Ann found Chuck eating hardened leftover cheese from her dinner plate. Chuck pressed a fork into the cheese trying to scrape off whatever he could.

"Chuck. Can I make you something?"

"No, no, honey, it's fine. I was just cleaning the plates because I hate seeing food go to waste."

Ann knew nothing was going to waste. Chuck slipped the plate into the kitchen sink.

Ann explained, "I didn't eat that because it dried up and got hard. Plus, there's really not much there."

Initially, she thought he was cleaning the plates to make it easier for when she washes the dishes.

"You sure I can't warm anything up for you?" Ann asked.

"No, honey. I know how to warm things up as well," he smiled. "Thank you, though."

Chuck knew Ann was concerned about him.

Ann and Christina used to cook together, getting dinner ready for their husbands. Food filled their bellies while conversations filled the air. Ann was upset at herself because she unintentionally neglected Chuck in the process of intentionally neglecting George. From that point on, whenever Ann prepared any dinner for herself, she fixed a separate plate for Chuck and left it in a corner of the kitchen with a note and his name on it, hoping Tommy or George wouldn't discover it.

Chuck never bothered to get rid of Christina's personal items. Everything was stored in their bedroom. Nothing had been touched or moved since she died. The room looked the same exact way it did for the past two years ago. Chuck felt that getting rid of her stuff would be akin to betraying his wife; trying to forget her. So he left everything alone. One day, not long after Christina's death, Chuck almost yelled at Ann when she attempted to clean his room.

"Ann!" he called out while passing in the hallway.

"Yes, Chuck?"

"I'm sorry. I didn't mean to startle you. You can leave the room the way it is. If you want, you can just pass a vacuum around it, but leave everything else alone."

"Sure, Chuck."

Ann didn't know why he appeared anxious, but she left the room alone. Chuck never slept in his bed since Christina passed away. Chuck didn't know how to cope with the rush of sadness and pain that came upon him when he entered the room. The only time he went into the bedroom was to get something he needed.

One day, Chuck walked into the room with his head down, in an attempt to avoid seeing anything of hers, and headed straight for the closet. He pulled a shirt off of a hanger. From the corner of his eye, he saw a teddy bear. Chuck picked it up and tried to recall where it came from. Then he remembered the day he went with Christina to a carnival in Kansas City.

They approached the ladder balancing game, which Chuck mastered during his youth.

"I bet you can't do that anymore," Christina challenged him.

Chuck chuckled, "Come on babe, you don't really think your man has lost his touch, do you?"

"Only one way to find out."

Chuck didn't want to be bothered. "Let's go to the roller coaster. I don't want to spend money on this."

"See, I knew you couldn't," Christina dared one last time.

Chuck pulled out his thick wallet and heavy set of keys, handed them to Christina, and approached the game attendant.

"It's only a dollar a try, or three attempts for $2," the attendant said.

"Come here, babe," Chuck told Christina.

She approached, pulled out two dollars from Chuck's wallet, and handed it to the attendant. Christina changed her role from doubter to cheerleader.

"You can do it, babe. Just concentrate."

"I know. I got this."

Chuck climbed onto the rope ladder. It was laid out horizontally, and the goal was to climb across to the other end without falling over. The tricky ladder flips easily, throwing the contestant to the mat below. The second he got on, Chuck flipped and fell off.

"Oh babe, what happened? I thought you got this," Christina laughed.

"Better balance this time," the attendant advised. "Stretch your –."

"I know kid, I know. I've done this before." Chuck grabbed the ladder, and got on slowly and carefully. Chuck trembled and shook as he tried to gain his balance. He moved forward and grabbed the next step. He did it again. The ladder continued to shake.

"Come on, babe. You can do it!" Christina yelled.

The attendant wanted Chuck to win and wanted to give advice, but didn't want to be rebuked, so he remained impatiently silent.

Chuck was two steps from the end.

"Come on!" Christina yelled.

Chuck was now one step from the finish. The ladder rocked harder as he got closer to the finish line. Chuck eyed the prizes below. He knew he was going to win. The shaking got worse. He refocused on the ladder. He paused, trying to gain control. He lowered his body onto the ladder, but the shaking wouldn't stop. Chuck was about to fall over again. He looked to the ground, saw how close he was to the finish line, knew he had seconds before going over again, and leapt in a desperate attempt to touch the finish line. Chuck was airborne, headed for the soft mat below. He was frustrated because he was so close, and didn't have the energy or drive to give it another attempt.

"Good job, sir. What would you like?" the attendant asked.

"You got it, honey. You did it!" Christina cheered.

Chuck was confused.

"Yea, babe. He said you got it. I want that teddy bear," she pointed.

Chuck hobbled off the mat and to the attendant, who held three stuffed animal prizes.

Christina tried to decide between two bears, one decked out in luau attire, and the other holding a heart.

Chuck whispered to the attendant, "I touched the line?"

"Yea," the attendant responded. "It was by a hair, but you got it. Technically, we're not supposed to give a prize to jumpers, but you were practically there. All you had to do was stretch out your hand and you would've touched the line."

Chuck smiled. "I still got it."

"Yes, sir, you do."

"Give me five," Christina hollered and held her hand up high.

Chuck's eyes welled with tears. He squeezed the bear and threw it aside. Chuck was filled with anger. He turned around looking for something to take his rage out on. This was his way of replacing the pain and sadness. Chuck grabbed the closet's sliding door and slammed it shut with such force that the top came off its hinges. He turned around like a madman, lifted the mattress from its corner, and threw it off the bed. He stormed out of the room and slammed the door shut. Chuck held onto the doorknob and pushed down until the knob broke off. He didn't want to enter the room ever again. Chuck realized he was being watched. He caught a glimpse of George and Ann staring at him down the hallway, by the living room. Ann watched with tears in her eyes. She knew the pain Chuck was going through. George, on the other hand, wondered why his father was acting psychotic. Ann wanted to comfort him and tell him everything was going to be ok, but she knew it was a lie. Everything wasn't going to be alright, and that's life. Sometimes things are great, other times they aren't. What bothered her was that she still had George, but they acted as if they were dead to each other. Chuck experienced an uncontrollable separation, while Ann and George went through an intentional parting. Ann envied Chuck. His separation seemed more bearable than the pain of lovers drifting apart in the middle of an endless ocean, with neither one reaching out to the other.

Chuck wiped his face as he walked past them. George realized Chuck missed Christina.

Chuck mumbled, "I'm ok," before coughing and going outside into the cold night. George loved Chuck. He would do anything for the man who took him in and raised him as his own. Seeing the once invincible man losing this battle bothered George. It showed in his face. Ann placed a hand on George's shoulder, hoping the gesture would be a rekindling of what they once had. Her touch caught George off guard. He shrugged her hand off his shoulder, and walked away into their bedroom. He didn't want his soft side to be seen. Once in the room, George cried like a baby. Ann rushed into the kitchen and started washing dishes. She needed a distraction. She washed and wiped as fast as she could. She shoved dishes into the dish rack. Some still had grease and food stains. A cup slipped from her hand and broke into pieces. Ann fell to her knees and cried. She left the water running. George heard the commotion, but his heart and pain was with Chuck. Ann's cries agitated him. It took his attention away from feeling pity for Chuck.

Chuck's coughs worsened over the next few months. They went from simple coughs to full blown assaults on his lungs. Chuck watched as one of his customers drive off the lot. The dust irritated his throat. He started to cough. The attack was so bad and lasted so long, it tired Chuck to his knees. When it was over, he spat orange mucus. Chuck went into the restroom to wash his mouth. He coughed again, splattering blood spots all over the sink.

Later in the day, George used the restroom and washed his hands; he ran out looking for Chuck.

"Chuck," he called out. "Chuck."

"Yea, son," Chuck replied from underneath a car he worked on. He let out another cough.

"What's going on?" George asked.

"What do you mean?"

"I found blood on the bathroom sink."

"Oh, that's nothing. My throat is irritated from this cough, that's all."

"Have you seen a doctor?"

"Doctor? With what insurance?"

"Dad," George softened his tone. "You need to go to the doctor. Let them take a look."

"I'm fine son, don't worry about it."

"Ok, you know what? I'll take you."

Chuck pulled himself out from underneath the car. "Now, why you wanna go doin' all that for? What you all worried about? Your old man ain't that old yet."

"Exactly, which is why I'm concerned. I'm taking you to the doctor tomorrow morning."

"Who's gonna open the garage?"

"Screw the garage! It doesn't exist without you. We can put a note on the door, until we get back."

The doctor came into the room with Chuck's lab results.

"So, it says here you've been a smoker for over 20 years?"

"Yes. I was on and off, until the past couple of years or so," Chuck shifted in his chair.

"You also work at an auto shop?"

"Yea."

"How's the ventilation?"

"Ha?"

"Is there good air flow, or are you breathing in the fumes?"

"What? I don't know," Chuck was frustrated. He knew the doctor was about to give him bad news, but first wanted to find the source of blame before giving the results.

"Doc, what's goin' on with me?"

The doctor took in a breath. He handed the paper over to Chuck and said, "This is the part of my job I least enjoy."

The paper trembled in Chuck's hand. He didn't know what he was reading, what was relevant, and what wasn't. There was too much writing on the paper.

"Tell me, damn it! What is this?" Chuck threw the paper aside.

"I'm sorry to have to tell you this, but you probably knew it was coming…"

Chuck looked into the doctor's eyes as if he wanted to rip his throat out.

"The results, unfortunately, indicate that you have a stage four malignancy of the lungs."

"What the hell is a malig-acy?"

"It's cancer, and it's stage four, the final stage."

Chuck dropped his head. George stood in the corner with his arms crossed. Tears streamed down his face.

"The cancer left, virtually, no place on your lungs untouched. Frankly, I'm very surprised you're doing as well as you are right now. This would have knocked anybody else off their feet."

Chuck looked around. He noticed George in the corner, quiet and crying. George looked away, pretending to stare at a poster of the lungs. Chuck pulled out his handkerchief and coughed into it several times.

"Well, son, I guess the good news is I'll be joining my Christina, soon."

George turned to Chuck with red and wet eyes.

"I thought you didn't believe –."

"Hell. How am I supposed to die believing I won't see my Christina anymore? I don't believe in hell, and if I don't have Christina, I'll be in hell."

Chuck got up and headed for the door. He turned to George and placed his hand on George's shoulder.

"It's been over two years," Chuck's eyes welled with tears.

"This is the toughest crap I've ever been through, and I want it to be over with. I need to be with Christina."

George hugged Chuck and buried his face into Chuck's shoulder. They held each other tightly. Chuck tried to pull away, but George wanted to hold on a little longer. George finally let go, and wiped his eyes with his sleeve. Chuck turned to the doctor.

"Doc," Chuck said as he held out his hand for a handshake.

"You don't gotta feel bad about this. Keep doin' what you do, and as long as your heart is in the right place, your patient's prayers will be with you; and so will mine."

"You should check into the hospital, George. You're in bad shape."

"Doc," Chuck smiled. "I ain't spending the last few days, or weeks, or whatever I have left in no hospital bed."

The auto shop's hours were inconsistent. Chuck was virtually couch-ridden from the medicines he took. George spent a lot of his time at home to care for him, even though Ann offered to help so George could work at the garage. Chuck insisted on George attending to the shop. His desire to help the traveler returned.

"Who's running the garage?" Chuck asked, hoping the question would remind George to open the shop.

"No one."

"Son, why don't you go to the shop, spend a few hours, and I'll be here when you get back. Trust me, I ain't going nowhere," Chuck said as he stretched out on the living room couch with his bloodied handkerchief in hand.

George looked at the handkerchief and said, "The garage will always be there. You won't."

"Son, the world ain't gonna stop spinnin' when I'm gone. Everything will continue. The customers need you, and you gonna spend your time watchin' your old man lay here? Who's gonna pay the bills when I'm gone? You've gotta think for a moment. Everything I ever did was for you and your mom; to take care of my family and make sure they're happy. When I say things, it's not for my benefit, it's for yours."

George was saddened at Chuck's repeated mentioning of his mortality, so he decided to take his father's advice and go to the shop; to escape the doom and gloom discussion.

Chuck tried to visit the shop as often as he could. He showed George how to handle some of the most common vehicle issues; checking for leaks, breaks, fluid and oil changes, tune-ups, and more. One lonely day, and the third day in a row without a customer, George decided to close the shop early. He became impatient with the lack of business and wanted to spend some daylight hours with Chuck and Tommy.

Tommy played with Chuck in the living room. They played hand-slap, where one person tried to slap the hand of the other, while the other had to move it out of the way before getting slapped. Chuck received the short end of the stick the entire time. He was too tired, weak, and slow. The sudden movements of the game wore him out.

"Come on, Chuck. Stick out your hand," Tommy pleaded.

"I'm tired, son. We can continue later."

"Come on, Chuck. I'm not finished yet."

Chuck coughed. His cough continued and sounded bad.

"Leave Chuck alone," Ann called from the kitchen. "Go outside and feed the chickens."

Tommy bolted out the front door.

"That boy's full of energy," Ann said.

Chuck didn't respond. He relaxed and immersed himself into the couch. His coughing eased.

"Can I get you some water or something?" Ann asked.

Chuck didn't respond. George pulled up. He saw Tommy running toward the chicken coop and called out, "Don't go far. We're gonna go somewhere soon."

"Where?" Tommy yelled.

"Somewhere in town. Just don't go far."

George came inside and saw Chuck resting on the couch.

George felt he had to explain why he was home so early. "The shop was dead. Not a single customer came in for the past three days. I wasn't gonna spend any more time there, not today, not in this nice weather."

Chuck was quiet.

"Ann, can you put some lunch and snacks together?"

Ann didn't respond. She continued washing the dishes. She didn't know what plans he had in mind, and didn't appreciate last minute rush requests. George walked over to Chuck.

"This man's knocked out. He's in a deep sleep."

George watched him.

"Pops," he whispered.

Chuck was asleep and at peace. His right arm rested on his chest and his left arm dangled from the couch.

"Dad," George whispered. He shook Chuck to wake him up.

"Dad."

Chuck's right hand slid off of his chest. George was concerned. He paid attention to Chuck's abdomen and didn't notice any movement. George became upset.

"Dad," George said softly while gritting his teeth.

"Dad!" He kneeled down by the side of the couch and grabbed Chuck's hand. Tears filled his eyes. George slammed his head against Chuck's chest.

"DAD!" he roared into Chuck's chest. George slammed his fist on the couch. Ann stood over them.

"Why now, why now?" he cried. "We're supposed to go out today," he cried. "You said you wouldn't leave me. It's all because of this damn garage," he kicked the coffee table behind him.

George lost interest in day to day activities. Tommy was older and played outdoors more often. Ann practically became non-existent, except when their, once tolerable, habits annoyed each other.

"Why the hell is there toothpaste on the damn sink?" George yelled.

He knew Tommy committed the offence and would typically clean up after him, but he didn't want to do it anymore. He wanted Ann to realize the sink needed to be cleaned, and that she should clean it. George packed on extra weight since Chuck's passing and became lethargic. Any kind of physical activity annoyed him, even wiping the counter.

"ANN!"

"WHAT?"

"Why are you yelling?" George stormed out of the bathroom to confront her.

"Because you yelled at me!"

"That's because you didn't answer, Ann. Don't piss me off."

"You don't piss me off."

"Answer me when I call you, damn it."

Ann returned to the kitchen and said, "Ok, King George. As you say, sir."

"Your damn son is leaving a mess everywhere he goes," George said.

Ann turned around. If she hadn't been frustrated at George's behavior, she would've laughed.

"My son?" she asked with a smirk. "Wow, George. Now he's my son?"

"Yea, why the hell are you asking like that?"

Ann resumed what she was doing, feeling some relief that George was finally getting annoyed with Tommy. George was beginning to feel the anguish of a relationship that wasn't going his way.

George forced himself to visit the shop every so often. He needed to make some money to pay for the mandatory bills. Lucky for them, both the house and the shop were already paid off. George held a cold can of cheap beer in hand. Wherever he was, whatever he was doing, a can of cheap beer accompanied him. George left Chuck's old clunker parked outside the shop as a sign to passing vehicles indicating the shop was open. George turned Chuck's vehicle on a couple of times a week, just to make sure it was still working. He didn't allow anyone, himself included, to drive the car. He didn't want Chuck's clunker to die. It was the one thing he could control in this uncontrollable life. It was his way of keeping a part of Chuck alive. He worked on it for hours on end, inspecting, removing, replacing, and repairing one thing after another. One day, George worked on it so long that he lost track of time. It was dark outside and there were no lights on except for a street lamp nearby. It flickered, occasionally turning off for a few seconds before struggling to come back on. Chuck knew it was late, but didn't realize how late. With one slow and successful repair after another, it neared midnight. George closed the shop and headed for his car. He pulled on the driver door handle, but it was locked. He wondered why the door was locked when he always left it open. He inspected the bed of the truck before pulling out his keys to unlock the door. Suddenly he heard a noise; the sound of steps walking on gravel. He left the car door open hoping the dim interior light would help him see what was outside. Instead, it blinded his vision from seeing across the car. The hairs on the back of his neck stiffened. He reached for the glove compartment and pulled out a flashlight. The sound of the steps continued. They were light, as if a child were walking, slowly. George couldn't handle the suspense any longer.

"Hello?"

The sound stopped. George looked around with the flashlight in hand. The steps resumed. George's heart rate increased. He pressed his back against the car to ensure nothing could attack him from behind while looking out in front.

"Anyone need help out there?"

The sound stopped again. George reached into the car and pretended to get something else from the glove compartment.

"If you need help, say something. I don't want to shoot you on accident."

The steps continued. George got in the truck. He tried to conceal his fear. He attempted to insert the key into the ignition, but couldn't find the entrance because he kept looking outside. He took a quick look at the ignition and went for it again. The keys fell from his hand.

"Damn it. Who the hell is out there?"

George's anger helped replace some of the fear that filled his body. With the new found courage, he picked up his keys, entered it into the ignition and turned the car on.

"Suit yourself," he said while slamming his door and locking it.

George drove in a circle, wanting to see who or what was out there. The headlights landed on a four legged creature a few feet from the car. It was a dog; a skinny gray dog. George had a moment of déjà vu, but couldn't remember where he had seen the dog or experienced this moment. He only recalled a graveyard with lots of trees. The dog didn't look lost. It didn't look worried. It didn't look frightened, and it didn't look hostile. George lowered his window and snapped his fingers.

"Come here, buddy. You lost? Hop in the back. I'll take you home."

The dog sat and watched George.

George became agitated. It was late and this dog was in the middle of nowhere.

"Come here you stupid dog."

The dog didn't move. George rolled up his window and sped toward the dog, trying to scare it off. Again, the dog didn't move, nor did it look concerned. It sat there as if calling George's bluff.

"You better move, stupid dog."

George realized the dog wasn't going to move. He made a hard turn, skidding across the gravel, and sending waves of dust in the air. The dog watched George race off the parking lot and disappear into the night.

3

It's been three months since the Carson's adopted Sparky, and Tommy just turned 16. Sparky never got sick, like George assumed. In fact he appeared to be exceptionally healthy, growing to his full size since being adopted. George became concerned at the rate of Sparky's growth. Sparky was the size of a large full grown German Shepherd at adoption, and within three months he tripled in size.

Ann spent much of her time out of the home, away from George, looking for a new start after being a homemaker for so long. Ann ran into Elizabeth during a job interview in Kansas City. It was a long-overdue reunification. Elizabeth never knew what happened to Ann and George and was eager to hear about the turnout of their romance. They reminisced about their high school days and talked about Catherine. Ann explained the unfortunate turn of events with George and told Elizabeth about how she's been looking for a job so she can move out on her own. Elizabeth lived in Kansas City, and let Ann move in with her. Ann could attend job interviews without having to travel all the way back to Selkirk each time. She was also reprieved of George's annoying habits, and Elizabeth couldn't have been happier in the company of her high school friend. Elizabeth was a gracious host and allowed Ann to stay for as long as she wanted, hoping Ann would stay even after finding employment, as Elizabeth lived alone.

"There's no need to move out after you get a job. We can save a heck of a lot more if we split the rent and bills. Besides, I like your company."

"Thanks, Liz. I wish I could, but I can't stay too long. I have to get my own place so I can bring Tommy in with me. George is no good. He can't take care of my boy, especially since his father died."

"Oh, I'm so sorry to hear about your father-in-law."

"Thank you."

"Well, when it's time to find your own place, we have plenty of openings here. Hopefully we can be neighbors."

Tommy tried to bake a cake by using whatever ingredients he could find, as he tried to remember how Ann did it. George heard Tommy cracking eggs in the kitchen. Bits of eggshells fell into the cake batter while some of the egg white leaked on the floor. Sparky mopped it up with his tongue. He stood alongside Tommy hoping more eggs would fall. He rested his head on the counter and watched Tommy. Sparky slowly inched his large head closer to the bowl. Tommy rubbed Sparky's head. Sparky lifted his head and took a look inside the bowl. His large tongue fell from his mouth.

"Wait till I finish making the cake, then we can eat together."

Sparky looked at Tommy and lifted an eyebrow. He focused on the bowl again, and let his tongue hang. He slowly lowered his head and watched for Tommy's reaction. Droplets of spittle fell into the bowl.

"Stop, boy."

Tommy pulled the bowl away and headed to another counter when the bowl slipped through his fingers, shattering and splattering across the kitchen floor.

"Look what you made me do."

"What the hell is going on in there?" George yelled. "You better clean up that mess."

Sparky did the honor of cleaning up the mess. He brushed the broken ceramic pieces aside while licking up the batter.

Tommy and Sparky spent every second with each other. He was no longer the little kid George used to play with. Tommy was smitten with Sparky, and George was unintentionally shoved aside. George assumed Tommy's behaviors were typical of teenagers.

For George, life meant loss. He lost his biological father as a child. Then, it was his adoptive mother, Christina, soon to be followed by the person he admired the most, Chuck, and then came Ann, to which he still doesn't know what happened. Finally, it was Tommy, the last relationship he had. One reason George didn't try harder to get Tommy to school was because he was concerned about Tommy picking up teenage group think; parents are not cool to hang out with. George didn't want to lose Tommy to new friends, and he didn't want him to be busy with school and homework. But, he couldn't understand why Tommy changed if he never spent time with other teens. George hoped his relationship with Tommy would return to normal, after the honeymoon phase with Sparky. In the meantime, George distracted himself with other means, while noticing the bond between his boy and the dog growing day by day. George didn't want to connect with Sparky, since he was the cause of his newest problems, and Sparky didn't have the desire to bond with George; he had Tommy. George grew in frustration and resentment. He mistreated and misspoke to the dog whenever he got the chance, usually when Tommy wasn't around to defend him. Sparky never got upset or disobeyed George because he recognized the hierarchical relationship between George and Tommy. He remained submissive, and George abused Sparky's obedience.

George left the front door open every night allowing the cool breeze to flow through the screen door. Sudden and unexpected heavy rains poured over Selkirk. Tommy got the urge to use the bathroom. Sparky followed him and waited outside the bathroom door.

"Sparky, come here boy," George called out from the living room.

Sparky looked to Tommy for permission, hoping Tommy would tell him to stay.

"I'll be right out," Tommy told Sparky as he shut the bathroom door.

Sparky dragged himself to the living room. He didn't want to be away from Tommy, and he didn't like being around George.

"Go outside, boy," George pointed to the door.

Sparky whimpered.

"What is it, boy?" Tommy called from the bathroom.

Sparky looked down the hall, hoping Tommy would be out soon.

"Get goin', I said," George pointed to the door. "Don't make me get upset. I'll punish Tommy, and you guys won't be able to play."

George never punished Tommy, but Sparky didn't know what it meant. All he knew was George had bad intentions. Sparky hung his head and pushed against the screen door to go outside.

"Stay there until Tommy calls you back in."

Heavy rains slapped Sparky on his head. Sparky lowered his head, and hoped Tommy would call him back soon.

"Where's Sparky?" Tommy called out.

"He went outside in this heavy downpour. I don't know what we're gonna do with that stupid dog. Now he's gonna be all wet and make a mess inside the house. You better just leave him outside till tomorrow so he can dry off."

"Why he go outside? Sparky," Tommy called out.

Sparky rushed into the house and slid across the floor. He licked Tommy.

"Why you go outside, boy?"

Sparky looked at George and whimpered. Water covered the entrance floor.

"Mop that up."

Carson's Garage looked like an abandoned dump. Weeds, that Chuck used to pick, crept up around the base of the shop. No inventory had been ordered since Chuck's death. The snacks were indistinguishable due to blankets of dust. Countertops were covered with dirty papers and business cards. George checked the cash register once a week because of the lack of transactions. The repair shop never looked clean to begin with, as rusty tools and grease stains littered the floor. Chuck's clunker had also been neglected. Its original paint was gone. George kept the car parked outside, because he worked on other cars in the garage. George didn't want to start the car anymore. He didn't want it to run out of gas, and didn't want another problem to occur. It was the only way he felt he could keep a part of Chuck alive, and seeing his car every day reminded him of his dad.

The sun was directly overhead. It was an unusually hot and humid day. Outside, the sun baked any living thing, and inside the shop felt like a sauna. George heard the sound of a car squealing as it approached the shop. It was music to his ears. The car screamed for help because one of its belts stopped rotating and needed to be replaced. The customer waited in the shop while George looked for a replacement belt. Sweat fell from his forehead as he searched through the inventory of boxes. Most of the boxes were filled with used parts from old vehicle repairs. George never knew why Chuck had the habit of holding onto used parts. Chuck kept old parts as proof of having made the replacement. He prided himself on honesty and care for his customers.

Despite Chuck's concerns, the used parts were never needed. Therefore, George had to search through numerous boxes, old and new ones. Opened boxes and vehicle parts were scattered across the floor, on the desk, and on the storage boards that aligned the walls of the shop. The customer grew impatient from the wait and temperature, so he called a cab. He needed to get to the nearest town, out of the heat, and in the company of a cold shower, cold drink, and air conditioner.

"Excuse me," The customer called out.

George rummaged through the inventory and didn't hear the customer.

"Hello? Excuse me."

He walked into the garage.

"Yes, sorry about the wait. I'm still looking to see if I have the part," George said as he continued searching through boxes.

"It's ok. I just wanted to let you know that I gotta get to town, so I can leave the car here for you to take your time."

"Ok, but if I don't have the part, I can't fix the car. You could still drive it a few more miles to another repair shop. If you wait a few more minutes, I'll know if I have the part."

"No, it's ok. I'll just pray that you can fix it. I'll leave the car with you, and will be back tomorrow morning. If it's not fixed, then I'll take my chances driving into town. Sound good?"

"Sure, I suppose. I mean I haven't found anything and don't think I will."

"That's ok," the man walked out as the cab drove onto the parking lot.

George found a belt, but it was used. George compared the belt in his hand to the one in the car. Although it was used, it was in much better condition. He convinced himself, "At best, it'll work and help him for a while longer, and at worst, it'll still need to be replaced. If it doesn't squeal after I change it, then we're ok."

He grabbed a cold can of beer from his carry cooler. While sipping on his drink and figuring out the next steps to remove the belt, George thought about Tommy. He felt lonely and wanted Tommy's company. He wanted to teach the basics of auto repairs to his son. Tommy could help him get the shop back on its feet. A renewed relationship with his son was all the motivation he needed to improve the quality of the shop, and his life. He thought about how to make it happen. The plan distracted him from the repair. George threw the can at the trash bin and missed. The can spilled on the floor, wetting the boxes that surrounded it. George didn't care. He needed to get home and work on his idea. There was plenty of daylight left, and they could return to the shop to continue working on the car together.

"Tommy. Tommy. Boy, where are you?" George called out as he entered the house.

No one responded. He heard laughter coming from behind the house. George went around and saw Tommy chasing Sparky in the yard. He couldn't believe they were playing in the extreme heat. Tommy's shirt was drenched in sweat. He caught Sparky and threw his arms around Sparky's neck to wrestle him to the ground. Sparky gently shook his head sending Tommy to the floor. Tommy laughed. Sparky quickly approached to make sure Tommy wasn't hurt. He licked Tommy's face.

"Damn, that dog is enormous," George said. He still couldn't get over the size of the dog. "Tommy!" George yelled.

"Yea George?" Tommy replied without looking back.

"Get over here."

"I'm playing now."

"Boy, I said get here."

The alcohol in his system was in no mood for disobedience, especially if it interfered with his new plan.

Tommy dusted off his pants as he came over.

"Let's go, you and me to the shop to work on a car together. I can teach you new things, things that'll help you earn money. It'll be fun. Then, maybe we could go into town and get some ice cream."

"Ouu, ice cream. I want some."

"I know, I want some too, but we have to make some money so we can afford it."

George turned and headed for the car.

"Come on, boy," Tommy told Sparky.

"Where's he going?" George asked. "He needs to stay here."

"Sparky can help us too."

"No. Sparky has to stay. Put him up in the house."

"I don't want to leave Sparky behind. If he can't go, I can't go."

"What?"

George became upset. Sparky felt George's hostility toward Tommy, so he moved in closer. Tommy had never seen George angry at him before.

"Sparky has to come too," Tommy tried to hold his ground.

Sparky whimpered. George knew Sparky's company would be counterproductive to his plan.

"Put him in the house. It'll only be a couple of hours. We'll be right back."

"I can't go anywhere without Sparky."

"Boy!" George yelled and pulled Tommy by his arm.

Sparky barked.

"Shut up, you. Tommy, son," he let go of Tommy's arm, relaxed his tone, and pat his son on the head. "Listen, please. I promise you, this will just be a couple of hours. I can't take Sparky with us because he'll scare the customers away."

"No he won't. He's the bestest dog ever."

"I know. And because he is such a good dog, he will stay home and protect the house, just for a couple of hours, while I use your help. Ok?"

"Oh, I guess."

Tommy dropped his head, "Come on boy, I gotta take you inside."

"I'll be right back boy, I promise."

Sparky whimpered as the front door separated him from his best friend. It's the first time they've been separated since Sparky was adopted. George was surprised that Tommy listened to him.

The short drive to Carson's Garage felt like it took forever. Tommy looked out of the passenger window.

George tried to initiate a conversation about the help needed at the shop. He noticed Tommy wiping a tear from his face.

"Son? Are you crying?"

"Leave me alone!" Tommy protested.

"You've gotta be kidding me. We're gonna be away for just a couple of hours."

"I don't care. I love Sparky!" he shouted.

"Calm down," George demanded. "Don't talk to me like that. I never spoke to my father in that tone, and I won't take that from you."

"Leave me alone," Tommy said, turning his whole body to the window.

They arrived at the shop. George showed Tommy around, but he was uninterested.

"You see son, the dog would distract you from what I need. I'm getting old," George said despite being in his 40's. "You're growing up to be a strong young man, and I need you to help your old man out. I need you to work the shop like I did with your grandpa. Look at this mess, I can't clean and work on this all by myself."

Tommy crossed his arms, "I don't see no mess."

George laughed.

"Son," he placed his hand on Tommy's forearm. "Just imagine, father and son –."

"It's hot in here."

"You're right. Let me get a fan. I'll be right back."

George pulled out a small fan from the cupboard and turned it on, facing it toward Tommy. The fan circulated hot, humid, and dusty air. Nonetheless, it gave Tommy the impression of a cooler environment.

"Just imagine," George continued, "Father and son, working together, fixing nice folks' cars, then those nice folks pay us. You know what that means, son?"

"No," Tommy still kept his arms crossed staring at the candy on the shelves.

"It means we make lots of money. You know what we can do with lots of money?"

Tommy didn't answer. He was distracted by the candy, and tried to tell them apart.

George continued, "We can pay all of our bills, right? Then, with the extra money, we can take nice vacations. I never been on a nice vacation, have you?" George asked despite knowing the answer.

Tommy walked over to the candy.

"Tommy, we could go swimming in places where the water is as clear as –." George didn't know how to finish the sentence. He was distracted by Tommy's inattentiveness. He wanted to shout to get his attention, but knew that wouldn't work. Another idea came to mind. "Tommy!" Tommy turned around, feeling genuine excitement coming from his father. "Guess what?" George asked with a big smile on his face. "We could take Sparky with us. He'll jump in the waves with the two of us, all three of us swimming together – can you feel the excitement, boy?"

Tommy uncrossed his arms and smiled.

"You mean, I could be with Sparky?"

"Of course," George got happy. "We'll never leave him alone. He's part of the family."

For the first time, George felt an affinity toward Sparky, if he could regain his son in the process.

"Yea," Tommy agreed, "He is part of the family. I love him. He is my best friend."

"Yea," George agreed. "But, there's only one way to get there."

"Get where?"

"To our dreams; where we can go wherever we want, and do whatever we want, with Sparky. But it all starts right here. You and me, alone without Sparky, so we can fix cars quickly and make money."

"But, I need my dog," Tommy protested.

"Tommy, boy get a grip. Didn't you hear a word I said? You and I need to get this garage back on its feet, make some money, and then we can do whatever we want."

"When am I gonna see Sparky?"

"When we go home, damn it. Did you understand anything I said? Do you know what I need from you?"

"I don't know," Tommy refused to understand George's point. He crossed his arms again, "I want Sparky."

"YOU'LL HAVE SPARKY! YOU CAN HAVE HIM!" George yelled. "When we get home, he's all yours." George took another deep breath and tried to explain further. "Come here, son. Look at the snack stand. Would you want to buy something from here?"

Tommy shrugged his shoulders.

George answered, "I wouldn't. There's dust on the packages, most of them are probably expired... I mean, it's disgusting."

"Look at the chairs, what's wrong with them?"

Again, Tommy shrugged his shoulders.

"Come on, boy. Take a look. Tell me one thing wrong with them. Just one thing, and we'll go home early today."

"Umm, they're ugly?"

"What do you mean, ugly?"

"I don't know. They're just ugly."

"Exactly. So, let's start here. What I need you to do is take these chairs outside, dust them off, make them nice and clean. There's a vacuum cleaner in the shop. Find it and vacuum the chairs. When you're done with that, let me know. I'll be working on that car."

Tommy never did a single chore in his life.

"When do we go home? Sparky is alone."

"We go home when we're done with our tasks. The faster we get done, the faster we go home."

Tommy turned around, sad-faced, and kicked a chair before dragging it outside.

"And, it has to be clean. Don't be fast and messy just to get home sooner. If it's not clean, we're not going home."

"Leave me alone."

George heard the vacuum start while he loosened the belt from under the hood. He felt good, despite the rough start. A minute later, Tommy stormed into the shop, wiped sweat off his forehead, and looked visibly upset.

"I'm finished. Can we go now?"

"Hold on, son. Hold on. I said a couple of hours. But first, let me check the chairs."

George went outside and found two of the four chairs in their original, filthy condition.

"What's this? Where are the other two?"

"I got tired. I cleaned them and put them inside."

"Ok, ok. No big deal. We can take breaks. Let me see the clean ones."

George followed Tommy inside. His eyes landed on the chairs from afar. George had to take another deep breath. He didn't say a word. He rubbed a finger against the cushion of the seat. His finger was covered with dirt.

"This is the clean one?"

"Yea, I cleaned these two. I'll do the others later."

George smiled to control his frustration.

"Ok...Sparky. I think that's what you need, him by your side."

"Yea, that's what I been tryna tell you."

"Ok. I'll get him for you. I think you guys are gonna play and run around all day, but if you say you'll get more work done while he's around, then I'll bring him."

"Yea, just bring Sparky."

"Ok, ok. I'll get him. You stay here and keep working on the chairs, and rest when you need to. I'll be back with Sparky, ok?"

"Yea, I can go with you."

"No, no. Tommy, you stay here," he said with the fake smile still on his face, "I'll get your friend. I need you to finish cleaning the chairs, ok?"

"Ok," Tommy said as he got sad again.

George hesitated to open the front door as he tried to figure out what to do. He wanted to make Sparky disappear for good. Sparky scratched against the bottom of the door, excited to get out and see Tommy. He didn't realize George was alone. George finally came to a conclusion. He opened the door. Sparky blew past him toward the car. He circled around the car searching for Tommy.

"Sparky. Come here, boy." Sparky turned his large head sideways, curious about George.

"Hey, you wanna be free?"

Sparky barked. He wanted to know where Tommy was.

"Free boy, don't you wanna be free? No collar around your –."

Sparky barked.

"No one will be in control of you. You'll have the world all to yourself. Whatcha say?"

Sparky tilted his head and whimpered.

"Come with me. I'll take you wherever you wanna go. I can take you to a dog park, and you can have fun with all the little female dogs you want."

Sparky growled. He wasn't being aggressive and didn't show any teeth. He wanted to know what George was really up to.

"Come on, boy. Let's get in the car."

Sparky stood still while his ears moved around, scanning for sounds in the distance; a screeching hawk, critters in the grass, and the wind blowing things around in the backyard.

"Sparky!" George's tone firmed. "Let's go. Get in the car."

Sparky sat in place and stared at George.

"Sparky, get in. We're gonna go to the shop to see Tommy. Let's go."

Sparky's tongue fell out of his mouth. He ran and jumped into the bed of the pickup with the elegance of a rabbit. George was astonished. How could something so big jump so high and easily into the back of a pickup?

George wanted to drive Sparky far away, through roads with twists and turns, so he wouldn't find his way back home. The short drive took longer than expected. Sparky stared out into the vast emptiness. George opened the window that connected to the bed of the pickup.

"You excited, boy? Freedom waits for you, and my son waits for me."

Sparky barked.

"Oh, you understood that part, ha?"

George turned on a long road with no turns coming up in the distance. He thought about how excited Tommy would be to see Sparky. He also thought about how devastated Tommy would be to learn of Sparky's runaway and disappearance. But, he would get over him in time. Doesn't everyone get over their pains? George thought about the hardship he's been through, and realized he's not ok. He hasn't been able to move forward. He thought about Tommy and realized Tommy may never get over this loss. Suddenly, George missed Chuck. He became emotional. He made a hard and sudden turn. The vehicle skidded and barely caught a road, nearly going into a ditch. Sparky slid across the bed. George searched the backseat for his cooler. It wasn't there. He felt the urge for another can. He looked in the rearview mirror and watched Sparky peacefully going along for the ride. George also thought about how much Sparky loved Tommy, and the intelligence he's seen from him. "Dogs have emotions too," he thought. George shook his head to gain clarity. "They're animals. They don't have emotions. Emotions are only for humans," he thought.

George pulled into the lot of Carson's Garage. Tommy ran out of the shop.

"Where's Sparky?" he asked excitedly.

George sighed. He looked down. "Sparky…"

Tommy approached the pick-up. His smile turned into a frown. The bed was empty.

George tried to explain, "Sparky…"

Tommy opened the door to look inside.

"There he is!"

Sparky jumped out, nearly knocking Tommy to the floor. Tommy embraced him as if they hadn't seen each other in months. Sparky licked him all over.

"Surprise!" George said. "Sorry, son. I wanted to tease you."

Tommy was so overwhelmed with happiness, he didn't hear his father.

"What do you say, son?"

Sparky ran off and Tommy chased him. George watched, helpless and hopeless about his plan.

Ann walked into the home as if she still lived there. She kept a copy of the keys to the house. She ignored George, who lay on the couch. Ann called out to Tommy. George pretended not to notice her. He hoped she would return to live with them, even though they rarely interacted. He was used to her company and hated being alone, but said nothing about it.

"Where's Tommy?"

George pointed to the back. Ann didn't know what that meant.

"Where's Tommy?" She reiterated.

"Outside. Don't you see where I'm pointing to?"

"Do you even care what your son is doing? How would you know if he hurt himself, or something?"

"Don't give me that crap, Ann. Ever since you got him that damn dog he's not cared about anything.

George sat up, readying himself for an argument. He slicked his hair back.

"Don't get up. You were doing fine before. I heard about a technique to get people calm. If you're standing, sit, and if you're sitting, lie down."

Ann went outside to look for Tommy. She was suddenly seduced by the carpet-like dark green grass that fell beneath her feet. The grass waved back and forth with the wind. The air was fresh from recent rains. Blue skies and spots of white puffy clouds overtook the horizon. Ann missed the scenery. She enjoyed every moment of it. She forgot what she came for. Butterflies fluttered by. She watched them fly across the grass toward the trees. That's when she broke from her intoxicated state. She was looking for Tommy, and there was no sign of him. They must be playing amidst the trees or by the cliff. The chickens were busy clucking and pecking for food. They scattered when Ann passed by. Their startles scared Ann as well. She didn't remember the chickens being so fearful before, and thought their behavior was odd.

Tommy sat on the ground, holding onto a burgundy colored hen in his lap with Sparky by his side. He stroked the hen to calm her. The lower half of his t-shirt was soiled from the hen's muddy feet. Sparky's eyes and head were in constant motion as he looked at Tommy, the hen, the horizon, back to Tommy, and then the hen again. The chicken's head jerked in all directions concerned about why it was brought to this unfamiliar area. The hen caught sight of a hawk floating over the cliffs.

The cliffs were an unusual sight for the area. A wide and deep canyon suggested a large river passed through millennia ago, or maybe it was caused by an earthquake amidst the flat lands. A mixture of dirt, rocks, and weeds lined the walls of the canyon that dropped about a hundred feet to a creek below. The creek swelled to raging rapids during the rainy season. The other side of the canyon wall rested about a hundred feet away as well.

The hen's attention was fixed on the hawk. Sparky watched the hawk continuously dip into the canyon and jet out high above. Tommy, on the other hand, focused entirely on the hen. His hands were small. It was difficult for him to maintain control of the hen when she squirmed. The hen's restlessness resumed. She didn't feel comfortable with a natural predator hovering above her, and she didn't like the energy coming from Tommy, as his heart beat nervously. Tommy continued stroking the back of the hen, trying to keep her calm. He tucked away her wings into his abdomen. The hen tensed each time Tommy moved. She readied herself for flight. She tried to free her wings from Tommy's small hands, but his grip was firm. Sparky watched the hen. He didn't know what was about to transpire, but loved the excitement emanating from his owner. Tommy stumbled back up to his feet. Sparky stood, ready to follow. The hen began to cluck.

"Be still, girl."

Tommy tried to comfort the hen as they approached the cliff. The hen became increasingly alarmed. Her clucking intensified. Sparky barked. The hawk screeched. Tommy came to the edge of the cliff. The hen looked down at the hundred-foot drop below. The hawk screeched again. The hen tried to loosen herself from Tommy. She was panicking. The hen clucked aloud and wriggled as she gave one final grand attempt to free herself. Tommy almost lost control. Sparky barked and bounced around from side to side, eager to see Tommy's plan. Tommy pulled the hen away from his stomach, and held on as tight as possible. The hen yelled at the top of her lungs. She looked up at the hawk and down into the canyon. Tommy rocked his arms back and forth, and began the countdown.

"3 – 2 –."

The hen continued to struggle, and was able to free one of her wings.

"1."

The hen was airborne. She flapped her wings in a desperate attempt to guide herself to safety. She glided toward the center of the canyon. Sparky barked from the edge of the cliff. Tommy jumped around and clapped his hands in excitement. The hawk blew past their sight and headed straight for the hen. Suddenly, she changed course, turning back to the cliffs. Sparky barked at the hawk, cheering it on to catch the hen. They got a complete view from the edge. Tommy and Sparky watched like crazed sports fans waiting for the outcome; the hawk intercepting the hen, or the hen crashing into the side of the cliff. Sparky's thundering barks echoed throughout the canyon. It shocked Tommy. He's never heard him bark that loud before. Tommy continued to cheer and clap. He stopped jumping because he was too close to the edge. Their wide eyes took in what was about to transpire. Tommy's eyebrows pushed up against his forehead. His arms pumped rapidly like the pistons of an engine. Small rocks and dirt escaped into the canyon from underneath them. The hen advanced closer to the cliff. The hawk sensed danger approaching and knew it had to catch the hen immediately, or redirect itself. The hen didn't show concern for the dangers of smashing into the wall. Death is imminent from her natural predator, but the danger from the canyon was hidden. It didn't have claws and a beak ready to tear at her flesh, and it wasn't chasing her. To the hen, the canyon was ready to house and protect her from the hawk. The hawk pulled up and away. The hen felt a sense of relief right before it crashed into the canyon, popping in an explosion with feathers blowing off in all directions. The hen rolled and tumbled down until it was caught by a large rock near the canyon floor. Its feathers swayed in the wind. The hawk shot back into the canyon.

Tommy stretched his head forward to see what the hawk was up to, when the earth suddenly gave way from under his feet. Rocks and dirt slid into the canyon. Tommy dipped straight down like a building pulled in a demolition. He yelled in horror. Tommy turned and grabbed the ground he once stood on. The fear and panic that was in the hen was transferred to Tommy. He held on to the edge of the cliff and tried to maintain his balance. The tip of his left foot rested on a rock protruding from the canyon wall. Sparky barked and dove in after his owner. Tommy stretched out his hand while holding on the edge with the other. Sparky swallowed Tommy's hand and pulled. Tommy didn't budge. His hand came out of Sparky's mouth covered in saliva. Sparky panicked and dove in again.

"Come on buddy, lift me up. You can do it," Tommy urged.

A female voice shouted in the distance. "Tommy. Where are you?"

"MOM! MOM! I'M AT THE CLIFF!!!" Tommy yelled at the top of his lungs.

Ann was unable to make out the words but heard sounds of desperation. Sparky made another attempt to lift Tommy, who slid lower into the canyon. The rock beneath his foot loosened. Tommy searched for another resting spot for his right foot, but didn't find one. He couldn't rely on the other rock for full support. Tommy's small biceps trembled as he tried to pull himself up. He stretched his arm out to Sparky. "Come on Sparky," he pleaded in a fainting voice. "Lift me out. YOU CAN DO IT!" He cried. "MOOOOOOM!"

Sparky's barks intensified. The dog grew in panic. Sparky dove in and clamped down on Tommy's arm again, without wanting to hurt him. Tommy didn't feel a pull. He felt his arm slipping out of Sparky's mouth. Tommy hung his head and cried. Sparky hopped around like a rabbit, whining and barking. The pain and worry in the dog's eyes were evident. Tommy's right foot descended lower into the canyon. He knew his life would be over soon; he knew he was about to die, but hung on as tight and as long as he could.

"TOMMY!" The distant voice called out.

"Mom!" Tommy cried. He felt a renewed sense of energy and drive to stay alive.

"Sparky, damn it. Lift me up!" His grip slipped. Tommy panicked and yelled.

Sparky channeled Tommy's energy and became angry with him. His anger turned to rage, a feeling he's never felt before. He barked again and again, pumping himself up. His barks rattled the canyon walls. Dirt and debris fell to the bottom of the canyon floor from the echoes of his thunderous sounds. Massive amounts of adrenalin flooded his veins. Tommy knew what was coming. Sparky understood what he had to do. Tommy extended his left arm and closed his eyes. Sparky puffed up like a hulk dog. He stepped back, zoned in on Tommy's arm, and attacked. Tommy yelled at the top of his lungs as Sparky bit down. The pain was unbearable. His teeth sunk into Tommy's arm. He dug his paws into the ground and pulled, creating impressions along the way. Tommy cried and yelled. The pain stripped him of any energy to pull himself out. The dead weight caused further tearing of his arm. Tommy's left foot lifted off the rock. The rock loosened and fell to the bottom. Sparky pulled. Tommy cried. He couldn't take it anymore.

"Let go, boy. Let go."

Sparky stopped for a quick second, deciding whether or not to be obedient to his master. He continued to pull knowing if he were to let go, Tommy would plummet to the bottom and share space with the hen. Tommy was half-way out. He finally felt relief that he wasn't going to die after all. He wanted to rejoice, but the pain in his arm was all he could focus on. Sparky continued to pull until Tommy was completely out of the canyon. He dragged him away from the edge.

"Let go, boy. Let go," Tommy moaned.

Blood dripped out of Sparky's mouth with Tommy's arm still in it. Sparky didn't let go. Tommy was nearly faint from the pain. Sparky stopped pulling. The ordeal was over. Tommy lay flat on his face without a trace of energy left in his body. His right hand trembled like an Alzheimer's patient. His left hand – remained in Sparky's mouth.

"Let go," Tommy moaned with his face down in the dirt.

Sparky's rage aired out. His enormous size diminished back into the large, overgrown German Shepherd, but he still held onto Tommy's arm.

"Let go, buddy," Tommy's voice escalated.

Sparky didn't listen. Something in his mind overrode Tommy's instructions. Sparky was confused. He was intrigued by the taste of blood in his mouth. It reminded him of something familiar and pleasant, but he didn't know what. All he knew is that he wanted the taste to last.

"Sparky, let go. Get off!"

Sparky knew he was supposed to let go, but he didn't. His jaws didn't open and release as his best friend commanded. There was nothing in the world Sparky wanted more than to please Tommy and ensure his happiness. However, the taste of Tommy's blood, and how it made him feel, became an equal competitor. Sparky felt anxious and moved around nervously, tugging Tommy's arm around with him. Tommy lifted his face off the ground and cried,

"Let go of my arm, Sparky. I'm safe."

Ann burst through the brush.

"Tommy!" she yelled. "Oh my God, Tommy! What happened?" She ran toward them.

Ann saw Sparky standing over Tommy from behind. She knew Sparky would never hurt her son, however she couldn't make out what she was seeing. That was, until she gained proximity and saw Tommy's arm in his mouth.

"GET AWAY FROM HIM YOU SON OF A BITCH!" she yelled.

Ann pulled off a shoe and threw it at him. The shoe missed its target. Sparky's anxiety increased. He felt Ann's fury coming at him. Tommy's arm was still in his mouth, and he didn't want the sensation to end. Ann pulled off the other shoe and whacked Sparky on the butt. Sparky ducked. He let go of Tommy's arm and ran a few feet away. Sparky watched Ann kneel down and comfort her son. He turned his head sideways, wanting to be a part of the comforting process. Ann turned to Sparky and continued to yell at him.

"What the hell did you do to my son? You're supposed to be his best friend. You're supposed to protect him. What did you do?"

Sparky whimpered, lowered his head, and ran off into the forest.

"Mom," Tommy said in his faint voice. "Leave him alone. Sparky saved me."

"He what? Oh my God, let's get you some help. Can you stand?"

Tommy turned over on his back and rested his injured arm on his chest. Blood covered his shirt. "He saved me," Tommy whispered as he tried to catch his breath.

"Baby," Ann looked confused. "How did he – what are you talking about?"

Tommy sat up.

Ann continued, "Come on. Let's get you to the hospital. Can you walk or should I call an ambulance to come here?"

"I can walk."

Tommy stood up. He placed his good arm over her shoulders.

"I almost fell over the cliffs."

"You what?"

"Sparky pulled me out."

"You almost fell in?"

"Yea, and Sparky helped get me out."

"Is that why your arm is torn to shreds?"

"Yea. Don't be mad at him. He saved me."

They entered the house.

"Hey. What's all the ruckus?" George yelled from the living room.

Ann turned the kitchen sink on full blast.

"Don't waste water!" George yelled.

Ann rushed past the living room toward the bathroom. She came back with gauze and scotch tape. "Quick George, call the ambulance."

George shot off the couch to see what was happening.

"What the hell, boy. What happened?"

"No time for questions, George. For God's sake, your son is bleeding to death. Could you please call the ambulance?"

George saw Sparky sitting outside the door with blood stains on his chin. George gave him a good stare before rushing to the living room phone. Ann wrapped Tommy's arm with the gauze, and used scotch tape to hold it together.

"They wanna know what happened, Ann," George said as he covered the receiver.

"Just tell them he was attacked by a dog. We'll figure out the details later."

"Attacked?"

George walked to the door, looking for Sparky. Sparky wasn't there.

"Hello? Mr. Carson?"

"Yes, umm, it looks like he was attacked by a dog."

"We're on our way…"

"Ok, thank you," George hung up the phone.

George walked into the kitchen. There were blood-stained rags and napkins in the trash. Tommy's arm looked like a poorly wrapped Christmas present. Wrinkled tape held pieces of gauze and paper towels together.

"They're on their way," George said.

"George, I'm gonna take Tommy home with me, after the hospital. I'm packing his bags."

"Whose bags?"

"Tommy. He can't stay here anymore," Ann said as she headed toward Tommy's room.

"Ann. What are you doing?"

He followed Ann into Tommy's room. Tommy leaned back against the kitchen counter. His face was pale, drained of any trace of blood. He took an occasional glance at the door, looking for Sparky, but didn't have the energy to keep his neck turned. He threw his head back and closed his eyes.

"It's not safe for him to be here any longer. He's gonna live with me."

"Look, Ann," George said as he maintained his composure. "I'm getting rid of that stupid dog. I never liked that mutt in the first place. Tommy's fine here. And, what the hell happened anyway?"

"Tommy said Sparky saved him from falling over the cliff. I don't know what happened. All I know is I saw my son's arm in Sparky's mouth."

"What the –?"

"I think Tommy is trying to protect the dog. He doesn't want Sparky to get in trouble or sent back to the shelter."

"Well, he'll be going back. I'll have him stay outside, and call the pound so they can come and get him."

"That's fine, George. You do that," Ann continued stuffing a duffle bag with clothes, socks, and underwear.

"Look, Ann. Please, calm down. It was a freak accident. That's not gonna happen again."

"You're right, George. It's not, because he's gonna move in with me. I'm gonna enroll him in school, get him cleaned up, and keep him away from you and that dog."

"ANN!" George yelled. "You can't just take him from me like that."

"We'll see. And if you try to stop me, we can let the police decide."

"Police?"

"Yea, police," Ann got up and looked George in the eyes. "I'll call the police and let them decide."

George rubbed his forehead. He didn't know what to say or do. Tommy wasn't moving in with anyone, yet. He needed to go to the hospital first, so he decided to drop the conversation.

Ann sat beside Tommy in the hospital bed.

"Mom, I miss Sparky."

"Oh honey, forget the dog for now. Let's take care of that arm."

"But, I love him. He's my best friend."

"Once we get outta here, you can visit him as often as you'd like. Ok? I have a neat, little apartment in the city. You'll love it there, and you can make lots of friends."

"Will Sparky and I have our own room?"

"Sparky will stay with dad. There's no room for him, and the managers won't allow me to have a dog."

"What? I can't leave Sparky, oh, no way," Tommy turned away.

"If you don't come to live with me," Ann tried thinking of something clever, "...they'll take Sparky away, and take me away, and your dad too."

"Take Sparky where?"

"To the pound."

"What's the pound?" Tommy asked impatiently.

"Son, stop being so dramatic. The shelter. We have to take him back to the shelter."

"The shelter? No, Mom, no. Never."

"Tommy, grow up. The dog nearly killed you. The police will take him away, and that's final."

Tommy became upset. He started pulling the tape off of his arm to expose the wound. He was looking for a way to hurt himself.

"What are you doing?"

"I'm gonna kill myself. I won't live without Sparky."

He continued to tear at the bandages and tape. Tommy turned his attention to the needle in his arm. He grabbed it. Ann jumped up and placed her hand over the needle.

"Nurse," she called out.

Tommy pulled his hand out from underneath Ann's and slapped her. Ann stood straight. She couldn't believe what just happened. She was overcome with rage, frustrated with George, Sparky, and now Tommy. Ann started slapping him back.

"Stop, Mom, stop," he cried out.

Half of her slaps were blocked. She stopped slapping him and grabbed his hair. Tommy cried. Ann yelled.

"You little bastard. You slapped me? You slapped your mom? You like slapping your mom? You ever do that again, I'll kill you."

The nurse sprang into the room.

"Ma'am. Ma'am. Get off him."

The nurse grabbed Ann from behind. She let go of Tommy's hair.

"Go ahead. Kill yourself. Do me the favor."

Tommy sat back in his bead, breathing heavy, and looking up at the ceiling. He was upset and lost the desire to injure himself.

"Do I need to call the police?" the nurse asked.

"No, it's ok. You can call his dad and tell him to pick up his son. He can keep him. I'm done."

4

Sun rays bounced off the morning dew sitting atop the blades of grass gently swaying in the wind. The early spring hosted perfect temperatures and weather, while late spring mixed beautiful days with hot and muggy ones because of the lurking summer. Today happened to be one of the perfect days. George left the front door open allowing fresh air to flow throughout the home. Sparky sat in front of the screen door. He squinted his eyes as the gentle breeze caressed his face. Tommy watched cartoons in the living room, taking occasional glances at Sparky during the commercials. Sparky appeared thinner than before.

"Hey, boy."

Tommy got off the couch and sat beside him on the tile floor, rubbing his ribcage.

"What's the matter, boy?"

Sparky turned and let out a whimper.

"You hungry? Come on, let's get some food."

Tommy jumped to his feet. George was snacking in the kitchen, eating whatever he could find. He overheard Tommy's conversation with Sparky. Tommy looked inside the refrigerator.

"You just fed him," George said with a mouth full of food.

"He's skinny. He needs to eat more."

"I tol' you boy, he already ate. You can't feed him dog food and human food. We can't eat dog food, he'll get used to our food, and soon we won't have anything to eat ourselves. Take him outside to his bowl and let him eat some more."

Tommy listened and went outside with Sparky to feed him. Since the dramatic day at the canyon Sparky always walked alongside Tommy on his left side. He felt guilty, and the need to protect Tommy from any harm. Sparky's height reached Tommy's shoulders as they walked side-by-side. The dog food was kept in a large galvanized container inside the shed behind their house. Tommy opened the door, but it wouldn't open all the way, jammed by misplaced items behind the door. The space in the shed was large enough for one person, given all the junk inside. Tools, sharp objects, nails, shovels, pieces of wood, and the lawnmower were scattered all over. Some of the items looked organized on shelves or stacked in a corner, while others were thrown around. Tommy had to watch his footing as he reached for the cover of the canister. Sparky waited outside the shed. Tommy removed the top, which had been placed loosely over the canister. Out came a rat. Tommy fell back, banging his back against the wooden door. The top of the canister flew across the shed. Sparky barked outside and nudged the door trying to make his way in. Tommy looked around for the rat. It was in a corner. The rat stared at Tommy with glaring reddish eyes. It wanted to get out, but Tommy was in the way. The door cracked open again. Sparky wanted in, but couldn't fit. Tommy was paralyzed with fear. He was afraid to move, thinking the rat might attack him. Finally, the rat turned away looking for another way out or a place to hide. Tommy got up. Sparky forced himself in. The rat was terrified. It scraped and scratched the corner trying to make a hole to escape from. Tommy wanted to get out, but Sparky blocked his way.

"Let me out, boy."

Sparky backed up and Tommy rushed out.

"There's a rat in there. Get it, boy."

Sparky poked his head in and jumped in the air like a startled cat. The rat ran out from underneath him. Sparky chased and caught the rat just a few feet away. A snap of the jaws and a shake of the head was all it took. Sparky stood by his kill. Tommy approached. He was excited for Sparky. His dog had a choice between two meals.

"Go on. Eat, boy."

Sparky looked at the dead rat, looked at Tommy, grabbed the rat in his mouth and dropped it off by the side of the house.

"No rat? You want your regular food?"

Tommy cautiously reentered the shed, inspecting the corners before looking into the canister. Rat feces were mixed with the dog food. He scooped out the food with Sparky's bowl and set it outside the shed. Sparky smelled the food, but didn't take any interest.

"Come on, boy. Eat up."

Sparky smelled it again, and pulled back. Tommy sat beside the bowl of food and picked out the rat droppings, throwing them aside.

"There, now you can eat."

Sparky stuck his head inside the bowl. He licked up a couple of pieces and chewed. He chewed and chewed. He grounded the food so finely that it mixed with his saliva and was swallowed without any effort. Tommy could tell Sparky didn't enjoy it.

"You wanna eat something else?"

Sparky barked.

"Ok, boy. I'll get you some. I'll get you some today."

George pulled up to a red building. The sides of the building were lined with bricks that looked like it was built in the 1800's, while the front was remodeled. Tommy looked out of the passenger window, and Sparky remained chained to the bed of the pickup. George didn't want to take any chances with Sparky in the middle of the city.

"Go out and ask your mom for some money."

"Mom?"

"Yea. This is where your mother lives. She's on the third floor, room 310."

Tommy was confused. George didn't tell him where they were going. Tommy thought they were going to the supermarket, and wondered what they were doing in front of this unfamiliar building.

"Son, go outside, walk into that building," he pointed, "take the stairs to the third floor. You with me?"

"Yea, third floor," Tommy reiterated.

"Yes. When you get to the third floor, find door number 3-1-0 and knock on it. Your mother lives there. Ok?"

"Ok, but why are we visiting mom?"

"We're visiting mom to borrow money from her."

"Borrow money?"

"Yes. Don't you want your allowance?"

"She already gave me my allowance."

"Yes, but now, because you need more food for your dog, you need to ask for a little more. Understand?"

Tommy shrugged his shoulders.

"Ask your mom for some extra money. Tell her you need more dog food, and tell her there isn't much food at home. We could use some extra stuff in the kitchen. Got it?"

"Yea."

Tommy jumped out.

"Come on, Sparky."

Sparky jumped around in excitement, eager to get his leash unlocked.

"No, boy. Leave the dog in the truck. Go and come back quick. We'll be here."

"But, it'll be fast," Tommy pleaded.

"Boy, hurry up and get in there. Leave the dog alone. He's not allowed inside. We'll be here."

"Ok, Sparky. I'll be right back."

Sparky lay down to rest. A couple of minutes passed and Tommy came out followed by Ann. Tommy sat in the truck, closed the door, and rolled the window down.

"Why are you doing this, George?" Ann asked from the passenger window.

"Doing what?"

"You know what. Don't put him in the middle of this. Just call me and tell me what you need, and I'll try to help. You don't need to involve him."

"I don't need help. Your boy needs some extra money, that's all."

"And you don't have a few dollars to get some extra dog food?"

"Look, Ann. Please don't complicate things –."

"No, you don't complicate things, George. I told you. It's very simple. Call me and tell me what you need. Don't involve my son."

"Well, your son needs some damn money, and I don't have any extra. That's why we're here, ok! If you don't have it, spare me the speech so we can leave."

"I have some, George. I have some. I'm just asking you," Ann reached into her pocket. "Actually, I'm begging you, please don't put him in the middle of this anymore. Whatever he needs, I want you to tell me. It hurts to have my son begging me for money like a homeless child."

"How much do you need?"

"I don't know," George looked straight ahead. "Ask your son."

"George, tell me what you need. This boy don't know nuthin' about no shopping."

"Just a little bit for the dog food is all."

Ann pulled out a few bills.

"Here's some for the dog food, and here's some extra for whatever else you need."

"Grab the money, boy."

Tommy took the crumpled bills and shoved them in his pocket.

"You gonna thank your mom?"

"Thanks, Mom."

"You got it, anytime you need."

"You got a job?" George asked as he continued to look straight ahead.

"Yea, God bless Elizabeth. I'm not making much, but I'm staying with her for free so I can save up."

"Thanks, Ann." There was a brief moment of silence. "You know, it'd be good if you'd move back in–."

"Life is full of if's, George. We need to work on fixing what's in front of us while we have it, so we're not living the rest of our lives wondering about 'ifs."

"Here we go with the lecture again. Thanks, Ann. We're gonna get goin' now."

Tommy was excited. He ran out to get Sparky's bowl and brought it to the pickup. George went inside. Tommy jumped to the back and tore the bag open. The dog food poured out. He caught some of it in the bowl while the rest spilled on the floor. Tommy pushed the bag up against the seat to stop it from spilling. He placed the bowl on the ground eager for Sparky to eat. Sparky sniffed the bowl. He knew Tommy was excited about getting him new food, and didn't want to disappoint him, so he ran off to the backyard. Tommy grabbed the bowl and chased after him, leaving a trail of dog food. Sparky waited by the shed. Tommy set the bowl in its usual spot.

"Wait. Before we play, you have to eat so you can get some energy."

Sparky pretended to be excited about the food. He scooped up a mouthful, allowing most of it to fall out of his mouth while eating a few pieces.

"Yea, boy. There you go. Eat up. You're gonna be big and fat again."

Sparky forced down a couple more pieces while Tommy patted his head. Sparky pretended to have his full. He got up and jumped around wanting to play with Tommy. Tommy was happy to see Sparky energized. Sparky stepped on the side of his bowl, scattering the rest of the food across the ground. Tommy didn't care. He was happy to see Sparky with the energy to play.

They went inside after a few minutes. Tommy looked for the remote control. Sparky sat by the screen door and looked out. A car turned onto the road that led to their property. Sparky stood, his ears perked up and his tongue rolled out of his mouth.

"What is it, boy?"

Sparky barked.

"What you barking at?"

Tommy walked to the door and saw the postal car driving toward them. The postal man delivers mail to the nearby residences on a weekly basis.

"It's the mailman," Tommy said while rubbing Sparky's head.

"Come, boy. Let's watch some TV."

Tommy took a seat on the couch. He turned the TV on and flipped through the channels. Sparky sat by the door, keeping his eyes on the mailman who exited the postal vehicle.

"Damn it," the mailman said.

Sparky stood up and pressed against the screen door. He wanted to go outside.

"Where you going?" Tommy asked.

The mailman tried to free himself from a rosebush. A piece of mail fell into the bush, and when he attempted to retrieve it, his leg and shorts were hooked by a few thorns.

"Damn thorns," he mumbled as he approached the front door.

Tommy wanted to see what Sparky was so excited about.

"It's just the mailman, Sparky."

Tommy nudged Sparky aside. Sparky wanted Tommy to unlock the screen door so he could go out. The mailman approached. Sparky whined. He wanted out.

"Whoa. Your dog has gotten mighty big since the last time I was here."

"Yea, he's a big dog," Tommy rubbed Sparky's head.

Tommy turned the handle to open the door.

"Would you mind holding your dog back? He looks a little excited."

"Who, Sparky? No, he don't bite. He's a nice dog."

"Would you mind holding him back? Don't let him out until I leave," the mailman insisted.

"Stay, boy. Don't go out."

Tommy opened the door, and Sparky pushed his way out. Tommy nearly fell over as Sparky blew past him to get outside. Sparky jumped off the porch and stood behind the mailman.

"Easy, big dog," the mailman said.

Sparky didn't do anything. He watched the mailman. The mailman turned to Tommy.

"You see. If the dog wanted to attack me, I would have been in big trouble now. That's why you have to be very careful with your dog, and when someone asks you to hold him back, or not let him out, you have to make sure you do your best not to."

The mailman was frustrated with Tommy, but felt at ease because of the distance Sparky gave him. He handed the mail to Tommy.

"What the –." the mailman became startled.

Sparky licked the mailman's bloodied calf.

"What's he doing?" the mailman moved his leg away.

"Sparky, come here."

Sparky stopped licking. The wound was clean. He watched the mailman's calf to see if more blood would flow. A spot of blood formed where he was pricked by the thorn. Sparky attempted to lick his leg again.

"What the…" the mailman laughed.

"He likes you."

"No, I think he likes my blood," he laughed again. "You got yourself a vampire dog. Wow. He's weird."

"Vampire dog?"

"Yea, he licked the blood off my leg, and he's at it again," the mailman laughed.

Suddenly, the mailman felt sharp teeth digging into his leg.

"HEY!" the mailman yelled in horror.

The mailman slapped Sparky on his muzzle. Sparky let go. Tommy came in between them.

"Whatcha doing, boy?" Tommy asked. "Get inside."

"Get that damn dog away from me," the mailman said as he hurried toward his vehicle.

"He's a nice dog. He don't hurt nobody."

"Be careful with that dog, son. I'm telling you, he's not right. I was joking about the vampire thing, but you ought to get him checked out. He's gonna hurt someone."

The lettering on Carson's Garage faded and parts were chipped off. The front of the store faced south, the direction in which the sun leaned throughout the spring and summer days as it coasted from east to west. The letters were originally red, and now looked like a dirty burgundy. The morning temperature was moderate, indicating a hot and humid day was upon them. Large dark clouds were off in the distance. Unpredictable weather patterns were commonplace. George pulled up to the shop. Tommy accompanied him, and Sparky was in the bed of the pickup. The doors of the pickup squeaked every time they opened or closed. George immediately started working on an old brown sedan for a customer who was in no hurry to get the car back.

"Leave the dog, and watch me!" George yelled. "You gotta learn how to do these things."

Tommy walked over to George and asked, "When you gonna teach me to drive?"

"You already know how to drive. It's simple. Gas is go, brake is stop, and the wheel is to turn. I didn't teach you how to walk, did I?"

"I dunno," Tommy shrugged his shoulders.

"Watch me so I can show you how to fix a radiator. Bring that toolbox behind you, over here," George pointed.

He dragged the dusty toolbox off the table by its handle and it opened, spilling most of the contents clanging on the floor. Sparky ran inside to see what the ruckus was about.

"Boy," George mumbled from underneath the car.

Tommy threw everything back inside the toolbox. Sparky helped with some of the items that rolled around. He nudged and pawed them back. Tommy dragged the toolbox to George. George searched for a tool.

"Watch while I work on this radiator."

"What's a radiator?" Tommy asked.

"The radiator is the part of the car that keeps everything cool, so it doesn't overheat."

"Overheat?"

"Yea, boy. If the car gets too hot, it'll stop working. So the radiator keeps things cool, so it doesn't get too hot and stop working. Get it?"

Tommy shrugged his shoulders.

Sparky came up from behind Tommy and pressed his muzzle against Tommy's back to get his attention. Tommy rubbed Sparky's head and ears. Sparky ran off, and Tommy gave chase.

"Hey, boy. Get back here and watch me. This is why I don't want that dog here."

Tommy returned. Sparky didn't want to get him in trouble, so he left the garage and walked the perimeter.

"Get me a can from the cooler, will ya?"

Tommy grabbed a can of beer for his father. George sipped and worked. Tools turned, parts rotated, things fell out, and new parts were put in. There was grease all over the garage floor, which blackened the tools and stained George's clothes. George called for Tommy to join him under the car. He pointed and lectured. He instructed Tommy to perform some of the actions, which Tommy did surprisingly well. George was suddenly overcome by an odd sensation. Claustrophobia set in. He's never had an issue working in tight spaces before. He stopped working and wondered where this feeling was coming from. The bottom of the car felt too close. George took in a deep breath, picked up his can, and pulled himself out from underneath the car. George gulped down the remaining contents of the can. He grabbed another can from the ice chest, and sat on a chair in the waiting area. Chuck came to mind; Chuck's sickness came to mind; Christine came to mind; her accident came to mind; Ann came to mind; Tommy came to mind. He looked back inside the garage to make sure Tommy was ok. Even Catherine came to mind. George looked at his arm and found a bruise. His body was suddenly overcome with a cold shiver. His bowels started to move and his stomach made noise. George rushed to the bathroom. He didn't know where the bruise came from. He didn't remember hurting himself. It had to be leukemia, a blood cancer with symptoms of unexplained bruising. George had a friend who died from leukemia over 20 years ago. He remembered his friend was fine one day, had a bruise on his face the next, and then was in the hospital fighting for his life.

George's bowels were relieved, but he stayed on the toilet shivering and worried. He took deep breaths to calm himself. It helped, somewhat. George wiped himself clean and exited without washing his hands. He walked the perimeter of the garage, looking up at the sky, wondering if God was really there, and if He could help him out of this feeling. His mind calmed. Then he remembered moments earlier, under the car, when the wrench socket slipped from his hand and landed on his forearm. It didn't hurt, which is why he didn't remember, but it must have caused the bruise. George was so happy that his eyes flooded with tears. He didn't have cancer. He thought about the countless people victimized by the horrible disease. He thought about Chuck and started to cry. He walked into the weeds to disappear for a while. He didn't want Tommy to see him crying. He didn't know how to explain the feelings he just experienced, or why they came in the first place. How do you explain the terrible fear that runs through your veins and fills your body with tremors and panic? How do you explain the feeling of doom to someone who looks up to you for stability and security? Everyone knows physical pain; the difference between a dull pain and sharp stabbing pain. People can relate to these as everyone has experienced pain several times over. But, how do you get someone to relate to a feeling they've never felt? If you tell them it feels like the world and everything around you is closing in, and you can't breathe, and you think you have a horrible disease, and will die from it, they'll think you're crazy and need to see a psychiatrist. How do you explain to someone, without sounding like a freak, that you're suddenly overcome by thoughts of dying alone, or your greatest fears feel like they're coming to fruition?

George continued taking deep breaths. He heard Sparky barking inside the garage. Then he remembered something. A sense of urgency overcame him. His shoes pounded against the gravel as he stormed his way to the garage. He headed for the cooler and pulled out a can. George chugged the drink down as if he were dying of thirst. Seconds later, he threw the empty can aside and grabbed another. He went into the waiting area, pulled out a seat and plumped himself on it, sending out an explosion of dust from underneath him. He tossed his head back and gulped. He wanted to ensure the feeling would never return. Numbing himself, he thought, would get rid of the feeling for good.

George closed his eyes. He heard Tommy calling out to him.

"How do I...?"

George opened an eye.

"Can't you see I'm trying to rest, boy?"

Tommy was under the car and George was in the waiting area.

"I need help. I want to fix the car."

George went into the garage. He became excited at Tommy's new enthusiasm for auto repairs.

"What do you need?"

"Nothing. I think I got it. Come check, George."

George sat down and lay on his back. He felt the fluids coming back up. George sat up and let out a loud burp. He lay down again and went to check on what Tommy did. George tried to clear his vision by blinking multiple times. He tested the tightness of the screws.

"You gotta be kidding me. You're not as stupid as I thought you were."

"Thanks, George."

"How did you know what to do?" George asked.

Tommy shrugged his shoulders.

"Good job, son." George tapped Tommy on his shoulder. "I gotta get back inside the waiting area. See if you could tighten it up from the top, under the hood. I'll be back to check it out."

George went into the waiting area, and helped himself to the snack rack.

Half of the rack was empty. George tore open a chocolate bar and downed it with his drink. He chewed and sipped; his mouth full of old chocolate and alcohol. Sparky was bored and wanted to sleep, but couldn't. He decided to leave the garage and walk around the shop.

Sparky tried to entertain himself amidst the tall weeds behind the shop. He jumped over and ran around dense brush. Sparky froze in his tracks. His ears perked up. Sparky drew his head closer to the ground. He remained in that position for a few seconds before sinking his head deeper into the landscape. Suddenly, he jumped straight into the air like a startled cat. A mouse ran across his paw. The tiny critter had a hard time running away through the thick and dense landscape. Sparky watched it run back and forth looking for a way to get around the obstacles. Finally, the rodent managed to disappear. Sparky was alarmed. The mouse was right in front of him. Where did it go? His ears perked up and listened for any movement. He lowered his head to the ground again, maintaining absolute focus and silence. Sparky quietly brushed weeds aside with his paw and large head. He searched for the hiding mouse. He saw what looked like the back of the mouse, but it didn't move. Sparky pressed on it. The mouse squealed and jetted off from under his paw. It found open terrain, scurrying as fast as it could. Sparky gave chase. He zoned in and dove on the mouse like a missile. Sparky covered the mouse with its paw. There was no movement. He lifted his paw and the mouse took off again. The game of dog and mouse resumed. The mouse realized it was safer amongst the brush. It turned around to go back, but saw the giant predator coming at it. The tiny mouse's heart pounded as it turned back and raced for the garage. Sparky pounced on it. He felt the critter moving under his paw. Sparky lifted his paw, and saw the mouse trying to pull away. It was trapped. Sparky covered it up again, breaking its bones. Sparky felt the resistance stop. He lifted his paw. The mouse remained motionless, taking in its final breaths. Sparky sniffed the mouse. When his wet muzzle touched the belly of the mouse, it gave one last ditch effort to get away. One unbroken leg did all the work in the attempted escape, sending the mouse in circles. Sparky grew tired of watching circles in the dirt. He pulled back and dove in for the kill. The mouse squealed inside Sparky's mouth. It was disgusting. Sparky spit it out. He tapped the unmoving critter. Sparky got bored with it and went back to the garage.

Tommy came out from underneath the car, retiring from whatever he worked on. It was quiet. No one was around. He walked out of the garage. George's car wasn't there. Sparky was nowhere in sight. Tommy looked around and called out to Sparky. He turned the corner and saw Sparky running at him.

"There you are, boy. There you are," he rubbed Sparky's head. "Where's George? Sparky? Where's George? Where is the car?"

Sparky looked west, toward home, and barked.

"We need to go home, boy. You need to eat."

George went home after the beers were finished. He was too tired and drowsy to do anything, but relax on the couch with the remote control and more beer. He didn't have any intention or thoughts of returning to the garage.

Without hesitation, Tommy decided to take the customer's car home. He tried to turn the car on, but to no avail. He turned the key again and again. The car clicked, and that was all. Tommy hoped his work would have brought the car back to life, but it didn't. It wasn't just the radiator that needed repairs.

Another car pulled onto the lot. Tommy ran out, excited that George came back. It wasn't George. His excitement for going home vanished, but was replaced with a sense of awe. The newest and nicest car Tommy had ever seen approached the garage. It was a white two-door sports sedan with a rounded front, black rims and tinted windows. The passenger window lowered.

"You guys got a bathroom here?" a young, well dressed man with jet black hair shouted across his female passenger to Tommy.

She shouted back, "What the hell?" She was upset that he opened her window instead of his. "Roll down your own window."

She rolled up her window. The driver got out of the car.

"Where's the bathroom?"

Tommy pointed to the restroom on the west-side of the garage. Not long after the driver entered the restroom, he shouted, "DAMN IT! What the hell is this?" The man burst out of the bathroom. "Who runs this God forsaken place? There's no toilet paper, the water runs cold, there's no paper towels – I mean look at this place," he huffed.

Tommy didn't respond. He didn't understand what the frustration was about. The man walked back to his car, opened the door, and just before getting in, yelled, "I had to stop my shit from coming out as soon as I saw there was nothing to wipe my ass with!" He got in and slammed the door. The car sped off, and its wheels shot pebbles in the air. One caught Tommy on the side of the face.

"Ahh," Tommy yelled falling down and covering his face. A huge cloud of dust loomed.

The car disappeared behind the cloud. The screeching of its tires was heard racing down the road. Sparky barked at the car in the distance.

Few cars passed every hour along the quiet Route 96. Some drove at extremely high speeds, taking advantage of the long stretch of open road. The sun began to set on

Selkirk. Tommy was getting tired of throwing sticks for Sparky to fetch. Sparky was even more tired, having to do all the running. Despite Sparky being low on energy, he retrieved the stick every time Tommy threw it. Tommy sat down with his back pressed against the garage. Sparky came to rest beside him. Tommy noticed Sparky's ribs again. He was concerned. Tommy rubbed his side.

"Are you sick? Why you getting skinny?" Tommy asked as he swatted a fly from his face.

Sparky barked.

"We'll take you to a doctor, and they'll fix you right up," he assured Sparky.

As the minutes and hours passed, the flies faded and mosquitoes came out. Tommy was annoyed with the flying insects.

"Let's go inside, boy."

Tommy and Sparky went inside the car he worked on earlier. It reeked of cigarettes. The seats had holes from cigarette burns. The weather outside was warm and muggy. It was warmer in the garage and hot in the car. Tommy wanted to leave the passenger door open when he noticed a mosquito flying around. He slammed the door shut.

Sparky squeezed through the front seats making his way to the back. He moved around, trying to find a comfortable spot. Tommy wiped the sweat off his dirty forehead. He lifted the front of his shirt to finish wiping his face. Sparky finally settled down. Tommy dropped the passenger seat down as far as it would go. Sparky lifted his head and rested it against Tommy's seat. Tommy rubbed Sparky's head. He exchanged hands whenever one hand got tired from the petting. After several long minutes, Tommy's petting slowed. Sparky's eyes closed. Tommy's hand fell off of Sparky. His breathing became heavier.

It was just before midnight. The temperature outside cooled down, but the warm mustiness remained inside the garage and the car. Sparky's ears began to move. It picked up on a distant noise. His eyes opened and his head lifted. Tommy felt Sparky moving.

"What is it, boy?"

Sparky barked as he looked out the window. Tommy didn't see anything. It was completely dark.

Tommy yawned and asked again, "What is it?"

Sparky barked again and nudged at the door. Tommy opened the door to let him out. Sparky ran to the garage door and stared out into nothingness. Tommy followed him. He didn't see anything. Sparky barked toward the east. Just then, Tommy saw lights appear in the distance. It was a vehicle. But why was Sparky interested in this one? The vehicle lights approached, becoming larger and brighter. The sound and weight of the vehicle rumbled the ground it drove on. It was massive and dark. Its engine growled as it downshifted to reduce its speed. It signaled to indicate it was about to pull into the Carson's lot. Tommy and Sparky watched the towering truck make its way onto the gravel. The truck stopped and turned off its headlights, leaving the parking lights on.

The driver freaked when he noticed Tommy and Sparky standing by the entrance of the garage. He regained his composure, rolled down his window, and yelled out, "Is it alright if I spend a few hours here just to catch some quick shut-eye? I'll be on my way real soon."

"Umm, yeah," Tommy shrugged his shoulders.

"Thank you," the driver said as he rolled up the window. Then, he noticed Sparky's size. He rolled down the window, again. "Is that a dog?"

"Yea. This is Sparky, my dog."

"How did he get so big? I've never seen a dog that big before."

"He's my best friend."

"I bet he is," the driver said while rolling up his window.

"Wait," Tommy shouted. "Could you help me start this car? I think it needs a jump."

"What?" the driver asked as he rolled the window down again.

"Jump. My car," Tommy pointed inside the dark garage, "needs a jump."

"Y – Yea," the driver said nervously. "But not right now. I'm very tired, and I can't locate my cables. Perhaps in the morning, after we catch that shut-eye."

He didn't want to get out of his truck in the middle of the night, inside a dark garage, with a weird kid and his oversized dog in the middle of nowhere. The truck driver watched Tommy and Sparky until they went back inside. He remained on the lookout, uncomfortable at the situation. Perhaps, a parent was inside and asleep. He pulled a bat out from underneath the passenger seat and took it with him to the back, where a twin sized bed awaited him.

Tommy and Sparky went back inside the car. They traded seats. Tommy rested in the back while Sparky tried to comfort himself in the front. The mosquitoes vanished, so Tommy decided to open a window. He felt a sense of relief knowing that when daybreak would arrive, he would get the car started and go home with Sparky. The truck driver, however, had other intentions.

5

Tommy rubbed his eyes open. Sparky's tail slapped against Tommy's face.

"Where are we, Sparky?"

Sparky barked. He nudged the door. Tommy opened it to let Sparky out. He realized they spent the night in the car, in the garage.

"Jump," Tommy said. He ran out of the car. "We need a jump. Where's the truck?"

Sparky barked. The lot was empty. The truck was gone.

"Where did he go?" Tommy shouted. "He was supposed to give us a jump, Sparky."

Sparky barked again.

"How are we gonna get home now?"

Sparky barked. He bumped Tommy and ran away. Tommy chased him to the back of the garage. He couldn't find him. Tommy knew there was only one place to hide, amidst the brush.

"I'm gonna find you."

Tommy saw a figure a dozen feet into the brush. He focused as hard as he could. Something was there, but he couldn't tell what it was. Tommy's head moved across his neck like a camera lens zooming in.

"Sparky? I think I found you."

Tommy saw a pair of eyes staring back at him. He knew it wasn't Sparky because the eyes looking back scared him. "Sparky, come out. I don't wanna play anymore." Suddenly, Tommy was tackled from behind. He fell forward, nearly falling into the brush. Sparky barked and jumped around.

"Boy, you scared me."

Sparky let out a whimper and rubbed his head against Tommy's hand, apologizing for scaring him. Tommy looked back into the brush, but didn't see the eyes. There was nothing there. Tommy took off.

"You're it, Sparky."

Sparky gave him a few seconds to hide. Tommy was out of sight. Sparky's tongue hung as he lazily explored the area. He picked up on Tommy's scent. Sparky looked ahead and saw Tommy peeking around the corner.

"You found me," Tommy called out, which meant it was Sparky's turn to run and hide again.

Sparky ran at full speed into the garage and hid behind the car. Tommy turned the corner. He tried to catch his breath.

"Where are you, boy?"

Tommy entered the garage. Sparky peeked from behind the car, oblivious that half his head was visible. Tommy saw him, but pretended not to. He walked toward the back of the car. Sparky walked toward the front from the other side. When Tommy stopped, so did Sparky. When Tommy resumed, Sparky continued to get away, circling the car on opposite sides.

"Where are you?"

Sparky stopped when he reached the front of the car. He was hungry, and didn't want to continue walking in circles. Tommy caught up.

"There you are," he pointed.

Sparky's ears perked up. He ran out of the garage. Tommy followed. George recklessly drove onto the lot at high speeds. He braked and skidded on the loose gravel, nearly hitting Sparky. Sparky stood his ground, as if he knew the car would miss him. Dust polluted the lot. George got out of the car. His eyes were red, and he swayed from side to side as he walked toward Sparky.

"Get in here, Sparky," he commanded the dog.

Sparky didn't move. He looked to Tommy for orders.

"George, why did you leave us last night?"

"Shut up, boy. Be a man. I s – spent countless nights here all alone w – working on cars in the late of the night until my f – fingers bled," George raised his hand, looking for blood. "Get in the car y – you stupid dog."

"Stop calling him stupid. I don't wanna stay here anymore."

"Tell your s – stupid dog to get in the car, Tommy."

"Let's go, Sparky," Tommy said. They walked together toward George's car. Sparky jumped in the back, "There you go, boy." Tommy straightened the passenger seat and was about to get in when George shoved him in the chest. He closed the door.

"You stay here, boy. Run this damn shop and make some money before comin' home. We're behind on our bills. All you do is play with your dog. Get in there, c – clean the place up, and wait for customers." George walked to the driver side and said, "Oh, and call M – Mr. Wilson, tell him to come and get his damn car."

"The phone doesn't work."

"Well, I'll call him from home. Did you fix it?"

"Yea, I fixed the part you told me."

"D – did the car start?"

"No."

"Good, that means you have something t – to keep you busy."

"I don't wanna stay here. I don't wanna be alone," he reached for the passenger door, again. George ran back around and pulled Tommy from his shoulders, sending Tommy to the floor.

Sparky barked.

"Shut up!" George yelled.

"Stop being mean, George. Let me in. I don't wanna stay here. I'm bored and scared."

"So, that's what it is. You're a ch – chicken. Too scared to be alone, ha? Well, now you know how I feel."

"What?"

"Ever since you got this damn dog, I've been all alone. Your mom left me, and th – then you."

George slammed the top of the car, and scared Sparky. He started barking.

"Shut up," George yelled.

Sparky barked louder.

"George, I get scared here at night. A truck came here last night. I was scared; I thought he might hurt us."

"A truck? What did he need?"

"Nothing, he just wanted to stay for the night."

"Well, you had n – nothing to worry about with that bear over there," he said pointing to Sparky.

Tommy got up. His eyes watered. He went for the door again. George pushed him back. Sparky dove to the front and barked wildly, scraping at the door handle.

"You shut up, you," George said.

Sparky barked louder. His teeth showed. He bumped and shoved his head against the passenger window, cracking it. Sparky pulled back and continued to bark, hoping George would come to his senses before he'd have to take matters into his own hands. For the first time, George became afraid of the dog. He knew Sparky was capable of bursting through the glass at any second.

"Tell your dog to calm down."

"It's ok, boy," Tommy said as he wiped a tear from his face. Sparky stopped barking, but continued to growl.

"Work on that car. I'll pick you up for supper."

George opened the door to get in. Sparky tried to push his way out. George shoved him back in.

"Go to the back."

Sparky went to the back seat and stared at Tommy, wondering when he would get inside the truck. George put the car in gear. Sparky whimpered. He sped off.

George left Sparky to wander outside. He stayed inside and continued to drink. Every time he thought about Tommy being alone at the shop, he gulped down more beer. Each time he thought about how he shoved Tommy aside, he tipped the can to his lips, and when he remembered the tears in Tommy's eyes, he finished the can, crushed it with his hand, and went to the kitchen for a new one. George opened the refrigerator, and tried to gain his balance by holding onto the door. He thought about going back for Tommy. He took a step away from the refrigerator and lost his balance. George quickly reached for the refrigerator handle and caught himself.

"Nope," he burped. "That b – boy can handle him – self. He'll be alright."

George saw Sparky walking back and forth in the yard. Something caught his attention. Sparky didn't seem as big as he used to be. He was still tall, but appeared to be losing his mass.

"Hope you die," he mumbled. He looked in the refrigerator. There was a hard piece of cheese on one side, cold cans of beer on the other, half a loaf of bread in the middle, and oatmeal packets in the right corner. George grabbed the oatmeal, thought about it, and threw it back inside. There were rotting vegetables in the vegetable drawer. He closed the refrigerator and opened up the cabinet right beside the refrigerator. He burped aloud before pulling out a can of tuna. Sparky entered his line of sight again. He walked to the chicken coop with something in his mouth. George watched to make sure Sparky wouldn't harm the chickens. Sparky lowered the object in his mouth to the ground. He stood and looked around, making sure he wasn't being watched. George's curiosity grew. He watched closely and saw Sparky's bowl by the coop. Sparky slowly turned his head to the house. George moved out of the way to avoid the dog noticing him. He stumbled, and fell against the refrigerator door, scraping his back.

"Damn it," he said, upset at himself for making noise. George struggled to pull himself back up. He wanted to see what the dog was up to. He slowly approached the window and peeked. Sparky wasn't looking back anymore. He used his paw to lift the side of the bowl, tilting his food into the chicken area.

The chickens scrambled for the dog food. A rooster ran into the crowd of hens giving off a loud sound, like that of a warning. The hens moved aside, but continued to pluck at the food scattered across the ground. George was astounded. Sparky was starving himself to feed the chickens. Why? Sparky turned again toward the house. George hurried to get out of the way, stumbling and banging his head against the refrigerator handle; unconscious.

Night fell on Carson's Garage. Tommy stood outside on the lot, looking in the direction of his home, and wondering when George would arrive. He was also worried about what to tell George, as not a single person stopped by, not even to use the bathroom. The longest and loneliest day of Tommy's life finally set with the sun. He was hungry, thirsty, dirty, smelly, and tired. Worst of all, Tommy missed Sparky. Each passing moment felt like a stab in his chest. Each passing minute drew a darker drape over the light in the skies.

Tommy stood like a statue, hands on his hips, staring out into the west, where the last glimmer of light remained. The annoying flies that looked for any sign of moisture on his face and nostrils took a break and made way for the mosquitoes. Tommy batted the mosquitoes away from his face. He's had a fear of mosquitoes ever since he was a child. When it was time for bed, Ann scared him by telling him the mosquitoes were out to get him if he didn't fall asleep. He ran inside the garage and rolled down the steel door as fast as he could. He raced into the car and slammed the door shut. Worried and alone, he locked the car doors. It was completely dark. He lay face up in the back seat, staring at the stains on the ceiling before the car light went out.

"Sparky, I wish you were here with me. I wish you were here," he whispered.

Tommy didn't want to speak aloud, fearing someone might hear him. He thought about the man in the monstrous truck returning and hurting him, now that he was without Sparky. Tommy closed his eyes and tried to sleep, hoping the night would pass quickly.

Tommy awoke in the middle of the night. There were no working clocks and he didn't have a watch. He heard a sound, that of light footsteps. He cautiously lifted his head to see who or what was out there. The garage door was still closed. Who could it be? Tommy saw a blackness in the middle of the dark garage. The shape paced back and forth in front of the car. It looked like a dog. Tommy got excited.

"Sparky," he called out.

Tommy turned the car's interior light on, but still couldn't see out of the car. In fact, he became blinded by the light and lost sight of the object. He squinted his eyes, trying to relocate what he saw. Sparkling eyes appeared. It stood still and stared at him. Tommy became nervous. If it was Sparky, he would have barked and came to the door.

"Sparky," he called out one more time. "Say something, boy. Say something."

The image approached the car. It became visible as it drew closer to the car's light. It looked like a dog, but much smaller than Sparky. Tommy's heart rate increased. The dog placed its mouth on the passenger door handle and lifted. Tommy's heart felt as if it were going to burst out of his chest. The door opened. Tommy was shocked because the door was locked. He didn't move. The dog walked onto the passenger seat. It was lean and clean, and its gray coat shined. It didn't give the impression of aggression or harm.

"What do you want?"

Tommy turned the light off and lowered himself into the back seat, hoping, if the dog couldn't see him, it would go away. Tommy realized no matter how quiet he could be, he couldn't stop the thumping of his heart. The dog should be able to hear his chest beating. The car light came back on. Tommy was terrified. Who turned on the light? Suddenly, the dog growled. He dashed into the backseat, and attacked Tommy's stomach.

"AHHHHHH!" Tommy yelled.

Like a bullet, the dog's head pierced Tommy's flesh and tore out his organs.

"AHHHHHH!" Tommy yelled as he woke up drenched in sweat. He sat up and continued screaming.

His heart pumped against his chest cavity. Tommy realized it was a nightmare. His breathing calmed. The light of day was visible through the shop window. He unlocked the car doors and got out. Tommy opened the garage door, squinting at the new day's light. He looked around in relief, taking in the fresh morning air. Tommy only enjoyed a few seconds of reprieve when, to his left, he saw the same dog that attacked him a minute ago. The dog sat and stared at Tommy. Tommy's heart barely caught rest before it started racing again. The dog got up and walked off into the brush, out of sight. George pulled into the lot.

"Get inside, boy. We're gonna have some breakfast."

Tommy ran into the car before George could change his mind. He locked the door and strapped on his seatbelt, ready to go. He gripped the sides of the seat, as if preparing for a roller coaster ride. He made sure no one could pry him out of the car. Tommy's mind and heart were set on seeing Sparky, and getting out of Carson's Garage. He forgot to express his frustration about spending the night alone, and the horrible nightmare he had.

George noticed something disappear from around the corner of the house as he pulled up. He got out of the car to see what it was. His biggest fear was a predator attacking his flock of chickens. He turned the corner, and nothing was there.

"Tommy, boy. Go around the corner and meet me in the back."

"What?" Tommy asked. He heard his father, but didn't understand why he was asking him to go around the house.

145

"Listen. Go around the house from the other side and meet me in the back. Holler if you see anything."

"Ok, but where's Sparky."

"He might be in the back of the house playing hide-n-seek, let's find him," George motivated Tommy.

They circled the house. George immediately noticed a white envelope laying on the grass. He picked it up and saw that it was mail belonging to him, but didn't know why it was outside. He shoved the envelope in his pocket and continued to search. Finally, he turned the corner to the back of the house and ran into Tommy.

"I didn't find him, George."

"He must be in the shed," George responded. "Why don't you take a look?"

"Ok, George, just be quiet. I want to surprise him."

The door creaked as Tommy pushed it open. There was a hissing sound inside. Tommy got scared. He didn't want to investigate.

"George. Sparky don't sound like that. Can you check?"

"No, boy. Push the door open all the way, and step back."

George was scared too. Tommy pushed the door and jumped back, but it didn't open all the way.

"Come on, boy. You can do better than that."

Tommy used his foot to push the door open and ran back. A possum stood right beside the canister and hissed again. Its sharp teeth scared them. George didn't know how to get it out. They backed away from the door to allow it to run out. Instead, it looked for a place to hide. George searched for something to throw at the possum, hoping it would get scared and run out. The possum felt surrounded with Tommy and George standing outside the door. George found a couple of golf sized rocks. He threw one and missed. It fell behind the possum. It hissed, looked back at the rock, and took a couple of steps closer to the door.

"Tommy, get back. He wants to get out."

"Get it, George. Hit it. Kill it," Tommy urged and stomped his foot.

"Tommy, step back. He's afraid to come out."

"Good, that'll show him he can't mess with us."

"Tommy!" George yelled. "We want him out of the shed, now step back."

Tommy took a step back and continued to intimidate the possum.

"Some more, son. Take a few more steps back."

Tommy took a couple steps back. George launched the second rock. It hit the possum on the back. It jetted off out of the shed and toward the trees.

"Yay," Tommy chased the possum. "Take that." Tommy turned to George. "Where's Sparky? We could chase the ugly critter and show him who's boss."

"He's probably wandering around somewhere."

George pulled the letter out of his pocket and tore it open on his way back to the house. Tommy walked the perimeter of the house, looking for Sparky and calling his name. Tommy searched the mini-forest and headed toward the canyon. There was no sight or trace of Sparky, Tommy made his way to the cliffs. He remembered the tragedy that nearly took place. He stood for a moment, looking at his arm. He remembered Sparky's heroism. Tommy felt a sudden rush of energy. He needed to find his best friend. He needed to find all that mattered to him.

"Sparky! Sparky!"

Tommy made his way back, across the yard, to the other side of the property, where the road connected the other residences. Blooming honeysuckle wove its way through the chain linked fence that separated the property line from the road. Tommy took in a deep breath. A sudden rush of sweet scent filled the air and overwhelmed his nostrils. He sneezed and continued to search, making his way around the fence to the roadside. He looked left and didn't see anything. He looked right and saw the postal car. No one was inside. Tommy turned back toward the house. Concern and worry set in.

Tommy cried out, "Sparkyyyyy! Sparkyyyyy!"

Suddenly, from around the corner of their house, and running at full speed, he saw his favorite being in the world. Sparky, looking larger than life and energetic as ever, ran across the field toward Tommy.

"Yay, Sparky."

Sparky leapt into Tommy's extended arms. Tommy hugged Sparky tightly around his neck, planting kisses wherever he could. Sparky licked Tommy back. Tommy rubbed Sparky's back. They couldn't get enough of each other.

"Come on, boy. Let's get you something to eat. I've been worried about you."

Tommy ran his hand across Sparky's rib cage and stomach. He stood back and took a look. He didn't notice any protruding ribs. In fact, Sparky looked fuller and bigger than ever before. With excitement, Tommy examined the other side of Sparky and noticed the same thing. Sparky wasn't skinny anymore. Sparky wasn't sick.

"You're better," Tommy clamored. "You're better," he dove in and hugged Sparky again. "What's that on your chin? Tommy noticed some redness.

George finished making breakfast. He sat on a flimsy wooden chair at the dining table in the kitchen. He positioned the chair to face the living room television. Tommy bolted through the door with Sparky right behind him.

"You found the dog," George said unenthusiastically.

"What's for breakfast?" Tommy inquired.

"Sit here," George tapped on the dining room chair. "Make sure the dog doesn't eat anything off the table. There's your eggs and toast." George pushed Tommy's plate closer to him. "Juice is in the frig, and there's some chicken in the pot right there on the stove."

"George, Sparky isn't sick anymore," Tommy said while stuffing his face.

"That's good, boy."

"No bacon, George?"

"No, boy. No bacon. Why have bacon when you can have chicken? That's why we have so many of those lil guys out there. The eggs and meat on this table is from our own yard. There's nothing healthier or fresher."

"George, Sparky isn't sick. He's not skinny anymore."

George stopped eating. He had a moment of déjà vu.

Tommy continued tearing into the eggs with his fork, causing the yolk to bleed all over his plate. George looked at Sparky. Sparky watched Tommy eating, which made him happy. Sparky's attention was completely on Tommy.

"The dog's gotten bigger – and fatter," George said as he pulled his chair back to take a better look at Sparky. "Boy, wasn't your dog skinny just a day ago?"

"Yea, he was. Not no more," he patted Sparky on the head.

George was confused and couldn't figure out why the dog looked plumper.

"So, what we got planned for today?" George asked.

"Are we going back to the shop?"

"No, we'll take the day off and spend it together, with your dog if you want."

"Yes. I'm not leaving him behind no more. Sparky and I will play outside."

"Ok, that's fine. But, what will you and I do?"

"I dunno," Tommy shrugged his shoulders. "You could come out and watch us, if you want."

George swallowed the lump in his throat.

"Watch you guys play outside?"

George got up from his chair, grabbed his dishes, pushed the chair in, and set the dishes in the sink. Tommy continued to eat while petting Sparky. George went to the frig and pulled out a can.

"Go ahead, do whatever you want. This is your day off. We'll go back to the garage tomorrow." Tommy scarfed down the rest of the food, grabbed the toast, and ran out of the house with Sparky tailing him.

George kept the bathroom window open, as a natural vent. He sat on the toilet and overheard Tommy and Sparky playing in the yard. George felt disappointed. He lifted his pants, left the bathroom without washing his hands, and headed for the yard. George passed by the chicken coop, and was suddenly overwhelmed by another sense of déjà vu. He stood there, staring at the chickens, trying to recall what bothered him. George watched the chickens cluck, chatter, peck at each other, and the ground. Two hens chased after a third, trying to pick off a piece of grass from its beak. The third hen was oblivious to the grass that protruded from her mouth. George saw the chickens pecking at brown chunks of hard food. The hens were smashing their beaks against the food on the ground attempting to break them into smaller pieces. He opened the gate and went inside. George bent over to pick up a piece, and fell over. The hens scampered away. George sat on the ground examining what the chickens were picking at. His eyes widened, and his memory returned.

Dog food! Son of a bitch, that's dog food."

He grabbed a couple more pieces and shoved them in his pocket. He finally had something to incriminate Sparky, hoping Tommy would understand the need to discipline the dog.

"Boy, get over here," George yelled as he tried to stand up.

Tommy continued to play with Sparky. He didn't hear George calling him.

"BOY!" George yelled at the top of his lungs. "Get over here."

Tommy ran over with Sparky trailing him.

"What, George? We're playin'."

"What's this?"

George pulled out the food from his pocket. Tommy took a closer look.

"Looks like Sparky's food," Tommy said.

"What's it doing with the chickens?"

"Ha?" Tommy looked confused.

"What you mean, ha? What's Sparky's food doing in the chicken area?"

"I dunno."

"Well, let me tell ya. While you and I've been working our asses off to buy this dog food, he's been dumping his food in the chicken coop for the chickens to eat, like he's too good to eat his own damn food."

"What?"

George continued, "He hasn't been eating his dog food. That's why he's so skinny."

"No, George, look." Tommy tapped Sparky on the side. "He's not skinny. He eats."

George was confused. He was skinny yesterday. How did he grow so fast in one day?

"Well, maybe he's sharing his food. But, that's not the point, Tommy. Look. This is dog food, and I found it here in the chicken coop. Look," George pulled Tommy by the arm and brought him to the fence. "Take a look on the ground. There are still some pieces, right there. And look over there, more pieces."

"Let go of my arm," Tommy pulled away.

"Boy, don't you dare make me," George pointed a finger at Tommy.

Sparky barked.

"You're hurting me."

"That's because you're not listening. And how was I hurting you by grabbing your arm?"

"Don't, ok. Just don't," Tommy whined.

"Son, if this keeps up, we're gonna have to get rid of the dog. He's too expensive to keep and we don't have enough money."

Sparky barked again.

"I can ask mom for more. She gives me allowance money."

"No, we gotta get rid of the dog. He's caused nothing but trouble, and heartache ever since you got him. I'll tell your mom to take him back to the pound."

"NO!" Tommy yelled.

Sparky barked.

"Shut up," George yelled at Sparky.

Sparky barked again.

"If you don't stop…"

"Leave him alone, George."

George slapped Tommy. Sparky barked and jumped in between them, bumping George to the ground. Tommy was upset. He soothed his face with his hand.

"Forget the pound," George grumbled. "It's the graveyard for you."

Sparky towered over George and growled. George looked away. He didn't want to challenge Sparky, not in the position he was in. Sparky looked as if he could swallow George's head whole. George brought himself back to his feet. He felt the need to reassert his dominance, otherwise Sparky would gain control of the Carson kingdom. By controlling Tommy, George would regain supremacy. He walked up to Tommy.

"Look at what your dog did to your dad. What's it gonna take to show you he's not a good dog?"

"He's a good dog, he's the best dog. You're a bad dad. You're the one that needs to go," Tommy yelled.

153

George felt like a ton of bricks fell on his chest. He didn't know what to say. Sparky made his way in between them. George and Sparky engaged in a stare-down. George finally decided what needed to be done, but kept it to himself. He stormed off. Tommy and Sparky watched him go inside. Tommy turned away to go and play. Sparky didn't follow. He was concerned.

"Let's go, boy. We can play."

Sparky stared at the house. He growled.

"Come on, boy. Let's go."

Sparky's focus on George drowned out Tommy's calls. Sparky didn't hear him. George came back out with a rifle in hand. Sparky growled louder and barked. George aimed the rifle at Sparky. Sparky's barks were thunderous. The hairs on Tommy's arms rose. Those were the barks he heard during the incident at the cliff. He's never heard Sparky bark that ferociously since that day. George fired a shot.

"NOOOOOO!" Tommy yelled.

Sparky ran off into the trees. Tommy went after him. George took aim again, but didn't shoot. Tommy came into his line of sight.

"That's right, you damn dog. Now you know who's in charge."

George looked at his rifle and kissed it; his chest pumped out in victory as he made his way into the house. The rifle was his new friend, taking third place to beer and the remote control. He set the rifle across the dining table. George stroked and petted the gun like a pet, giving it kudos every time he remembered Sparky running off.

The evening rolled around. Tommy and Sparky weren't back yet. George finished supper. He tossed the dishes in the sink and headed over to his trusty couch, picking the remote off the floor before lying down. There was a hard knock at the door.

"I just sat down, damn it."

The knock repeated, and it sounded angry.

"Come in. The door's open."

George wondered who, apart from Tommy or Ann, it could be. It was too late for the postal man.

"Open the door," a male voice requested. "I'm Officer Myers from the local police station."

George jumped off the couch. He straightened his shirt. The police must have been tipped off by one of the neighbors regarding the gun shot. George became nervous. He placed the rifle under the coffee table before opening the door.

"Good evening, officer." Behind the officer stood a postal worker he's never seen.

6

George noticed another officer leaning against the patrol car with his arms crossed.

"Good evening, sir. I'm Officer Myers and standing behind me is the manager from the postal office. And there," Myers pointed, "is Officer Matthews."

George raised his hand to greet the postal manager and Officer Matthews.

"The reason why we're here is because we're looking for the postal worker who services your area, Mr. Grimes, and we're wondering if you or anyone in your family may have seen him today."

"Mr. Grimes? I don't know. I mean – ." George stuttered.

The combination of nervousness and alcohol didn't help at the moment.

"I haven't seen him for a couple of days, I think."

"His postal vehicle is parked right outside the fence, there. It looked as if he might've serviced your home, and the neighbor's in front of you."

"No, officer. I haven't seen him. I haven't even received my mail today."

George suddenly remembered the letter he found outside.

Officer Myers noticed a torn envelope on the dining table behind George.

"Mind if I come inside?"

George didn't want the officer in his home. As a matter of fact, he didn't want anyone in his home, apart from Tommy. Visitors and guests meant tidying up the house and acting formal. He preferred to be left alone, with his can, remote control, and – George panicked but tried not to let it show. He went directly to the coffee table and used his foot to make sure the rifle was tucked underneath. The postal manager approached the door and looked inside the house. Myers walked around the kitchen, looking around at the cabinets and floors before coming out to the living room. He glanced at the torn envelope, not wanting to make it look obvious that it was of his primary interest. Myers continued looking around, standing above the envelope.

"Mind if I take a look at the envelope?"

"S – sure," George replied, again, wanting the officer away from the coffee table.

"Was this part of today's mail?"

"Oh, that? I don't know. I actually found it outside, on the grass."

The postal manager's curiosity intensified. He wanted to hear more, and so did Myers.

"Outside? What was it doing outside?"

"I wondered the same myself. I could show you where I found it," he approached Myers.

"Ok, in just a minute. Mind if I keep looking around?"

"Umm, you know the house is a real mess, and I gotta get it cleaned before my son comes home."

"When's your son coming home?"

"He should be here any moment, just went outside to play with the dog."

Myers looked down the hallway for any sign of Mr. Grimes. He didn't see anything suspicious, so Myers headed outside with an eager George following him out, and shutting the door behind them.

"Right around there," George pointed. "This is where I saw the letter."

Myers and the postal manager both looked around the area searching for any clue. The postal manager went to the chicken coop and watched the chickens play.

"Don't wander off too far," Myers called out to the postal manager.

The postal manager heard noise coming out from amongst the trees. It sounded like a large animal. The postal manager became startled and hurried back to the patrol vehicle. Officer Matthews entered the patrol vehicle and started some paperwork. Sparky appeared from amidst the trees with Tommy right behind him. Myers looked up.

"What in God's name?"

"Oh, they're here. That's my son and his dog," George said.

"How'd that dog get so big?" Myers asked.

"I don't know, but I'd sure like to get rid of it. Could you imagine? All the money we make goes into feeding that bastard."

"I could imagine," Myers said with awe.

The postal manager heard noise coming from behind. Startled again, he turned around. Someone was approaching.

"Hi, I'm the neighbor over there," an elderly lady said.

"You scared me," the postal manager said.

"Sorry, didn't mean to. Well, I just saw you guys here, and wanted to see what was goin' on."

Tommy went inside the house wondering why the police were here. He wanted to confront George about shooting at Sparky, but he was concerned the police might be here to take Sparky away. Sparky followed. Officer Matthews looked up and saw Sparky from behind.

"What the hell is that?"

He got out of the car and saw the neighbor standing by the postal manager.

"Ma'am, how can I help you?"

"I was just telling him that I'm the neighbor over there," she pointed.

"Actually, we'll be over your house in a minute. If you wouldn't mind returning home?"

"I'll just stay here since I walked all the way over here already."

Matthews turned his attention to George and Officer Myers.

"We done here, Myers?"

"Yea, for now." He turned to George, "Well, thank you for your time. I might be back if I have other questions."

"O – Ok, thank you for coming."

George went inside the house.

"Tommy, have you seen the postal man?"

"What? No," Tommy said while heading toward his room.

George followed them to the room, making sure Tommy understood the question.

"The postal man, did he come by today? Have you seen him?"

"No, George. We didn't see the postal man. I don't like you. You tried to kill Sparky."

The neighbor addressed Officer Matthews, "I wanted to complain about something, but not while they were out here."

"What about?"

"Earlier today, I heard a gunshot, a loud one, and I'm pretty sure it was from here."

"A gunshot?"

Myers and the postal manager approached the conversation.

"Yea, and it was loud."

"Did you call it in?"

"No, I don't know why. I guess I was waiting to see if something else was gonna happen. I thought, maybe they were hunting or shooting at a coyote or something, but when I saw you guys here, I knew something was wrong."

Myers tried fitting pieces of the puzzle together. "The letter was found outside, a gunshot was heard outside…," he mumbled.

Matthews added, "And the kid and his grizzly just came back from the woods."

Myers rushed to the car, "Let's go. We gotta get a search team going."

"Oh Lord," the postal manager covered his face. "How am I going to break this to his family?"

Matthews placed his hand on the postal manager's shoulder, "Break what? We don't know anything yet, so don't say anything to anyone until we find out what happened here."

"Don't you guys want to stay here and call in for the search team? I mean what if they try to hide the body?"

"There's no body," Matthews responded. "No one is dead. There's no evidence of anything. Understand?"

Myers turned his attention to the lady. "Please, come inside. We'll give you a ride back."

"No, it's fine. I live right there."

"Ma'am, you're the one who said you heard a gunshot from here. You sure you wanna take your chances walking back?"

"Ok, I'll take the ride."

The four of them got into the police car and drove off.

"Aren't you gonna check the home for a gun?" the postal worker asked.

"Everyone in Kansas has a gun. We'll need a warrant to check inside the house," Myers said. He turned around to the postal manager in the back seat. "We don't wanna jump to conclusions. We still have no clue of what happened to your employee, but, that's what we're gonna find out. Make sure you don't say anything to anyone, otherwise it could ruin the investigation as well as get you into trouble."

"He's gonna hide everything, by the time you get back. He's gonna get rid of the gun, the body –," the postal manager shrugged his shoulders and looked out the window to avoid eye contact with any of the officers.

"Please, let us do our work. We'll get all this figured out." Myers responded.

"I'm thinking, if I were his family member, and was looking for him, and know that the police drove away after finding clear evidence, it would make me very unhappy, to say the least."

"I understand, believe me I do. But, we have rules to follow. And if we don't, we'll do Mr. Grimes and his family a disservice," Myers explained.

It was near midnight. George fell asleep on the couch. An empty can of beer rested on George's stomach. The can tilted and rolled off, falling to the floor. The TV was on and the volume was high. Sparky was in the room with Tommy. Tommy was sound asleep. Sparky rested on the floor at the feet of Tommy's bed, but couldn't sleep. His eyes were open, and he felt uneasy. Sparky fidgeted, trying to find a comfortable position to rest in, but it wasn't the position his body was in that kept him awake; it was the state of his mind. Sparky couldn't take it anymore. He needed to wake his best friend from a deep sleep. He licked Tommy across the face. Tommy squinted. He petted Sparky on his head. Sparky continued to lick his face.

Tommy woke up, "What is it, boy? It's sleep time."

Sparky whimpered quietly, and walked to the door. Tommy tried to fall asleep. Sparky whimpered and came back to Tommy. He licked Tommy again, and continued whimpering before walking to the door again. Tommy sat up. His head was spinning. Sparky approached him again, placed his paws on Tommy's thighs, and licked his face.

"Ok, boy. What is it?"

Tommy got and followed Sparky out of the room, down the hall, and to the front door. Sparky walked with caution, careful not to make noise. Tommy walked with heavy feet, thumping his way down the hallway. Sparky stopped and turned around, hoping Tommy would walk quieter. Tommy saw George sleeping in the living room, and lightened his footsteps. Sparky stopped by the front door.

Tommy whispered in Sparky's ear, "Where we going?"

Sparky looked worried.

"Ok. I'll be quiet."

They made it outside, into the cold. Tommy had on sweats and a t-shirt. He hugged himself while following Sparky to the entrance of the cellar. Sparky scratched at the lock. The doors were wooden and old, laying flat across the ground. Tommy removed the lock. He lifted one of the doors open, and Sparky disappeared into the darkness of the cellar.

"What are you doing in there?"

He found the light switch and flicked it on. He saw Sparky sitting calm and relaxed. There was something behind Sparky. Tommy got closer, squinting his eyes and wrinkling his forehead, trying to make out what it was. Clothes and shoes became visible. He stepped into a sticky puddle. Tommy looked down and saw the puddle extended to where Sparky was. He focused on the object and realized what he was looking at.

"Ahh," Tommy yelled.

Sparky dove at Tommy, knocking him to the ground. Sparky licked Tommy's face to prevent him from yelling. He whimpered and licked Tommy until he stopped yelling. Tommy got up and ran for the stairs. Sparky caught him from his ankle.

Tommy turned around, "Come on, boy. Let's get outta here."

Sparky whimpered aloud. He cried. He went back to the body and licked the blood from the ground. Tommy was confused. He didn't understand what Sparky was doing. Sparky walked to the corner of the cellar where another bag of dog food was stashed. He tore the top open and shoved the bag on its side, spilling the dog food. Sparky went back to the puddle and licked the blood.

"Sparky, did you do this?"

Sparky jumped up. He was excited that Tommy figured out what he was trying to tell him.

"Why did you do this, boy?"

Tommy noticed a mail pouch strapped across the dead man's chest.

"That's the postal man, Sparky. That's who the cops are looking for," he said feeling sick to the stomach.

Sparky, again, walked over to the dog food. He pushed the bag further, allowing more of its contents to spill out. Sparky came back, and again licked from the puddle of blood. The spilling of the dog food reminded Tommy of why George was upset earlier; Sparky wasn't interested in his food, and that's why he was getting skinnier, but then Tommy looked at the half eaten carcass. He just saw Sparky lick blood off the floor.

"Oh, Sparky. Did you eat the postal man?"

Sparky ran around in excitement. He sprinted out of the cellar. Tommy waited by the body. Suddenly, there was a tap at the window. It was Sparky. Tommy pulled the window open.

"What you doing out there?"

Sparky stuck his head in and whimpered, while looking at the body below. Tommy wondered what Sparky wanted. Sparky continued to whimper and stomped his paw against the window seal, looking down at the body. Tommy looked at the body and back at Sparky, still confused. Sparky whimpered and stuck his upper body through the window trying to reach the postal man with his mouth. Tommy realized what Sparky wanted, but didn't understand why. The postal man laid upside down with his legs against the wall and his back to the floor. His face was darkened with dried blood. Segments of his backbone were visible through the chest cavity. Tommy grabbed the postal man by his ankle and extended it to Sparky's outreached mouth. Sparky clamped down on the ankle and pulled back, lifting the postal man like a rag doll. Sparky wanted to get the body out of the garage and hide it somewhere. He continued to pull. The postal man's body was nearly out of the window until it tilted sideways. His head was caught and pressed against the side of the window. Sparky couldn't pull him out. If he were to let go, the body would fall back inside. Tommy realized Sparky needed help. He wrinkled his nose and reached for the postal man's head, shoving it toward the opening of the window. Sparky pulled. The postal man's head bent so far into his chest, it looked as if it was going to break off. The body was finally out. Sparky carried it off into the woods. Tommy ran and slipped on the blood, nearly falling down on his way out of the cellar. He turned off the light and shut the cellar door without placing the lock on. It was dark outside. The light on their front porch and the shine from the full moon helped Tommy see his way as he tried to catch up to Sparky.

"Where we taking him, boy?"

Sparky growled while dragging the body. Leaves were swept under the body while twigs crackled under their footsteps. The darkness intensified amidst the trees. Tommy tried to keep up with Sparky. Sparky dragged the body as fast as he could. Tommy had to slow down and stop each time he came across large branches and other obstacles. Sparky didn't stop. He was on a mission. Tommy used Sparky's growling and the body's dragging sounds to find his way. Finally, the tree line ended, and the sounds stopped. The moonlight reemerged. Tommy saw the ground. He looked ahead, past Sparky. The darkness of the canyon was a few feet from where Sparky sat. Sparky rested. His breathing created large clouds of condensation as he stared off into the moonlight. Sparky didn't rest for long. He went to the other side of the body and shoved his muzzle into the postal man's crotch, nudging the body closer to the edge of the cliff.

"Sparky, be careful," Tommy yelled out.

He sprinted to Sparky and tapped him on the back to make sure Sparky's attention was received. Sparky barked.

"What are you doing, boy? You might fall over."

Sparky barked again. He resumed pushing the body to the edge. Tommy stared into the darkness.

"Be careful."

The postal man's head tipped into the canyon followed by his arms and chest. Gravity did the rest of the work. Sparky backed up and watched the darkness drag the body into its abyss. The body freed loose rocks and debris on the way down, thumping against the edges until the final plop at the bottom of the canyon's pit. Sparky's mission was complete. He was relieved.

It was a little past noon in Selkirk. The sun was at its highest peak, leaving no trace of shadows for the creatures to take respite in. The temperatures were beginning to pick up as summer approached. A quiet Sparky remained in the house, peering through the curtains as he watched George drive off with Tommy to the shop. Tommy, exhausted and sleepy from the night before, didn't have the energy to resist George, who wanted Sparky to stay home. He felt like a zombie, incapable of doing anything for himself except feeding. Tommy fell asleep during the ride.

"What's the deal, boy?"

Tommy didn't respond.

"Tommy. What's the deal? Why so tired?"

Tommy's head rocked from side to side. He looked faint.

"This is what happens when you're up all night with that stupid dog."

Suddenly, a flash of heat ripped through Tommy's body. His heart raced, and his eyes widened. Tommy and Sparky were quiet last night. They didn't wake George. How did he find out?

"Wha?" Tommy asked.

"Just know this. You won't get out of your responsibility to run this garage, unless you wanna go to school, and I don't think you want that."

Tommy didn't know what George was talking about, but he felt better, because George didn't say anything else about last night.

"All of your choices have consequences, just be prepared to handle them."

Tommy didn't register a word George was saying. He continued talking. His words sounded like mumbling. Images of the gutted body came to mind; the hollow and empty abdomen. Tommy shook his head to get the images out. George's words were becoming annoying background noise.

"Wha – hell – boy?"

Tommy shook his head again and slapped the side of his skull.

"What the hell are you doing, boy? What's gotten into you?"

"Nothing, George."

"Why are you rocking your head? You look retarded."

"Just tired."

George pulled into the lot. Tommy looked for Sparky, hoping he'd be sitting and waiting out front. George got out. Tommy stayed in the car wondering why Sparky didn't run to him from wherever he was. Tommy imagined getting out and throwing his arms around his best friend, and receiving licks in return. Then he remembered, Sparky was home.

"Let's get to work, boy," George called out from the garage.

Sparky slept on the kitchen floor, recovering from the night before. His ears perked up after hearing the sound of a vehicle in the distance, but he kept his eyes closed. He wasn't concerned because it didn't sound like George's car. However, the vehicle didn't continue on. Instead, it turned on to their road. Sparky got up and looked out of the living room window. He saw the same vehicle that was here yesterday when the officers stopped by. Officer Matthews got out and stood by the vehicle while Officer Myers approached the house. He pounded on the door.

"Open up, it's the police!" Myers shouted. Myers signaled to Matthews to check the perimeter of the house. Matthews walked around the corner. Myers pounded on the door again.

"Open up!"

Myers took a few steps back to examine the front of the house. He looked through the windows to see if anyone was inside. He took a few more steps back and saw Matthews standing by the side of the house. Matthews stared at the ground.

"What is it?"

He gestured for Myers to come over. Myers ran to see what intrigued Matthews. Matthews pointed at the window to the cellar. Myers squatted by the window.

"No way!"

Myers stuck his head inside.

"No way!" he yelled. "Did you see inside?"

Matthews approached, unsure of what to expect. He looked into the cellar and saw a pool of blood. Myers stood up and withdrew his gun. He felt like they were being watched. Myers looked up and nearly fell backwards. Sparky stared down on them from the kitchen window above their heads. Matthews looked up at Sparky.

"That must be our suspect," he said in his deep voice.

"The Carson's obviously know about this. That bastard, George, must've shot the postal man and then fed him to the dog."

"Why?" Matthews wondered. He looked into Sparky's eyes. "He looks like a gentle giant. Why would he do this? I've known dogs all my life, especially shepherds, and they don't do this kind of stuff; they don't eat people."

"He's not a normal dog," Myers responded. "I mean, look at its size."

Myers radioed back to the station, "Myers here, checking on the status of the warrant for the Carson's residence."

"One minute," a voice replied.

"We're not going in?" Matthews asked.

"No, not without the warrant."

The voice from the radio returned, "Looks like the request was submitted yesterday."

"Yes, it was."

There was an awkward silence for a few seconds.

Myers grew impatient, "The status!"

"Requests can take up to 72 hours, Officer –."

"I know that. I'm not asking for a training on warrants. What's the status?"

"It's not ready. There are no other notes."

"Add this note, and make it expedited, 'We have evidence of the disappearance."

"Do you want to add details? It might speed up the request."

The operator sounded interested in the evidence.

"Y – yes," Myers said. "Add that, 'We found a pool of blood inside the Carson's residence cellar."

"Officer, are you inside the Carson's home?"

"No," Myers replied. He became even more frustrated with the operator's inquiry, as if she were going to lecture him about searching without a warrant. He turned to Matthews, "Where do we get these people? Acting like we just got hired."

Matthews shook his head. He looked at the blood, and then to the kitchen window. Sparky wasn't there.

The operator returned, "Your request has been submitted. Please do not go inside the home, or anywhere else that's off limits."

"Ma'am, please don't tell me how to do my job. Just make that submission and keep me updated. We're on a hot one here," Myers ended the line.

"Matthews, time to look for the Carson's."

Ann and Elizabeth sat on a bench, one of many lining the sides of Main Street in Scott City. Locomotives passed back and forth not far from where they were sitting.

"I can't believe it's been such a long time since we used to hang out here," Elizabeth said. "My fat ass couldn't get on that train," she laughed.

"Yea, but you finally did," Ann added.

"Yea, after a few attempts. All because of Catherine," Elizabeth smiled.

"Yea, that girl was something else," Ann smiled. "I wish she were still around. Bet she could still bring fun and smiles to our little lives. Oh, the good old days."

"Meh, I'm not too sure about that," Elizabeth said. "You know, I think most people say good old days because they hold onto the good memories of the past. If you think about it, school was a stress, our families were a stress, and we lost a good friend. Not a whole lot good about that, if you ask me."

"Yea, I know what you mean. Like you said, I'm referring to the good times. The freedom of doing things and not really having consequences, you know? But I suppose Catherine would disagree."

"Ann, whatever happened to you and George?"

Ann didn't respond. She felt a sudden tensing of her shoulder and neck muscles. She stretched her neck by tilting her head from side to side.

"It's ok if you don't wanna talk."

"No, it's not that. Just, I don't know where to start. I mean, I have my own questions. My life hasn't made much sense to me."

"But, you guys were so happy. You and George." Elizabeth pointed to Old Town Cafe, "That used to be your favorite spot."

"I know," she smiled. "I know. Everything was great. We moved in with his parents. They had a decent house on a nice piece of land. I enjoyed the house and yard work. I had freedom. He would come home from work and eat, then we would go out, sometimes coming here, walk around the streets of Main St and KC; everything was so good."

"Well, what happened?"

"Strangely, it was the birth of my son."

"I – I don't understand."

"Not that it was my son that made things go bad, but well, George. When I was pregnant with Tommy, all I dreamt about was adding him to our love and fun. Wherever we went, we could take Tommy in a stroller with us. I imagined the three of us going to the parks, taking walks in the city and everywhere else with our beautiful son. I imagined my hands being held by Tommy's tiny palm on one side and George on the other. But, as soon as Tommy was born, George did a complete 180, like I never seen before."

"Like, what did he do?"

"He didn't become a monster. He didn't go from nice to being mean. He left me," Ann's lips quivered.

Elizabeth looked confused. "For another girl?"

Ann shook her head as she tried to get her emotions under control. She threw her hair back and wiped away a tear.

"No," Ann cleared her throat. "Not for another girl. He left me for Tommy."

"Girl, if you don't make sense of this story soon, I'm gonna go crazy."

"Once Tommy was born, George ignored me and sent all his love and attention to Tommy; I mean, like, 100%. All of it. He ignored the shit out of me, like I didn't even exist. I mean, it was nice and all seeing the two of them having so much fun together, and him being a good father, but I was completely forgotten about and pushed aside."

She took in a deep breath.

"Damn, just like that, ha?" Elizabeth asked.

"Just like that."

"How's your relationship with Tommy? Sounds like George has a lovely one."

"Psht," Ann sounded. "What goes around comes around. God sees to that. For some people, justice is served in this world, for others it's served in the next, and for some, they get it in both. George is getting his now. Tommy's doing to George exactly what George did to me. Justice is good."

"Wow, what happened with them?"

"Same thing. Same exact thing. As soon as we adopted Sparky –."

"Sparky?"

"Yea, oh. We adopted a dog."

"Gotcha."

Ann continued, "Speaking of, I just remembered I've been having nightmares about dogs; weird."

"So what happened when you adopted the dog?"

"Wait, about the dreams, it felt like déjà vu. It's crazy because there's nothing scary about the dream, yet it's the most terrified I've ever felt. When I see the dog, or even feel the dog's presence in the dream, it turns into a nightmare and I wake up before anything happens."

Elizabeth found herself drawn to Ann's story.

"Sometimes it's Sparky, other times it's this smaller, skinny dog, and other times it's just the feeling of a dog's presence. It's so weird. I'm getting goose-bumps just talking about it. Look," Ann showed Elizabeth her arm.

"Your dreams are so vivid. I wish I could remember my dreams with that much detail."

"I wish I never had these dreams. I wish we never got that dog." Ann thought for a second, "Never mind, I'm glad we did," she laughed. "But those nightmares, I tell ya. Sometimes after a nightmare, I just lay in bed, dead tired, wanting to go back to sleep, but I fight myself not to because if I do, I know I'll go right back into that dream. So, I have to snap myself out of it, think about something else, and then go back to sleep. Problem with that is, sometimes when I snap myself out of sleep, it takes a long time to fall back to sleep. You ever have that experience?"

"I think I know what you're talking about," Elizabeth said. "So, you don't like the dog."

"No, yea, I mean, I guess it's a love/hate thing."

Elizabeth tried to psychoanalyze, "Cuz your dream clearly shows you don't like the dog, unless there's something about him that scares you?"

"Well, you know what he did to Tommy."

"Yea, you told me about that, but that was because he had to save Tommy, right?"

"Yea. True. At least that's what Tommy said. That boy would do anything for that dog, even lie like that."

"Give the dog a break. He's a freaking savior. I would place him on a golden pedestal if I were you; saving my son? Heck. He'd be front page news."

"When I got there, he had my son's arm in his mouth and wouldn't let go. And ever since then, the nightmares began."

"That makes perfect sense. Obviously, that was a traumatic situation, not only for Tommy, but for you as well. To top it off, it looked like an attack to you, so the incident was recorded in your subconscious as a traumatic situation to be blamed on the dog. Had Tommy fallen off the cliff, you probably would've been having nightmares about falling."

"Well explain this, counselor," Ann laughed. "Who's the other dog?"

"What other dog?"

"You're not listening. I said my nightmares are sometimes with Sparky and sometimes with another smaller, skinny dog."

"The other dog is George," Elizabeth laughed. "You got dog problems. I'm not a dream interpreter. Let's get outta here. My butt's hurting on this hard bench."

George returned home without Tommy about a couple of hours after the police left the Carson's home. George heard Sparky's excited barks coming from inside the house. Sparky heard George's car approach and assumed Tommy was with him. George opened the door to come inside, and Sparky tried to nudge his way past him, wanting to get to Tommy. George closed the gap between himself and the door, and shoved Sparky back inside. George was still upset at Sparky from the prior encounter they had, and wanted to ensure Sparky knew who was in charge. Sparky seemed to have forgotten, or forgave George for shooting at him. Sparky moved aside and waited for George to enter so he could make another attempt to run outside. George slammed the door shut.

"You can't go anywhere today."

George headed toward the refrigerator and retrieved a cold can from the frig. Sparky sat by the door, calmly watching George go from the kitchen to the living room couch, remote in one hand and beer in the other. Sparky wondered how to get out. He knew Tommy wasn't outside the house, but wanted to find Tommy, and was frustrated at the continuous separation George enforced.

During a commercial break, George glanced to see what Sparky was up to. Sparky remained by the door, staring at George. George felt Sparky's frustration. Sparky didn't take his eyes off of George.

"So, this is what they mean when they say, 'dogging, ha?"

George knew the dog didn't have any fear of him and he didn't like that. It made him feel uncomfortable that there was another male living in his home who didn't respect his role as the alpha. It was not ok for George to feel uncomfortable or fear anyone living in his own home. The staring had gone on long enough. George couldn't take it anymore.

"What are you looking at?"

Sparky didn't turn away.

"I said, 'What are you looking at?' Don't look at me. Look the other way."

Sparky appeared relaxed, as if staring off into a calming ocean; looking straight through George. George tried to talk himself out of making Sparky look away, since Sparky didn't even bat an eye.

"I kicked him when I came inside," George thought. "Sparky knows who's in charge. If he tries anything –."

Sparky barked. George nearly fell off the couch from being startled. He spilled some beer on his shirt.

"What the hell was that for?"

George stood up pointing the remote at the dog, "You better stop staring. Go outside and play or something."

He wanted the intimidating dog out of his home and away from him. Sparky's tongue poured out of his mouth in happiness. He got up and turned to the door, waiting for George to open it. George saw how happy Sparky got at the thought of letting him out, so he decided against it. He didn't open the door.

"You can't go outside. If you listen to me and do as I say, I might consider letting you out later."

Sparky walked back to the same spot and sat in the same position, as if he never moved.

"Now, go to Tommy's room or do something, but get outta here."

Sparky remained defiantly motionless. George approached Sparky and stomped his foot. Sparky didn't flinch. George realized Sparky wasn't going to move. It became a game of chicken. George stared back at Sparky and tried to look angry, but inside he was getting nervous at Sparky's emotionless face. He gave up the staring contest and pretended to need something from the kitchen. He took the long route, passing by Sparky and extending his leg out, bumping Sparky along the way. Sparky stayed in his spot. He watched George, knowing George was up to no good. George opened the freezer. He pulled out a piece of frozen meat and placed it on the cutting board. George became increasingly frustrated at Sparky's silent resistance. He was also aggravated that he felt the need to pretend he was busy in the kitchen. George struggled between leaving the dog alone and his need to exert dominance. George tried cutting the hard, frozen meat, but it was hard as a rock. He stabbed it to try to break a piece off. He looked outside the kitchen window and remembered Sparky dumping the dog food. His frustration grew even more. The knife slipped off the meat, banging against the cutting board. George continued to stab and chop at the meat; aggravated stabs followed by reckless cuts. George held onto the meat with one hand while cutting with the other. He looked out the window. The knife slid off the frozen meat and sliced across warm thawed flesh.

"Ahh!" George yelled.

Sparky stood up, wondering what the commotion was about. George was in pain. He held his hand to his face. There was a deep gash across his finger. He saw white flesh, but no blood. In the midst of the pain, George was surprised that blood didn't pour out. He shook his hand trying to shake off the pain when blood rushed to the wound. Blood spilled all over the place; splattering against the floor, counters, and walls.

"Damn it!"

George looked at his finger. His hand was covered in blood. Sparky walked over to the blood-splattered wall. He sniffed it, and waited for George to look away. George focused on controlling the bleeding. Sparky licked the blood off the wall. George grabbed a soiled towel and wrapped it around his finger, tying it tightly. The pain began to subside. He grabbed the piece of meat that broke off. Sparky's attention was at the drops on the floor. George threw the meat at him, hitting him on the top of his head. Sparky ducked, and turned to George. Sparky wanted to be left alone to clean up George's bloody mess. George wanted to go to the living room and relax on the couch, but he had to get past Sparky to get there, or take the longer way. George could not allow his gains, shoving the dog, sacrificing his finger, and hitting him on the head, to go to waste by avoiding Sparky and taking the long way to the living room. He also felt if he tried to push Sparky aside this time, Sparky might retaliate. George thought about how to reduce the tension, while still clinging on to his perceived victories.

"That's your treat. Eat it," George said while pointing to the piece of meat he threw at him. "I was giving you your food. Any other dog would be excited for that. Go on and eat."

Sparky bent his head closer to the meat and sniffed. It wasn't tempting. Nonetheless, Sparky licked the meat, trying to work up a taste for it. George realized this was his chance to make his way to the living room. Sparky licked the meat across the kitchen floor, moving it like a hockey puck across an ice rink. He licked and licked.   George   walked   right   past   Sparky, unintentionally grazing him. Sparky stopped licking the meat.   He turned back to the drops of blood while George got comfortable on the couch.

George sat on the couch with his legs crossed on the coffee table. He held the can of beer in his left injured hand, and used the remote with his right. The rag on his finger started turning red. The wetness of the blood loosened the knot. George didn't care as long as the rag stayed on and blood didn't drip. Sparky finished licking all the stains he could find. Like a great white shark, he caught on to the scent of fresh blood. He turned around and laid eyes on the source; the bloody rag. Sparky turned to the meat and sniffed it one last time before approaching George. George ignored Sparky. He was satisfied at the result of the confrontation. George didn't mind his proximity.   Sparky didn't appear agitated. George   thought   Sparky   might   finally   want   his companionship, especially since Tommy wasn't around. Sparky sat beside the couch, next to George.   He lowered his head to sniff the rag. George tried to pat Sparky on the head while searching for a television program.   Sparky moved his head to avoid being touched. He had something else in mind.

"Stupid dog, you want me to be nice or not?"

Sparky   moved   in   closer   to   smell   the   rag, unintentionally bumping his head against George's can. As a reflex, George gripped the can tighter to avoid dropping the beer. The pressure pained his finger. He got upset and slapped Sparky with the back of his hand, denting the can and spilling beer across Sparky's face and the rag.

"Get outta here, idiot."

Blood and beer dripped on the floor. The dog didn't retaliate. He was too distracted by the rag. The dog licked the mess off the old wooden floor. George got up to change the rag, since it was soaked in beer. Just as he stood, the dog sniffed his hand.

"Get the hell away," George pulled his hand away.

The dog was dead set on one thing, getting more of that taste in his mouth. He charged at the hand like he did with the mouse in the weeds and the rat in the shed.

"What the hell are you doing?"

George slapped the remote against the dog's face.

The dog missed his hand. George remembered his rifle under the coffee table. Even under the intensity of the moment, George thought about Tommy and how to explain Sparky's death. He knew Tommy wouldn't accept any explanation of why his dog had to die, but George wasn't going to stand for Sparky's behaviors any longer. It was either him or the dog. George reached underneath the table, tapping around for the gun. The dog dove in again, biting George's hand. George yelled. He pulled away from the coffee table, trying to wrestle his arm free. George and the dog were face to face. George saw a focus and determination in the dog's eyes that filled him with horror. The dog lost self-control and was determined to take his hand off or kill him. Blood gushed from George's hand into Sparky's mouth. Sparky chewed, enjoying every moment. George screamed at the top of his lungs, punching Sparky on the head. Teeth tore through the bloody rag, into his skin, flesh, and bones. George wasn't sure about the outcome of the altercation anymore. He lay down with his back to the floor, reaching for the gun with his good hand. He was close, but Sparky's pulls to rip his hand off drew him further away. George extended himself. The dog continued to tear George's hand off his body, pulling, tugging, and shaking his head. George cried. He was pulled further away from the gun. He couldn't take it anymore. It was do or die, and he had to figure something out. He kicked the table as hard as he could exposing the gun. Sparky took another bite, clamping further into George's hand.

George yelled, "Let go you damn dog!"

He kicked the dog on the muzzle. The dog turned away. George couldn't tell what he was doing, but it looked as if he hurt the dog. George grabbed the barrel of the gun. He brought his injured hand closer to help lift the gun when he noticed he had no hand. The dog tore it off from the wrist.

"Ahhhh!" he cried in horror.

Blood poured. George couldn't believe what he was seeing. The dog was distracted with eating his hand. George got up, cradled his injured hand into his abdomen, and held the rifle in the other. He straggled to the door and went outside. George needed a moment to lift and aim the rifle in case the dog came out after him.

The dog finished devouring the hand. He looked around and sensed more blood. He found a soaked spot on the living room carpet. A streak of blood led to the door. He followed it, licking some of the trail on the way to the door. He jumped and tore through the screen, following the trail of blood that led around the house toward the chicken coop. The dog picked up the pace and turned the corner when a booming sound filled the air. A bullet zipped past the dog's head. He ducked and saw George getting ready to fire another shot. He ran back to the front of the house. George took aim, waiting for the dog to reappear. He struggled to hold the gun. His hand trembled. The loss of blood weakened him both physically and mentally. George felt a sense of urgency. He needed to get to the hospital, but the phone and keys were inside. He kept his aim, hoping the dog would reappear soon, but there was no sign of him. His muscle strength weakened and his hand trembled. The chickens were huddled at the other end of the coop, away from George. For some reason, the chickens became startled again. This time, they clucked and ran toward George. George drew his attention to the back of the house, but there was still no dog in sight. He looked back and forth from the front to be back. Suddenly, he heard a thunderous bark. Goose-bumps propped up on the back of George's neck and ran down his spine. The chickens squawked, jumped, and tried to fly away to no avail. Sparky emerged from the back. George turned and fired a shot that struck the shed. The chickens ran to the middle of the coop, not knowing who to keep away from. The dog approached with confidence. George gained control of the gun and fired another shot, striking the corner of the house. The dog picked up his pace, running toward George. George tried to control the rifle, knowing he had one final shot. He aimed, but the dog dove on top of him knocking the gun away. He clamped down on the injured hand. George yelled. The chickens squawked.

7

Sparky sprinted along the center of Route 96. He saw a car approaching from ahead, so he slowed to a jog and moved to the side of the road. Joe, the passenger in the car, turned up the radio.

"There's a pattern of major storm systems to occur in a few days with all sorts of high and low pressure areas throughout the region. It's expected to bring in tornadoes, heavy rains, hail, and flash flooding. Meteorologists are considering this accumulation of weather patterns as one large storm; the largest in over a century for the region. For now, enjoy the weather while it lasts. As always, this is your news and storm alert station, KDST."

"What's that?" the driver asked.

"What?" Joe wondered as he kept his attention to the radio.

"That," the driver pointed up ahead.

Joe squinted, "Must be a coyote or something."

"A coyote? No way. Look how far we are and how large it is from here. Looks like a freaking lion or something."

Joe chuckled. "Get closer and drive slow. Be careful. You don't wanna hit it in case it jumps in the way."

The car slowed as they approached. Joe rolled his window down. Sparky decided to get off the road and mix in with the brush and weeds, twisting and turning his way through. He watched the people in the car as they watched him.

"God, it's a dog," Joe said.

The driver tried to get a good look.

"That is a dog. Wow, that thing is huge."

"That's the biggest dog I've ever seen," Joe said

"You think it could take on a lion or a bear?"

"You and your lions. No way! Lions are much faster, and have bigger teeth, and 20 knife like claws. A regular sized bear, maybe," Joe said.

"Looks like a German Shepherd."

"Yup, that's for sure. One on steroids," Joe laughed.

The driver threw the car in reverse.

"What are you doing?" Joe asked.

"I want to check it out. Take out the camera and take a picture."

"Just keep driving. It's just a big dog. You act like you never seen a dog before, sarayee," Joe said referencing an inside joke.

"Not so fast. Things like this, that you'll never see again, you're gonna regret not capturing it."

"I'm not getting out, just to let you know."

"Of course not. That dog is capable of ripping this car in half, let alone me and you."

"Let's go. You're scaring me now," Joe said.

"Come on, get the camera."

Sparky didn't like the uninvited attention. He continued on toward Carson's Garage. The brush slowed him down, so he hopped back on the side of the road, behind their car, and ran off.

"Hurry, he's getting away."

Joe snapped a couple of pictures. "He's gone."

"Did you get a good shot? Let me see."

There were two blurry images. A tail was visible in the second shot.

"See, you took too long. I told you to get the camera and you kept delaying."

Sparky decided to take a break off the side of the road. He rested and watched critters scattering to and fro in front of him. A large bug crawled on his paw. He lowered his muzzle and licked it. The bug fell off and scattered away. Sparky wanted to take a quick nap. The soothing sounds of warm winds blowing across the terrain helped Sparky relax. However, the movement of tall and dry brush kept him awake. A long weed kept bending over and tickling his ear. Sparky's ear flicked over and over again. He was too tired to move to a new spot.

Sparky felt guilty about his food. He wished things could return to normal, when his dog food and other meats satisfied his hunger. He didn't understand why the change occurred, but he does remember the first experience, the day at the cliff. Sparky felt alone. No one would accept him for how he was, except Tommy. Since the day of the cliff, he never looked to Tommy, or his arm, as potential food. In fact, thinking of Tommy in that way was a complete turnoff. Sparky had occasional nightmares after the incident at the cliff about eating Tommy, and not a single bite or drop of blood pleased him. After those rare nights, Sparky woke up feeling sick and uneasy, like a person with a hangover. Sparky was concerned with another thing; Tommy didn't mind the killing of the postal man, but how would he react to the murder of his father? Sparky had no intention of showing Tommy what he did to George. Sparky's eyes closed. His chin rested between his paws. His ears lowered. He took in a deep breath and tried to rest.

No sooner than he fell into a slumber, Sparky's ears perked up and turned in the direction of the noise. He opened his eyes, but continued to lay low. Unlike the sound from the car before, this one created tension within him. Sparky needed to get to Tommy, quick. He needed his main source of comfort. Sparky crawled closer toward the road to get a glimpse of who was approaching. He kept himself glued to the ground. A black and white sedan zipped past him down the road. Sparky got up and ran into the brush. The car suddenly came to a screeching halt. It looked familiar; it was the police car. The passenger door flung open and an officer came out. He looked left, and then right into Sparky's direction. The officer walked toward Sparky, who tried to hide behind the thick brush and weeds. His fur blended well with the background. However, Sparky felt uncomfortable with the officer walking toward him. He crawled backwards, inches at a time, being careful not to give himself away. He remained as quiet as possible. The officer's steps and strides increased in speed and size. All the muscles in Sparky's body tensed, particularly in his legs. He was ready to make a dash, but remained patient and stayed low. The officer continued getting closer. Just as Sparky was about to dart off, the officer stopped and looked around again. He was only a few feet away from Sparky when he unzipped his pants. Sparky looked away. He didn't want to make accidental eye contact through the brush. The sound of fluid splashing against the ground continued longer than Sparky had hoped for. The zipper sounded again, and the officer ran back toward the police car. The car sped off. Sparky plowed through the brush in front of him, making for a straight dash to the road. He needed to find Tommy before the police did. He sprinted along the side of the road staying alert in the event he needed to dash back into the landscape.

"It's the police, open the door! We have a search warrant to enter," Officer Myers banged on the door while holding a gun in the other hand.

Officer Matthews also had his gun drawn, pointed at the house, from a few feet back.

"Open the door, it's the police," Myers yelled again. He signaled for Matthews to walk the perimeter of the house.

"Myers," Matthews called out.

He waved Myers down to come over to the chicken coop.

"Oh my. That's a lot of blood," Myers said. He shook his head in disbelief. "There's bits of flesh on the ground. It looks like someone tried to cover it up with dirt, and didn't do a great job. And, this body was clearly dragged away, that way," Myers pointed toward the trees behind the coop. "Matthews, this is fresh blood."

"I know."

"This means, we have two murders on our hands, now."

This isn't good," Matthews said.

"We might be getting another 'missing persons' call soon, and then we'll know who."

"Let's see where the trail leads," Matthews said.

"Why don't you follow that lead while I stay here in the event someone shows up," Myers said.

Matthews followed the trail. It led around the coop and toward the trees. The trail faded as debris increased. Matthews walked a couple dozen more feet before he lost the trail.

"I can't tell what happened from here. There's too much debris," Matthews shouted.

"It's ok, let's check the house," Myers responded. Myers opened the door. It was unlocked, and the screen was torn. He entered with Matthews right behind him. "Looks like the dog's on the loose." Myers went into the living room and Matthews took the kitchen. "Matthews. Check this out."

"Myers," Matthews called out, "You need to come here first."

Myers ran to the kitchen.

"There's blood all over," Matthews said.

"There's a piece of meat on the floor," Myers noticed. He looked on the counter and saw a knife on the cutting board. "Looks like someone sliced his finger."

"Yea, that might be true. There's drops on the walls and the floor. It looks like they tried wiping it up."

"But now, look at this, Myers said. "It gets weirder." Myers went into the living room and Matthews followed. "Look," Myers pointed to the carpet.

"How did a cut in the kitchen that didn't have a trail of blood suddenly turn into a pool of blood in the living room?" Matthews asked. "And, the coffee table was tossed around, like there was an altercation."

"That's likely," Myers confirmed.

"I think I'm feeling overwhelmed. I mean, I'm fitting together small pieces, but completing the puzzle is confusing the hell out of me," Matthews said. "I can't wait till we find out what happened here."

"Soon enough. We'll get some answers soon. Let's get out there and find some leads on where these people could be, starting with the neighbors," Myers said.

Sparky saw the garage from a distance. He barked as he got closer. Tommy heard the barks. He was overjoyed at the sounds. He rushed out of the garage to an empty lot. He heard the barks again. Tommy was confused. The barking continued and was getting closer, but he didn't see Sparky. Finally, Sparky appeared from around the brush and onto the lot.

"Sparky!" Tommy shouted with excitement.

Tommy ran toward Sparky at full speed with arms wide open. Sparky slowed down to avoid a high-speed head-on collision. Even then, Tommy was thrown back when they came together. They could not have been happier. Sparky licked Tommy all over his face. Tommy closed his eyes and laughed.

"I missed you so much, boy. I missed you so much, you don't know."

Sparky pulled away, wanting to play a game of tag. Tommy got up and chased him. Sparky ran into the garage. He tried to hide under the car. Sparky turned sideways to fit his head. The rest of his body stuck out like a sore thumb.

"I see a big butt, but I can't find Sparky," Tommy pretended not to see him.

He approached quietly, repeating, "I see a big butt, but I can't find Sparky."

Tommy slapped Sparky on his tail, startling him and causing his head to hit the bottom of the car. Sparky got out, happy and ready to chase Tommy. Tommy ran out of the garage. Sparky began to chase, and immediately came to a sliding stop. He saw his water bowl and needed a drink. Tommy returned to the garage, wondering why Sparky stopped.

"Hey, what happened?"

Sparky never stopped playing in the middle of a game before. It dawned on Tommy; George didn't drop him off. No one did. Sparky ran all the way from home.

"Hey, boy. How'd you get here? Where's George?"

Sparky let out a light whimper, and resumed drinking.

"Did you run here all the way from home?"

Sparky finished drinking. Tommy rubbed his head.

"You ran here all the way from home?"

Sparky got happy.

"Wow. Boy, that's great. Now you can come here anytime you want. If George leaves me here all alone again, you can still come."

It was late in the afternoon. Tommy felt hunger pangs setting in. He clutched his growling stomach. Tommy hadn't eaten a proper meal in more than a day. Tommy didn't have anything to work on, nor did he have the energy to play with Sparky. Boredom extended the afternoon. Tommy relaxed outside the shop door with Sparky resting his head across his lap. He gently rubbed Sparky's head, moving across from ear to ear. Sparky's ears perked up. Tommy knew what it meant.

"Who is it? George?"

Sparky turned his head toward the east and barked. Their house is located to the west of the shop. Finally, Tommy saw a car pulling into the lot. Tommy eagerly rose to his feet and dusted his pants off. He took a whiff of his armpit. "Phew," Tommy was disgusted. He stuck his finger inside his belly button and smelled it. "I need a shower."

Tommy showered once a week, usually at the command of his mother, or when his body odor became unbearable, even for himself. It was that time again.

The driver frantically pulled out a small boy from the back seat.

"Hold on just a little bit longer, son."

"The bathroom?" the man asked.

Tommy stood there as if he were frozen. The man moved and spoke too fast for his brain to grasp.

"The bathroom, where's the bathroom?"

The words finally registered with Tommy, so he pointed to the bathroom.

"Thanks," the man darted off with his son.

"We need to get home, Sparky. I don't wanna be here anymore. George can run his own shop. I wanna go home."

Sparky barked.

The man came out without having washed either of their hands. He was in a hurry.

"Thanks for the bathroom, but it's filthy in there. You're out of toilet paper and soap. Thank God he didn't have to do number two."

He placed his son in the back seat.

"Can you give us a ride down the road?" Tommy asked.

The man placed his son in the booster seat and looked at Tommy.

"Wha?"

"I need a ride. My dog and I need a ride down the road to our home. Our car doesn't work and I don't know where my father is. My house is –."

"Sorry kid, I have to run. I'm in a hurry."

The man closed the rear door. He tried to get to the driver seat, but Sparky stood in his way blocking his entrance.

"Can you call your dog?"

Tommy stood, speechless. He didn't know why Sparky stood so close to the man preventing him from getting in his car. Tommy regained some hope as there was more time to convince the man.

194

"Please, Mr., it's a quick ride. Like 5 minutes."

"Boy, I need you to call your dog. I'm in a hurry."

Sparky barked. The man jolted backwards.

"Call your dog, before I get upset."

Sparky barked again. The man jumped again. He was upset at his sensitive reflexes. He didn't want to show any fear. The man puffed his chest and, in a firm voice, called out to Tommy.

"Boy, call your dog, now!"

Sparky growled and got closer to the man. The man took a few steps back.

"Your dog, call your dog!"

Sparky growled and barked.

The man closed his eyes, frightened by the loud barks.

"I'll call the police if I have to."

Tommy realized what Sparky was doing. Sparky wasn't going to attack the man. He wanted to intimidate the man into giving them a ride.

"Sir, Sparky wants a ride."

"No. He's asking for trouble. He looks like he's about to attack. I have a gun, and would hate to shoot him."

"Sparky, stop."

Sparky stepped back, but continued to growl.

"He seems to listen really well. Now call him back to you."

"Sir, we really need a ride. I'm hungry, and I don't know where my father is. It's getting dark, and we need to be home."

Sparky barked. His barks continued getting louder and louder. The boy inside the car began to cry.

Tommy had to yell for his voice to be heard over Sparky's barking. "He's not going to let you leave until you give us a ride."

"Ok, get inside the damn car. Both of you sit in the front seat. I don't want any of you in the back with my son."

"How can we fit?"

"Figure it out. You want the ride. Pull the chair back."

"Sparky, get in the car," Tommy said.

Sparky got excited. His tongue fell from his mouth. He jumped into the driver seat making his way to the passenger side. Tommy sat on the floor hugging his knees. Luckily, he was skinny enough to fit in the tight spot. Spittle rolled off Sparky's tongue and onto Tommy's back. Sparky closed his mouth, swallowed the spittle, and withdrew his tongue again. The driver looked at Tommy. He was disgusted at the boy, their bathroom, the spittle that he allowed onto his back, and the stench. The driver lowered both of the front windows and sped off.

"How far you got to go?" the driver asked.

"Oh, not far. Just down the road there's a turn."

"Just keep me posted, I'd hate to miss it."

The rest of the ride was silent, except when Tommy provided directions.

"There's our home," Tommy pointed.

The man pulled off the road that led to their driveway.

"Ok, out you go."

Tommy tried to get out, but was squashed under Sparky. He reached for the door handle and opened it.

"Out you go, boy."

Sparky jumped out. Tommy grabbed the door handle and pulled himself up.

"Thank you, Mr."

The man didn't say a word and sped off.

Tommy approached the front door. It was surrounded by yellow tape that read "Do Not Cross". He ducked under it and went inside.

Moments later, a car pulled into their driveway. Sparky ran to the door and barked.

"Relax, boy."

Tommy looked out the window.

"It's mom!" he shouted. "Maybe she brought us food."

Tommy opened the door and ran out to her car, trailed by Sparky.

"Tommy? What's this police tape for? Where's your father?

"I don't know where George is. Mom, I'm very hungry. George dropped me off at the shop for like two days. I had nothing to eat."

Ann could see the paleness in Tommy's face.

"Boy, I told you. I told you to come and live with me. George can't take care of you. Let's go inside."

Ann looked in the refrigerator.

"Tommy, what's the police tape for? What happened?"

"Oh, Mom. Can you keep a secret?"

Ann turned around with a bowl in her hands.

"What kind of secret?"

"Well, you know the mailman?"

"What mailman? Our mailman?"

"Yea, the guy who brings us mail."

"What about him?"

"Well," Tommy said with a grin. "Sparky – kind of hurt him."

"WHAT?" she yelled.

"Relax, Mom. It's ok. I helped Sparky hide the body."

The bowl slipped from her hands. Glass and grapes shattered and scattered across the kitchen floor. She walked up to Tommy.

"Hide the body? Tommy – What are you talking about? She couldn't believe what she heard.

"Mom?"

Ann sat on the floor, and set her hand on a piece of glass.

"Mom, your hand is bleeding."

Ann looked at her hand and removed it from the glass."

"Tommy, honey, where's George? Where's your father?"

"I don't know, Mom. Why you crying?"

"Tommy, I don't believe what you're saying. You don't know what you're saying."

"About what?"

"About what? Tommy, about the mailman. You're lying. Sparky didn't hurt the mailman and you didn't hide anybody."

Sparky ran to the door and barked.

"What is it, boy?"

Tommy looked outside and didn't see anything. He opened the door to let Sparky out. Sparky ran to the cellar door and pawed at the lock.

"Mom!" Tommy got excited. "Come, look. Let me show you."

Ann jumped off the floor and followed Tommy, patting her skirt along the way to remove any glass or grapes that might have caught on. Tommy opened the cellar door.

"What are you doing?" Ann asked.

"The body, he's in there. I mean, he was, but – oh just go and see."

Ann went inside the cellar and turned the light on. Her breathing became heavy. She held on the handrail.

Ann turned to Tommy, holding her hand against her chest to calm herself down.

"Where's the body?"

"Over there," Tommy pointed toward the trees, "But you have to promise not to tell anyone."

Sparky barked at Tommy. Tommy looked back at him.

Ann grabbed Tommy by the shoulders and shook him.

"Where's the mailman?"

"Over there," he continued pointing. "We threw it over the canyon."

Ann ran her hand through her hair and pulled it back.

"I knew it," she mumbled. "I shoulda brought the boy home with me. I shoulda brought him home. Where's the police? Do they know about this? Have they seen you?"

Tommy shrugged his shoulders.

"Oh my, oh my. Come with me. Both of you, come with me. Let's get outta here. I have to hide you, otherwise the police will find you."

The old neighbor in the front heard Ann's car pull up. She knew the house had been sectioned off by the police. By the time she got outside, Ann was driving away. She went back inside to phone the police.

"Tommy, I'm gonna take you to my apartment until I can figure out what to do. In the meantime, I'm gonna drop the dog off at the shelter, where we got him from."

"No, Mom, no," Tommy slammed his feet on the floor in a tantrum.

"Tommy, we can't fit this dog anywhere. Everywhere we go, people will notice. He'll be on the news soon, and we'll get caught."

"I'm not going anywhere without Sparky. Never," Tommy crossed his arms.

"I gotta think. I gotta think," Ann said as she drove into a parking spot on Main Street's shopping strip. Old Town Café was across the street.

"Let's go inside, get a bite to eat."

Tommy tried to get Sparky out.

"Wait. Leave him here. He's got no leash or anything. It's unsafe, leave him in the car."

"Hey, boy. We'll be right back," Tommy said.

Sparky whimpered.

"It's ok, boy. We'll be right back."

He shut the door and followed Ann into the café.

"Welcome to Old Town Café. Please have a seat right here and let me know if you have any questions. Breakfast is served all day –."

"I know," Ann smiled, "Don't I know."

Ann looked around and saw a couple of people looking their way.

"Our best seller is the "Storm Breakfast," the waitress smiled.

"What is it?" Tommy asked.

"Glad you asked. It's two eggs, topped with your choice of meat, topped with two more eggs, and layered with cheese."

"Umm, sounds good. I want that."

"And for you, ma'am?"

"Nothing for me."

Ann looked outside for passing police cars. It reminded her of her high school days, hiding and running from authority. She scanned the diner to see if anyone noticed them. A male customer looked down as soon as she laid eyes on him. She still couldn't believe what Tommy told her.

"Tommy, tell me what happened again."

"I dunno," Tommy shrugged his shoulders. "Sparky called me to the basement at night. I went with him and he showed me the postal –."

Ann pressed her finger against Tommy's mouth, "It's ok son. It's ok. We can talk later."

Ann looked around the café again. She saw the man who looked at her when they first entered, looking at her again. Her heart rate increased. She looked away. Tommy's plate arrived. It was packed and piled high. Without hesitation, Tommy dove in and enjoyed every bite, swallowing faster than he could chew. His fork dripped with yolk and cheese in one hand, while he held tightly to a biscuit in the other. Ann wanted to see if the man was still staring at her, but didn't want to make it look obvious. She lowered and tilted her head as if pretending to stretch her neck. She noticed the man looking outside. It appeared as if he was checking out her car. Sparky was relaxed and motionless in the backseat. She turned to the man and saw him looking at her again. Ann got nervous. She started talking to herself.

"He saw the dog. He knows it's us. Oh my," Ann grew in panic. "Son, hurry up. We have to go. We have to go before the police get here," she whispered.

"I'm not finished," Tommy said with his mouth full of food.

Ann looked over to the man as inconspicuously as she could. He was talking to the waitress and pointing at them.

"Oh my God. Tommy, we have to leave."

Ann got up to get a to-go box from the counter.

"Can I help you with something?" the waitress returned.

"Yes, I need a to-go box, and the check. We're in a hurry."

"Sure, I'll be right over with that."

The waitress brought the to-go box, but no check.

"Ma'am," Ann said. "The check? We're in a hurry."

"Ok, I understand, but…"

Ann's heart nearly exploded in her chest. Why was the waitress stalling? What was she about to say? Were the police on their way to arrest them? Should they forget the check, the food, and make a run for it?

"…your check has been paid for by that man over there at that table. He'd like to connect with you, if that's ok. If not, it's totally fine, and I apologize for the awkwardness."

"Connect? Wha? I don't understand."

"Probably because –."

"Never mind," Ann said. "We have to go, let's go Tommy," she said while dumping the rest of his food in the box.

Ann's mind was overwhelmed with the postal man, the police, and hiding Tommy. They left the café in a hurry.

"Excuse me," a male voice called out from behind as they crossed the street.

Ann pretended not to hear.

"Ma'am?"

Ann got in her car and, before shutting the door, made eye contact with the man.

He waved his hand to her. She smiled, looked away, and drove off.

Ann slowed down before pulling into the Carson's Garage lot. She was being careful to ensure the coast was clear. There were no police or other cars present, so she drove in and parked. The garage was also surrounded with police tape that read "Do Not Cross."

Ann lifted the tape. The garage door was locked with a heavy duty padlock. The door to the waiting area was also locked. She knew no one was here, but wanted to get Tommy and Sparky inside until she could come up with a plan.

"Tommy, you got the keys to the shop?"

Tommy and Sparky came out of the car.

"Yea Mom, I do, but what happened to Chuck's car?"

Ann looked around and didn't see his car. "Maybe, your dad took it? Where the hell is he?"

Tommy pulled out a set of keys from his pocket and unlocked the door. Ann went inside. Tommy looked down at the lock on the garage door. He didn't recognize it, so he tried to unlock it with one of the keys. The first key didn't work. He tried another key.

"No, Tommy. Leave the garage door shut. We don't want anyone thinking it's open and coming in. We don't want anyone to know you guys are here."

Ann looked around. She became increasingly alarmed at the condition of the shop and wondered where Tommy would sleep; the sun was about to set.

"Son, are you ok to spend the night here with Sparky?"

"Yea, we're ok. I spent the night here before."

"You spent a night here before?"

"Yea, all alone. Mean George took Sparky away from me and made me spend the night all by myself. And then a dog ate my stomach."

"What? What are you talking about?" Ann was extremely stressed, and anything that didn't make sense added to her tension. "What dog, Tommy? What stomach?"

"I was in the car and he came in and killed me."

"Tommy, was that a nightmare?"

"It was a dream."

Ann felt relieved, and brought the conversation back to Tommy spending the night in the garage.

"He left you here, alone? God," Ann looked up, "Why would he do such a thing? That's so unlike him. He would die for you."

Tommy shrugged his shoulders. He tried to open the door that connected the shop to the garage, but it was also locked.

"What the –," he remarked wondering why everything was locked.

Tommy unlocked the door with his keys.

"Where you goin'?" Ann asked.

"To the car, to sleep."

"Is that where you slept last time?"

"Yea, Mom."

Ann felt a little better knowing Tommy was ok with spending the night here. She watched the two of them get cozy in the car and, for the first time, felt happy that Tommy had Sparky as a companion.

"He won't let nothing happen to my boy."

Ann got in her car and turned the headlights on. She shifted the gear into drive when she suddenly saw a pair of bright eyes looking at her from amidst the brush. She got nervous, not for herself, but for Tommy. The doors to the shop and garage were locked. Tommy had Sparky right beside him. The animal in the brush didn't appear large. For all she knew, it could be a fox or a small lost dog, but the eyes touched upon her deepest feelings of fear, and she didn't know why. She felt the way she did in her nightmares about the mystery dog and Sparky.

"They'll be ok. No one's gonna mess with them as long as Sparky's around. I have to get home as soon as possible, and talk to Elizabeth about this. I'll be back to get you outta here," she said to herself.

Ann drove off the lot.

Tommy woke up from the noon heat. He was completely exhausted, and the extra sleep couldn't have come at a better a time. Sparky sat patiently by the shop door, looking out into the quiet world. Tommy saw the top of Sparky's head through the window of the door that separated the waiting area from the garage. Tommy wondered how Sparky got out of the car. He yawned and stretched out wide, fists scraping against the ceiling of the car as he let out a loud moan. Tommy felt great. That was, until his stomach rumbled.

"Oh, man. I wish I could have that breakfast again," he said.

A car pulled onto the lot.

Tommy got out and greeted Sparky by rubbing his head. Sparky's attention was to the new arrival.

"Hey, son," an old man came out of the car. "You guys have gas? There isn't one around for miles."

"Oh yea. George wanted to get one, but he couldn't afford to," he said.

"You would do well with a gas station here. This is a perfect spot." An awkward silence ensued before the old man continued, "So, what you guys got going on here?" He walked into the shop to have a look around. He picked up candy, looked at the back of the labels, checked for expiration dates, and set them back. "This place looks like I run it," he laughed. "Where's the owner?"

"I dunno," Tommy shrugged his shoulders.

The old man continued to rummage through the half empty snack rack. He picked up a chocolate bar, tore the package open, and bit into it.

"What the hell is this? It's chewy and gooey." Spit dripped from the side of his mouth as he chewed the bar. "This damn thing gonna make me get new dentures. You better hope this crap comes off my teeth." The old man put his dirty finger in his mouth to clear out a piece of the chocolate bar that stuck to his molars.

Candies were mixed with chocolate bars in one large messy pile. Tommy watched the old man walk straight into the garage, looking around as if it were his own.

"Well, this looks like a place where we can get some good work done."

Tommy followed him.

"You're not much of a talker are ya?" the old man turned around and asked.

"No, I'm not."

"Don't seem too bright neither."

He continued walking around the garage. The old man found a car jack.

"Tell you what; I'll just roll this out to my vehicle, gotta fix a flat tire at home, and I'll bring her right back."

Tommy didn't say anything.

The old man dragged the jack out of the shop, across the gravel, and headed straight for his car. Tommy got worried and chased him down.

"Sir. Are you taking that?"

"Yea, boy. Don't you run up on me like that. You could get hurt, dontcha know?"

"Ah, no?"

"Hell na, you ain't bright," the old man chuckled.

He continued toward his car, popping open the trunk.

"Sir," Tommy placed his hand on the man's shoulder.

"Dontcha touch me, boy. I thought I warned you already."

"But, you can't take that. We need it for the garage."

"I told you, I'll bring her right back."

He bent down to lift the jack.

"Sir."

"Ahh," the old man moaned in pain, holding his lower back. "Damn it. God damn it. It's my damn back again."

Tommy tried to help the man stand straight.

"Dontcha touch me, damn it! Can't you see my back is out? Keep your damn jack. I don't need it."

He hobbled his way to the driver seat, sat inside and rested a minute. Tommy walked the jack back into the garage with Sparky behind him. The old man sped off in the direction he came from.

Teresa slowed the car as she pulled onto the Carson's Garage lot.

Soraya, the passenger, was worried.

"What are you doing here?" Soraya asked.

"Stopping. You said you needed to use the bathroom."

"Yea, but not that bad."

"Oh my God. What do you mean? You just asked me to stop when I see a restroom."

"I don't like the feeling of this place. Let's go somewhere else."

"Soraya. Would you get out?"

"Let's just go. I don't need to go anymore."

"Stop acting crazy. Wait here while I check for a restroom."

Teresa put the car in park. Tommy came out with Sparky by his side. Teresa saw Sparky and decided not to exit the car.

"Oh my God, Teresa, let's go. That freakin' dog could swallow me. I thought your dog was big."

"My dog is big. But this dog –."

"Could you please drive away?" Soraya pleaded. "I don't like the way that guy looks."

"He's just a kid," Teresa said.

"You're making this road trip very stressful for me. Just freakin' drive."

"You and your stress. Fine. But, don't blame me if you have to pee in your pants."

"Fine, I won't. Just get outta here."

Teresa shifted the gear back into drive and drove off.

Tommy watched, wondering why they stopped and left.

"They're weird," he said. Sparky confirmed with a bark.

"Tonight on the news at 10, police are on the search for a giant German Shepherd and its owners. Stay tuned for details."

Ann was shocked. The sense of urgency to get Tommy out of town increased.

"Your family is famous," Elizabeth said. "Will they come looking for you too?"

"I don't know. No one knows where I live, except George, and I don't know where he's gone off to."

Suddenly, she couldn't breathe. It felt as if the world was closing in.

"I'm dying," Ann said.

"What's the matter?" Elizabeth asked.

Elizabeth sat beside Ann, but Ann pushed her away.

"I need space. I can't breathe."

"I'm gonna call the ambulance," Elizabeth said.

"No!" The feeling intensified. She took deep breaths. "No ambulance, no police, no hospital," she emphasized.

Ann went out to the patio. She looked up at the sky, which released the choke she felt against her throat. The sensation began to subside. Elizabeth rubbed her back. Ann turned around.

"I gotta get my boy outta here," she said, grabbing her purse on the way out the door.

A car pulled in. It was an old pick up and looked as if it could use some service. The guy jumped out of his truck.

"Hey, man," he greeted Tommy. "Hey, I need to use a phone, man."

Tommy was disappointed. He hoped the guy needed a quick repair, which meant quick cash. He wanted money to buy another Storm Breakfast. But, that's not what the guy came in for.

"Umm, our phone don't work."

"It's real quick man, real quick."

The thin, pale guy was eager to get inside and make a call. His clothes were dirty and it didn't look like he had showered in some time. As a matter of fact, he looked like a 30 year old version of Tommy, except, he spoke fast, very fast; a nervous kind of fast. He was jittery and, occasionally, his facial muscles twitched. Tommy couldn't tell if the twitching was intentional or not, but it annoyed him. Why wouldn't he stop moving his head and neck like that?

"The phone doesn't work," Tommy said.

"Listen, I need a phone. Any phone. A pay phone. Something."

"I don't have a pay phone. And George always said, 'we ain't got no service in here.'"

"Let me check inside," the guy insisted.

He twitched his way past Tommy and Sparky. Tommy wanted the guy to leave. The guy headed toward the counter in the waiting area. He continued into the garage and headed for the desk, which was smeared with grease, fingerprints, and hand marks. Papers were littered across the desk. The guy pushed aside some papers as he reached for the phone sitting on the desk. He lifted the receiver, and gave Tommy a bad look. He put the receiver to his ear. It was silent. The guy tapped the hook several times. There was no dial tone.

"Damn!" he yelled. "Can I get a damn phone around here?"

Sparky barked.

"Hey, kid. I need a phone. I know you have one. How do you make calls?"

The guy got in Tommy's face. Sparky barked.

"I don't call anyone."

"Bull shit," the guy's spittle landed on Tommy's face. "This is a shop, ain't it?"

"Yea," Tommy wiped his face.

Sparky barked again.

The guy stepped in closer. His nose touched Tommy's. Tommy got nervous. Sparky felt Tommy's apprehension. Sparky came right beside Tommy, letting him know everything would be ok. Sparky's face was lined up to the guy's chest. The guy drew back.

"Take it easy, boy. That's a big dog you got there." He turned his attention back to Tommy. "So, what phone do you use to order parts and stuff? How do you call your customers to pick up their car?"

Tommy thought for a second. Good question. How did George call customers back? The guy didn't give time for a reply. His frustration increased with each passing second. He got close again.

"WHAT PHONE DO YOU USE?"

Sparky stood up on his hind legs and pushed the guy back, creating space from Tommy. The guy was taken completely by surprise, and Sparky's weight was overbearing. He fell backward cracking his elbow against the desk before landing on the floor. The guy quickly got up. Sparky saw blood trickling down his forearm. His tongue fell in excitement. Tommy loved it when Sparky was happy.

"You damn dog," the guy yelled.

He exited the shop and headed back to his pickup. Sparky looked to Tommy, as if he sought permission to play with the guy.

"What is it, boy?"

Sparky let out a pleading whimper and followed the guy.

The guy turned around.

"What's he want? I'm leaving."

"I dunno," Tommy shrugged his shoulders.

The guy continued to walk. He reached his pickup and noticed Sparky was even closer.

"Get your damn dog before –."

Sparky bit the guy's elbow and pulled him to the ground. The guy yelled. Tommy stood and watched.

"Get your damn dog off me before I kill him."

"Sparky!" Tommy yelled.

Sparky released his arm.

"Crazy ass dog. I'm calling the cops. I'm gonna get animal control to put this beast away," the guy yelled. "You're gonna get sued. I can't believe you let your dog bite me."

Sparky whimpered. He looked back at Tommy. His whimpers grew louder and louder as the man pulled himself into the truck. Sparky wasn't worried about animal control. His focus was on one thing, the great tasting crunchy elbow. Tommy became worried about animal control. It was enough that the police were already looking for them. He couldn't allow for it.

"Get him, boy."

The man pulled the door to shut it when Sparky suddenly jammed his head through the opening.

"What the – get the hell away. Get your dog, kid. He listens to you," the guy yelled while he struggled to push Sparky away.

Sparky bit the guy's arm and pulled him out of the pickup. The guy fell to the ground, waving his arms out in front of him to protect himself and cover up. Sparky fell on top of him. They rolled around on the ground. The man yelled. Tommy plugged his ears and turned away. He wanted Sparky to enjoy himself. Besides, he didn't care for the guy, and couldn't let him get away to tell everyone.

The man yelled at the top of his lungs, "GET YOUR DAMN DOG OFF ME!"

They looked like a couple of wrestlers, one atop the other, moving to the left and to the right, rolling around with legs and feet pushing against the ground surrounding themselves in a ball of dust. Blood dripped on the gravel. Tommy walked into the shop with his fingers in his ears. The man struck Sparky on his head with his free hand several times. It didn't faze Sparky.

Tommy's arms were tiring. He unplugged his ears. He heard a dragging sound against the gravel. There were no more yells or sounds of struggle. Suddenly, Tommy heard a car skidding across the gravel lot. He looked outside and saw a sports car racing up to, and nearly striking, Sparky. Sparky was carrying the body of the guy to the back of the shop. He released the body. A well-built, middle-aged man got out of the car. He saw the mauling victim laying lifeless on the ground.

"Get the hell away from him, you damn dog."

He reached into the car and grabbed a knife from the glove compartment. The man felt confident as he wrapped his hand around the sharp and large knife. He thought, "One strike anywhere on the dog, and it's over." The man was very upset and disturbed at what he saw when he drove by.

"Is anyone here?" he called out. "I'm gonna kill this dog unless you come out and take him away," he yelled.

Sparky took a step toward the guy, as if calling his bluff.

The guy yelled, "Get away, shoo."

He swung the knife at Sparky, who was still a few feet away. Sparky paid attention to the weapon realizing its danger. He growled.

"What are you doing?" Tommy yelled from the shop.

"Your damn dog just killed this man. What the hell are you doing inside? Didn't you see or hear anything?"

"Leave Sparky alone, that's his food."

"Food? You kidding me? You mean you knew he was killing him?"

"Sparky can't eat anything else."

The man was beside himself. He couldn't believe what he was hearing. This was not going to be a conversation of reason.

"Where's your dad? Who runs this place?"

The man pointed the knife in Tommy's direction as he spoke. Sparky growled again.

"Sir, could you please leave him alone? He didn't do anything to you."

"Are you alone? Who's here with you, I said?"

"No one. Just us."

"Ok, I tell you what. So I don't have to hurt the dog, why don't you tie him up to the back of that pickup and give me the keys. I'll drive him straight down to the animal shelter, and they'll take care of him."

"Take Sparky away from me? No way."

"Kid, you don't have a choice! This isn't going to end well if you don't do what I say."

Sparky's growl intensified.

"Sir, Sparky is gonna hurt you if you don't leave."

"Oh he will, will he?" The man walked toward Sparky. Sparky's growls continued, although he took a step back each time the man took a step closer. The man swung the knife from side to side. Sparky continued to back up. Tommy became worried. Sparky was on the defensive.

"Get in the back of that pickup, pooch."

Sparky looked to Tommy for direction. Tommy's worry increased. Sparky felt Tommy's concern. His best friend was in pain, and it was all because of this knife swinging man. Sparky stopped taking steps back. He lowered his hind legs as the man came closer. Sparky was in attack mode, ready to pounce on the knife and the man waving it. The man stopped approaching after Sparky stood his ground.

"Get in the pickup."

"Leave him alone!" Tommy yelled.

Sparky sprang at him. The man threw his left arm in the air, feeding it into Sparky's mouth. He swung the knife at Sparky, cutting his side. Sparky bit down harder. The man yelled. He swung again stabbing Sparky on the side. Sparky let go and jumped back to avoid further damage.

"Yea, get him boy. Get him!" Tommy cheered him on.

Sparky didn't want the risk. The man hoped the dog wouldn't continue the fight either. He was hurt. He wanted to leave, and call the police. But, Sparky couldn't let Tommy's cheers go unattended. The man walked backward toward his car, holding the knife out in front of him. Sparky followed.

"I told you to leave him alone. Now you'll be his food," Tommy cheered.

"If you don't want your dog to die, I suggest you call him off."

The shock and adrenalin in the man subsided, and fear kicked in. Fight was replaced with flight.

"You can't kill him. Sick him, boy."

Sparky attacked, unconcerned about the knife. The man gave his left arm again and fell backward, tripping over the dead man's body. Sparky was on top, shaking his head from side to side attempting to tear off his arm. The man yelled and stabbed Sparky again. Sparky whimpered and backed off. He looked to Tommy and felt disappointed that he let Tommy down by not killing the man.

"You ok?" Tommy asked.

The man felt emboldened. The return of adrenalin in his veins replaced the pain in his gruesomely gashed arm.

"You want some more?" the man yelled.

The pain returned in just a few seconds. He turned and made a run for his car. Sparky's instincts kicked in. His prey was fleeing and his back was turned. Sparky caught up just as the man opened his door. He jumped on his back catching the rear of his neck. The man yelled. Blood squirted all over his shirt. Warm, red fluid dripped across his chest. The man turned with every bit of energy he could muster and stabbed Sparky, again, although it didn't strike deep. Sparky jumped back. The man pulled himself into the car, pressed his hand against the side of his neck, and drove off. Sparky barked as the car pulled out of the lot and disappeared. Tommy ran and hugged Sparky to congratulate him.

"You're the best!"

Tommy rubbed Sparky's side. He noticed Sparky's coat stained with blood. He touched the wound, causing Sparky to whimper.

"I'm sorry, boy. I'm sorry," he hugged Sparky again.

Sparky's ears perked up. He pulled away from Tommy.

"What is it, boy?"

Sparky jogged out onto the road and looked in the direction the car drove off to, but there was no car.

"What is it, boy?"

Suddenly, they saw a cloud of dust rising to the side of the road amidst the brush. Sparky went after it.

8

Officer Matthews drove west on 96 toward the Carson's residence. He slowed down by Carson's Garage to take a quick look before passing. It didn't look like anyone had been there, so he drove on. Just as Matthews was about to pick up his speed, something caught his attention. He slammed on the brakes, coming to a skidding stop. Smoke from the burnt rubber clouded the back of the patrol car. Matthews put the car in reverse, keeping an eye out for what caught his attention. He kept in reverse, wondering if a piece of tin foil flickered the sun in his direction, or if it was something else. He arrived to a section of the brush that didn't look right. Matthews drove back a few more feet. The area appeared mowed down or trampled on, and the width looked like a car must have gone through. At night, it's not uncommon for tired drivers to veer off the long stretches of dark road. Matthews has seen his share of accidents, and illegal off-roaders. He parked the car and got out to take a look. Matthews walked cautiously amidst the sharp and pointy brush. Dry weeds crushed and crackled under his feet. Something shined in the close distance. He looked back just to make sure nothing was behind him. The patrol car was barely visible from where he stood. He proceeded to the shiny metal object. It was orange. He finally made out what it was; the trunk of a sports car. He rushed toward the driver side. The door was open and no one was inside. Blood was everywhere; the steering wheel, the seat, and even the head rest. The door panel was covered in bloody hand prints.

"What the hell happened here?" Matthews mumbled.

He looked around. With this much blood, a body must be nearby. Matthews noticed a spotty trail of blood. He followed it. Surprisingly, it didn't lead toward the road, where one would go to seek help. It was in the midst of the thickened brush.

"Why –?"

Matthews continued on the trail, moving aside weeds along the way. The trail thinned and finally vanished, as if the body was snatched straight up into the sky. Suddenly, Matthews felt he was being watched. In panic, he looked back at the car. No one was there. He turned to the road, and didn't see anyone. He looked around. Someone was watching him, and he knew it; he felt it. Matthews looked down. His foot rested on a lump. He removed his foot from the pile of debris. Matthews broke it apart with his foot. Revealing itself was the ribcage of a human being. Matthews drew his gun. He pointed down, looked around, and returned his focus to the person he stood over. He kicked aside more debris, and saw the face and eyes that stared at him. Goosebumps lined the bottom of his spine to his neck.

Matthews got on his knees and pulled back more debris. The man's internal organs and muscles were gone. Matthews covered his mouth. His insides started turning. Ants and other insects rolled in and out of the body. An animal must have eaten him, but someone covered him up. Matthews stood up.

"Couldn't have," he said to himself.

Matthews looked in the direction of Carson's Garage, which was just a couple hundred feet away. The top of the garage was visible from where he stood. He got on the radio and called for back-up.

The day was at its peak temperature. Sweat dripped from Tommy's chin as he busied himself on repairing anything he could find with the vehicle in the shop. It was too hot to play outside, and Sparky was hurting from the injuries. All he wanted to do was lie down and rest. Not long after relaxing, his ears perked up. He lifted his head and ran outside. Tommy stopped working, wondering where Sparky ran off to. Sparky saw a car approaching from a distance away. He barked and ran back for Tommy.

"What is it, boy?"

Sparky barked and ran into the brush behind the shop.

"It's too hot. Let's go back inside."

Sparky barked again and again amidst the brush. He continued going further in, and waited for Tommy to follow him. Tommy didn't want to enter into the dry, prickly, thick, and high brush, but Sparky called him there for a reason. Tommy knew Sparky wanted him to follow, and that it wasn't just for amusement. Sparky continued barking, letting Tommy know where he was as he went deeper into the brush, further from the garage.

Officer Matthews pulled into the lot. His car rolled over a bump just before stopping. He saw the shop door open, and drew his gun.

"Who's here? This place is off limits."

Sparky and Tommy settled by a rock and watched the garage. Tommy sat on a rock, disinterested in what was happening, but Sparky paid attention.

"What are we doing here, boy?"

Sparky whimpered while staring at the garage. Tommy stood up to take a look. He could barely see the car, and couldn't tell it belonged to the police. He got excited.

"Ouu, boy, let's go –."

Sparky jumped on Tommy, tackling him to the ground. He looked Tommy in the eyes and whimpered.

Tommy realized Sparky wanted him to be quiet. He lowered his voice, "What if it's mom?"

Sparky shook his head from side to side. He lowered his head coming face to face with Tommy. Sparky mustered all the energy, determination, and focus he could. Sparky's mouth shaped as if he smiled. Tommy was surprised. He'd never seen that facial expression before. Sparky sucked his tongue into his mouth and let out a "shhh" sound. Spittle sprayed onto Tommy's face. Tommy's eyes widened. He wiped his mouth.

"Did you just say, "Shhh?"

Again, Sparky focused and repeated, "Shhh."

"What? How did you do that?"

Sparky got off of Tommy and looked out at the garage again. Tommy stood on the rock to get a better look, now that he realized they were hiding. He recognized the patrol car and ducked.

"Wow, boy, wow. How did you know that?"

Matthews kicked the door open and checked every nook and cranny. The door that led from the shop to the garage was also wide open.

"Bastards were here."

He saw Sparky's bowl with water in it. Matthews looked under the car in the garage. He returned outside after clearing the shop. His final checkpoint was the bathroom. Then, his radio sounded.

"Matthews, this is Myers. I'm on an assault case for the rest of the day. Heard about another mauling you called in. What's your position?"

"Myers, I'm at the Carson's Garage. They were here."

"Who?"

"Them, the Carson's."

"Do you know who?"

"I don't. I'm still checking out the place. The dog was here too. There's fresh water in his bowl."

"The mauling you just called in, was that from their dog?"

"Who else could it be? Unless some large carnivores escaped from the Kansas City Zoo, deciding to take residence in Selkirk."

"There's lots of coyotes in the area. You reported the vehicle off-roaded. Maybe the guy got into a wreck, got out, and a coyote or two attacked him."

"Coyotes don't do this. This guy's interior was completely gone. I hate to think of it, but it's like we got a cereal killing dog on our hands; and with his size, he's very capable. I'll fill you in on the details later."

"You need backup to check out the place?"

"Oh," Matthews added. "The dead body was covered up."

"What do you mean?"

"They killed the poor bastard and covered him up to hide him."

"Wow, we got some case on our hands," Myers said.

"Hold on. Don't call for backup just yet. Let me check out this bathroom," Matthews said as he opened the door. It was completely dark and empty. The bathroom was for single use only, without a stall, so there was no place to hide.

"Don't call for back up. No one's here."

"Ok, well if you want, meet me at Herald's Gas Station about 20 miles east of you, right by Modoc. Help me finish this assault case so I can jump back on the Carson's case with you."

"Will do. Over and out."

Matthews looked out into the brush, frustrated about not being able to locate the Carson's or their dog. Like a horror movie, bodies continue piling up, but the culprits are nowhere to be found. Matthews looked in Tommy and Sparky's direction. Tommy freaked and ducked, thinking the police officer saw them. Sparky watched, undisturbed. Matthews kept his stare out into the vast terrain. He started feeling the same sensation as before, that someone was watching him. He turned around 360 degrees, looking for any sign of anyone. He saw nothing, but felt something. Goosebumps formed on his wrist and rolled up to the back of his neck again. His instincts told him there was something to find, but he hated the helpless and spooky feeling of being watched. Matthews wanted to help Myers with the assault case so they could return to the garage, together. Finally, he turned around and headed for the car. He tripped over the bump. He kicked the mound to level it out. The dust caused him to cough, as he waved his arms around to get it out of his face. He noticed a dark spot through the dust cloud. Matthews squatted and touched the gravel. It was wet.

"Ah, what the hell?" His hand was smeared in blood. "Damn – son of a –."

He looked around again before jumping into his car and speeding off. A minute after heading east on Highway 96, Matthews passed by a familiar vehicle. It was Ann's. She was headed to the garage. Matthews tried to get a look at the driver, but Ann pretended to be distracted, looking away as if she were reaching for something in the passenger seat.

Sparky ran to the mound in the parking lot and whimpered.

"What is it, boy?"

Sparky stood over the lump. Tommy came by and saw the blood they tried to cover up.

"It's ok. It doesn't even look like blood. Don't worry, boy. Let's play."

Sparky got happy. His tongue rolled out of his mouth. He lowered his back legs and got ready to jump in any direction, to run away from Tommy. Just as Tommy was going to chase Sparky, Sparky's ears perked up, and his head became erect.

"Not again," Tommy said.

Sparky ran to the road and barked. This time he didn't attempt to run away and hide. He barked, and jumped up and down.

"Who is it?"

Ann's car rolled onto the lot. Sparky chased the car from behind. She parked the car right in front of Tommy.

"Come on, son. Let's get outta here."

Tommy and Sparky rushed inside the car. They couldn't have been happier. Sparky took the back seat. His large tongue dangled while spittle dripped onto the carpet below. Tommy was excited about the Storm Breakfast. Ann drove back into town. Tommy noticed the Old Town Café to the right, but Ann didn't turn.

"It's there, Mom. The café," he pointed.

"No, honey. We're not going there right now."

"But, I want the Storm Breakfast."

"I know, son. I know. I got you a bag of chips and some chocolate for now."

"I hate chocolate," he hit the dashboard. "That's all I eat at the shop. I hate it."

"Son," Ann pulled the car over and parked. "You need to listen to me. The cops are looking for you and him."

Sparky sucked his tongue back into his mouth.

"If you care about him," she pointed. "You need to listen to me, otherwise the police will take him from you, and you will never see him again. Do you understand?"

Tommy was silent. He crossed his arms and looked away.

"Do you understand?"

Sparky whimpered.

"Yea, I understand."

"Then, turn around and listen to what I have to say."

Tommy turned to face her.

"Uncross your arms."

"Why?"

"Because, when your arms are crossed, it blocks your brain from taking in what I have to say."

Sparky whimpered. Tommy uncrossed his arms.

"That's my boy. I'm gonna get you and your dog outta here. You guys have to be as quiet as possible, and hide until I come back for you. If anyone sees you, or your dog, they'll call the police. Do you understand so far?"

"Yes," Tommy said. His defensive tone vanished.

"Sparky is a very, very large dog, and if anyone sees him, they'll call the police right away. So you have to hide him as best as possible."

"Where are we going?"

Ann looked around. She didn't know. She didn't have a plan. All she knew was that they couldn't stay at the garage any longer.

"I'm trying to figure that out, but we need to come up with a plan right away."

The ground trembled. The car rattled. Ann looked up. Her eyes lit up.

"Yes, that's it."

"What?"

"Tommy," she said with a large smile. "How do you feel about a train ride?"

"Train? Hmm, I dunno," he shrugged his shoulders.

"Tommy, this is so cool. How do you feel about running and catching a train with Sparky? You get to chase a train, hop on, get a free ride, and be safe with your dog, with your best friend," she turned around to pet Sparky.

Sparky enjoyed her touch and pressed his head against her hand.

"Good dog," she continued rubbing him. "You've been a good friend to my boy," she patted him. "So, what do you think?"

Tommy didn't respond.

Ann added, "When I was your age, my friends and I hopped on trains all the time. It was so much fun; you'll love it."

"Umm, ok."

"Ok. I'm gonna get you as close as possible. Then I want you two to get out, chase after the train, jump on one of those landings, and stay inside the car."

"But, I thought you said we're gonna catch the train?"

"Yes, you are. Didn't you hear the instructions I just gave you?"

"Yes, but at the end you said to stay inside the car."

Ann laughed, "Silly, not this car, the train car."

"The train has a car?"

"No, son, listen. You see the train? Each one of those sections is called a car."

Ann saw the puzzled look on his face.

"Tommy, what do you call those?"

"Umm, the train."

"Ok, that's right. After you hop onto the landing,

get inside the train and stay inside. Don't come out until the train stops, or until you hear me."

Tommy stared at the train as it passed by ever so slowly.

"Tommy," she grabbed his chin. "Did you hear me?"

"Y – Yea."

"I'll repeat it. When you get on the train, stay inside of it, ok?"

"Ok."

"And do not get out until –."

"The train stops," he completed Ann's sentence.

"Yes, my boy, yes. You listened. Don't get out until the train stops, or you hear me calling you to come out. Ok?"

"Ok."

Ann drove to where the road ended.

"Give me a kiss and go."

Tommy turned and pecked his mother on the cheek. He opened the door, but Ann grabbed his arm.

"Get back in. Stay inside," she said while looking in the rearview mirror.

A patrol car came down the road behind her. She watched in horror as the car drew closer.

"God, the dog is so big. He can't even hide."

Sparky whimpered and lowered his head as far as he could. The patrol car approached Main Street, where the café and other shops were.

"Turn you bastard," Ann said hoping the police car would turn away.

The patrol car stopped on the corner of Main St.

"God, please leave my baby alone."

The patrol car moved up and, suddenly, it turned, disappearing out of sight.

"Yes," she cheered. "Wait here. Let me check and make sure, before you go."

Ann got out of the vehicle and walked up to Main St. She saw the patrol car driving further away. She ran back to her car.

"Quick, let's get you guys out."

Tommy got out, and held the seat for Sparky to exit.

"Ok, boy. I want you to have fun. Take this bag of goodies. You won't be on that train too long before I catch up with you, when I think it's safe. Now jump on that train and have fun."

"Ok, Mom. Don't forget my Storm Breakfast."

"Ok, son. Go on now," Ann said as she fought back tears from streaming down her flushed cheeks. She felt a rush of emotions as her heart ached at the thought of sending her son off without her.

Tommy and Sparky ran after the train.

Matthews pulled into Herald's gas station. A man sat on the curb, by the patrol car, with his head buried in between his knees. He wore jeans, torn at the knees, and a torn t-shirt. His pants were torn for style, but the tears in his shirt had bad intentions written all over it. Officer Myers stood above him.

"I'm waiting for a social worker to take him to a motel," Myers said.

"What's his story?" Matthews asked.

"He got into an altercation with another man who took off, headed westbound on 96."

The man lifted his head, "It wasn't an altercation. It was a beat up. He beat me up. I didn't do anything to him. People are crazy nowadays," he put his head back down.

"So, you're stuck here for how long?" Matthews asked Myers.

"Hopefully, just a few more minutes. Let's take a walk," Myers told Matthews. "You stay right here so we can get you help," he said to the man.

They walked far enough to be out of earshot from the man.

Matthews said, "We need you on this case. If this is from the same dog, it's bad. We can't have maulings all over town. This is gonna freak people out."

"Yea, I know, I know. No information yet on the Carson's?"

"We got wind of the wife, the kid's mother. She lives separately in Kansas City. A couple of guys are checking out that lead. I'm staying in Selkirk till we get this thing figured out," Matthews explained.

"So, what's the deal with the mauling earlier?"

"I checked out the car. It was a nice, orange, sporty car."

The guy sitting on the curb lifted his head.

"And listen to this," Matthews lowered his voice. There was no one in the car. There was blood all over the driver seat, the driver door, all over, and I found this guy buried underneath the brush with his insides eaten."

"Covered up, ha? You think it's the kid or the dad?"

"Maybe both, but I can't find any of these bastards to know for sure."

"Wow, this sounds –."

"Oh, oh, and get this," Matthews interrupted. "I cleared a mound of dirt from the Carson's Garage parking lot only to find fresh blood underneath it," Matthews showed Myers his hand.

"Damn, what the hell is going on? Same person?"

"No clue. This is really making me anxious. If it's more than two people, I'm gonna flip," Matthews said. "When was the last time anyone was mauled anywhere around here?"

"I can't remember," Myers said.

"Maybe the guy found the dog on the side of the road, picked him up, and got attacked," Matthews added. "Or, maybe he got attacked at the parking lot, escaped the mauling, but was bitten so bad he lost lots of blood, and crashed only to have this man-eating dog catch up to him, with his crazed, lunatic owner. Or maybe the dog killed one person at the lot and – I don't know. This is becoming too much. We'll let the investigators put the pieces together. I need to find this damn dog before it's too late."

"Maybe we got a real life murdering dog on our hands, like in the movies. You're right Matthews. We need to catch this thing before it becomes famous for the wrong reasons."

The man with the torn jeans approached. Myers shouted, "Hey, hey, go back over there and sit down."

"My ass is sore from too much sitting."

"Well, don't come here. We're having a private conversation."

"I heard some of your private conversation. Did you say an orange car?"

"What do you know about an orange car?" Myers turned around giving the man his undivided attention.

"The bastard who beat me up had an orange sporty car. Guess he got what he deserved."

"You didn't say anything about it being orange. You said you didn't remember," Myers said.

Matthews intervened, "So, this guy in the orange car beat you up, and took off heading west on 96?"

"Yea."

Matthews turned to Myers. "Your suspect is my victim."

"We need to get the entire search team in ASAP," Myers said.

"Captain's organizing as we speak. Let's get something to eat. Ain't had a good meal the whole day."

Myers got inside his car. Matthews yelled out to him, "What about your guy?"

"If he wants a place to sleep for the night, he'll wait for the social worker," Myers looked at the man. "I'll catch up with them later. The Carson's are hiding the dog, and we need to find them before someone else is killed."

The end of the train approached. Ann was worried about whether they'd find a stretch of cars they could get on. She anxiously watched from the driver seat.

"Hurry, boy. We gotta get on," Tommy shouted as he ran in the direction the train was headed.

Despite the train's slow speed, hopping on a train was still a frightful event for both of them. It's not something they've ever done before. Tommy finally found a car in which the sliding door had a small opening, and a railing to grab onto. He reached for the railing and grabbed it, holding firmly, jogging alongside the train. Sparky barked in excitement. Tommy turned back to make sure Sparky was still with him when suddenly he tripped, crashing against the side of the tracks. He rolled and fell into a sitting position. He banged his elbow against the ground during the roll. Tommy clutched his arm to ease the pain. Sparky barked and whimpered, trying to comfort Tommy. Sparky licked him, assuring him everything was ok. Sparky looked back at the end of the train, which was getting closer. He barked. Tommy got up and hobbled alongside the train.

A slender man in a dark gray suit stood on the corner of Main St, where the police car turned earlier, watching the kid and his dog trying to get on the train.

Tommy was distracted by the pain from his elbow. He caught up to the same car he missed earlier. He kept trying to nurse his elbow. Sparky barked. He wanted Tommy to focus on getting on the train. Tommy grabbed the railing with one hand, then the next. He jumped and pulled himself up, landing on a thin walking strip alongside the car.

"Come on, boy. You can do it."

Sparky barked. He could easily hop on, but he wouldn't fit on the walking strip, and he knew it. Sparky ran up to the opening in the door and poked his nostril inside. He pulled back and barked at Tommy.

Tommy watched, trying to figure out what Sparky was telling him. Again, Sparky stuck his nostril inside the opening and pulled back, barking.

"We're running out of time, boy. Come on."

Sparky barked over and over. He stuck his nostril inside the opening yet again. This time he didn't pull back. Instead, he tried to open it by shoving his face in as deep as he could. Tommy finally figured it out what Sparky was trying to do.

"I got it."

Tommy pulled on the handle. The door was heavy and the handle rusty. He used all his weight to pull back, opening it a few more inches. He rubbed his palms against his thighs to relieve the pain in his hands from pulling so hard. Tommy grabbed the handle and pulled back again, moaning from the extreme effort and pain. The door screeched open a few more inches, wide enough for Sparky to squeeze through.

"Quick, boy. Get in," Tommy waved him on.

Sparky went back a few feet from the train before running and jumping into the opening. His head and front legs went through, but his rear hung. His hind legs bounced off each passing track. He pushed off the ground, but he couldn't muster the strength to pull himself up. Sparky let go and, like Tommy earlier, fell to the ground, rolling over a couple of times.

"Sparkyyyy!" Tommy yelled.

Tommy was about to jump off, but Sparky caught back up. The speed of the train increased as the front of the train approached the town's outer border. Sparky barked, needing a larger opening to jump through. Tommy grabbed the handle and pulled back some more. He couldn't get it to budge any further.

"Come on, boy," he waved Sparky on.

Sparky knew he couldn't jump through the opening. He barked. Tommy placed himself in the opening. He pressed his back against one end and used his legs to push the door further apart. It worked. The door screeched and squealed open a few more inches. Sparky barked for Tommy to get out of the way. He made a run for it. The train's speed increased again. Sparky jumped. The side of the door caught Sparky against his ribs. He whimpered. Most of his body went through the opening, but his legs hung. Sparky kicked and scratched the walking strip for dear life. Finally, he pulled himself through.

"Yes, boy. You made it," Tommy hugged Sparky around his thick and furry neck.

They finally took shelter inside the cold, empty, and dark trailer. Tommy remembered that they had to remain hidden. Shutting the door was a lot easier as he pressed his weight against the edge of the sliding door and pushed. It moved back to its original opening and stopped. For some reason, the door wouldn't shut all the way, leaving a gap of a few inches.

Tommy woke up to screeching sounds. The car jolted back and forth as the train increased in speed. Tommy got up, wiped the crust from his eyes, and peered out of the opening, curious to see where they were. The scenery looked familiar, open and empty land. He looked left to the east, where they hopped the train. He hoped to see Ann coming, but there wasn't a road in sight.

"Sparky, how far did we go?"

Sparky barked and wagged his tail. Tommy pried the door open a few more inches, enough to squeeze his thin frame through. The fresh morning air pressed against his face while the early sun soothed it like a warm towel. Sparky poked his head out. Tommy leaned against the train, enjoying the morning sensation offered to him. Tired, restless, and hungry, Tommy shut his eyes and crossed his arms while standing on the thin platform. Sparky decided to rest as well, keeping his head out and enjoying the breeze. The train rocked again, shaking Tommy out of his hypnotic state. Sparky lifted his head. Tommy held on to the railing. He wanted to rest, so he went back inside.

He leaned against the hard metal wall of the car. Tommy's head bumped against it throughout the rocky ride. Sparky rested his head across Tommy's knees. Tommy rubbed Sparky's back with one hand and ate a chocolate bar with the other. Tommy saw dried blood on Sparky's side. He rubbed around the wound to comfort him. Sparky lifted his head and looked back at Tommy's hand. Tommy stuffed the rest of the chocolate in his mouth to free his other hand to rub Sparky under the chin. Sparky lifted his head, turning it from side to side, enjoying every moment. Tommy pulled back Sparky's fur and saw the cut, which was a couple of inches long. Blood hardened over the wound, sealing it, but the wound was swollen. It was surrounded by a large area of red and purple skin. Although Sparky had eaten to his full a day earlier, he started thinning again.

"You ok, boy?"

Tommy tapped his side. He kissed Sparky on the head. Tommy rested his head on top of Sparky's. He was worried for his friend.

Matthews and Myers made their way to Scott City, questioning all the shop owners for any leads on the boy and his dog. Myers took one side of the street, and Matthews visited shop owners on the other side. Myers walked into the Old Town Café.

"Hi Officer," the waitress said. "How can I help you today?"

"Ma'am. I need to talk to the owner."

"Sure. Give me a sec. I'll get him."

The owner came out wiping his hands on a white towel.

"Hi – ya Officer."

The owner got close to Myers, as he wanted to talk quietly. A police officer entering his establishment and not sitting down to a table meant police business, and he didn't want his customers to be distracted from the enjoyment of their meal.

"What can I do for you?"

"Lookin' for a boy and his dog, very, very large dog."

Seen lots of boys come in and out of here, alone, with friends, or with family, but no dogs. Dogs aren't allowed in this establishment, you know. We have to keep this place sanitary and clean. Some people don't want pets around their food, and I get it."

"Would you prefer to come outside and have this discussion?"

"Sure."

The owner threw the towel over his shoulder and followed Myers out.

"We want members of the community, who have access to the public, to be on alert. There's been a couple of dog attacks, one that took place in the area of Carson's Garage, a small auto repair shop in between Scott City and Selkirk. If you see a kid and a large dog, and make no mistake about it that when you see the dog you'll know who I'm referring to, call me immediately."

"Did you say Carson's? Why does that sound so familiar?"

"Well, if you remember anything, here's my card. Call me. I need to interview some others. Someone must have seen them."

"Will do, officer. Thank you."

Myers walked away when the owner added, "Officer. Would that place be owned by George, or Jorge Carson from Selkirk?"

"How do you know Mr. Carson?"

"He used to work for me. That was quite a few years back, before he ran his father's shop."

"You haven't seen him since?"

"Oh, no. He comes here as a regular, at least once a week; can't get away from this place."

"When was the last time you seen him?"

"Hmm, maybe a couple of weeks ago. He should be coming in any day now. He's overdue for his Storm Breakfast."

"Storm breakfast?"

"Our most popular item on the menu, what he always orders."

"Ok, well I gotta look for more leads. You have my information in case you see him."

"Ok, but could you tell me what this is all about? I'd hate to lose a valuable customer."

Myers approached the owner and whispered, "His dog's been linked to a couple of maulings. That's all the info I have for now."

The owner noticed another police officer, Matthews, across the street, questioning shop owners as well. "Yal interviewing all of Scott City for a mauling? Ok, officer. I'll be in contact."

Officer Matthews came running across the street to exchange notes with Myers.

"What did you find?" Matthews asked.

"Not much. The owner knows George Carson from back in the day, but hasn't seen him in a couple of weeks, and George is a regular at his café."

"You think he's skipped out of town with the kid and the dog?"

"Probably. What did you get?" Myers asked.

"I came runnin' to tell you we need to track the train that ran through town last night."

"Why the train?"

Matthews pointed, "You see the guy right – there?"

There was no one in sight except for an old lady crossing the street.

"Well, anyway, there was a guy just there in a gray suit, well dressed fella. He said he saw a kid and a large dog hoping the train last night, headed west."

"That's how they're getting away. Did he mention anything about George?"

"No, he said it was just the kid and a dog."

"Where the hell is George?" Myers wondered. "Anyway, guess we got a train to catch. We'll have some answers soon. Good job Matthews."

The midday heat replaced the morning breeze, cooking the metal cars on the train. Tommy and Sparky sat beside the opening. They had to choose between getting burned by the sun or suffocating from the heat inside the sauna. They watched barren landscape roll by, acre after acre. Tommy was hungry. He crouched into a fetal position holding tightly to his stomach. Sparky went over to comfort him, putting his head besides Tommy's legs. Tommy was also very thirsty. He'd been losing fluids from sweating. His lips were dry and sealed. The candy bars and chips were finished, and there was no water in sight. Tommy closed his eyes, hoping the struggle would be over soon. He wanted a home to live in with his mother and Sparky. He wanted to eat, drink, and play with his best friend. He wanted the wound on Sparky's side to disappear. He imagined Sparky never having to be hungry or get skinny again. His hopes and imagination for the immediate future helped pass the time, thus he fell asleep.

Tommy moaned and cried in his sleep. Sparky whimpered, not knowing whether he should wake him up to the hell of the heat, thirst, and hunger, or leave him to the anguish of his dream. Sparky couldn't handle his best friend's cries. His heart ached, so he licked Tommy on his face to comfort him. Tommy forced one of his eyes open. He felt relief. His moaning and crying stopped. Sparky felt good about his decision to wake him. Tommy looked outside. The dry barren land had been replaced with a mix of greenery, rocks, and boulders. He saw a sign pass by. Tommy jumped up, startling Sparky. He stuck his head out, wanting to read what the sign said. Tommy recognized the words "Welcome to", but didn't know what the rest said. The train just entered Colorado Springs.

"Where are we?"

Tommy looked to the right. There was a long stretch of mountains far away.

"Sparky, do you think we could find some stores here?"

Sparky barked.

"Keep an eye out, boy. We don't wanna miss anything."

The sun was setting behind the mountains, bringing about a cool breeze. Tommy couldn't stand any longer. There was no sign of a store, or civilization, for the past couple of hours. Tommy's legs felt like noodles. He was dizzy. There was no space to sit on the thin walkway. Sparky watched Tommy, afraid he might fall over and off the train. Sparky's tongue was dry. He repeatedly licked his lips in the hopes of creating wetness to swallow. Tommy went inside the car. Sparky got up from his spot to sit beside Tommy. It was getting cold, fast. Tommy hugged Sparky's warm coat. They lay down together with their arms around each other. Sparky licked Tommy's face. Tommy squinted.

"Where's mom?" Tommy mumbled as his eyes closed. "I'm hungry."

Tommy's stomach growled. Sparky whimpered. He licked Tommy's face again.

Sparky's ears shot up. He heard a pounding noise coming from outside their car. The sounds were odd. He couldn't make sense of it. His ears went out of control, perked up as high as possible, swaying left and right like a radar antenna. The curiosity became overwhelming. He picked up on a variety of noises, including light ghostly whispers. Sparky wanted to investigate, but didn't want to wake Tommy. Sparky lifted his head and looked around. The noise stopped. Sparky lowered his head, but his ears remained on alert. Shortly after, the noises resumed. Sparky's head shot up again. He couldn't take it anymore, and wanted to ensure their safety and hiding. Sparky slowly rose to his feet, hoping not to wake Tommy. Tommy's arm fell off Sparky's back. Sparky stuck his head out from the door. He pushed as hard as he could through the opening, enlarging the gap inches at a time. There was finally enough space to fit through, but he couldn't fit onto the walkway. Sparky looked left and right. There was nothing but pure darkness. He continued to hear the noises. The moving of the train and the wind threw off his senses. As soon as the wind gusts settled, Sparky heard the noise again. He looked at the car attached to their right. Then he noticed a glimmer of light coming from underneath the door. The noises were coming from there. He barked. The sounds stopped. He continued to bark, and the light went out. Sparky barked for a few more seconds. He stopped to listen. There were no more sounds. Sparky kept his head outside. He was concerned about who or what was in the car next to them. He remained attentive to the car for a few more minutes before deciding there wasn't a risk.

"What is it, boy?" Tommy called out in a weak voice.

Sparky brought himself back inside. He took his place beside Tommy. Tommy patted Sparky on the head.

"Did you see a store?"

Sparky whimpered.

"Nothing? Something should be coming soon. I hope we see one soon."

Cold gusts of air poured in through the opening. The chills from the cold and hard metal floor made its way through Tommy's t-shirt and jeans. Tommy hoped the door would miraculously close. The night just began. The breeze blew Sparky's fur to and fro. Tommy closed his eyes tight, and curled himself up into a ball tucking himself into Sparky's underside. Tommy placed his hands in between his thighs hoping it would stop the shivering. Sparky licked Tommy on his head, rearranging his messy hair.

"I wish the wind could stop," he mumbled.

Sparky whimpered. He wanted to help, but didn't want to leave Tommy, who needed his body heat. Tommy couldn't handle the cold and shivers anymore.

"Ugh," he got up with a new found energy.

He pulled the door handle. It didn't budge. He pulled again. Tommy didn't have half the energy he did when he boarded the train. He went to the end of the door and pushed it with all his weight. It moved a few inches. He stood up and repositioned himself, again leaning his weight against the end of the door. It moved a few more inches. He continued to push. The remainder of the opening closed before stopping a couple inches short of shutting. Tommy went back to his original spot and crouched in the same position with Sparky. His shivering still continued.

Sparky woke up to an unfamiliar noise. Brightness shone through the door. The night was over. Tommy remained motionless, like a frozen corpse. Sparky got up and looked out of the small opening. The landscape was flat with a few homes in the distance. Some of the homes had farms while others had unused acres of land. Sparky looked around to see what the noise was, which was increasing in volume. Suddenly, a police jeep zoomed by the train, racing toward the front. He became alarmed. He turned to Tommy, who was still asleep. Tommy's head rocked from the motion of the train.

Myers pulled up alongside the motor unit at the front of the train. Matthews, on the passenger side, lowered his window. The train operator stared at the officers, wondering what they were up to.

"Stop the train," Matthews yelled as he gestured with his hand. "Stop the train."

The train operator struggled to open the small window in his cabin.

"What?" the train operator asked,

"Stop the train. We have to inspect the cars."

The operator shook his head in the negative, "I can't. I'm not allowed, unless I receive instruction from my supervisor."

"We're the police, and we're demanding that you stop the train."

"You guys can't just stop a 100 car locomotive anytime you want. You know the process. It's gotta come through your superiors to mine, and then to me."

"There's a murderer on board. We need to find and capture him."

"Then you should have definitely gone through the proper channels. What jurisdiction you guys from anyway?"

"Scott City."

"SC? Didn't we pass that place a couple of days ago? You guys drove all this way knowing you need to search the train for a murder suspect, and you didn't make the calls? Next stop is going to be in Colorado Springs."

Matthews turned to Myers, "He's not stopping."

"Oh, heck," Myers said. "Let's jump the train. I mean, it's not like it's moving fast."

Matthews stared at Myers and asked, "You don't wanna call this in?"

"By the time our guys speak to their guys, we'll be in Colorado Springs. Call it in, then let's jump the train."

Myers sped the jeep up and got well ahead of the train. They parked, got out, and waited for the train to approach. The operator waved his finger gesturing to the officers not to hop the train. The lead car passed.

"I'll get on this one. You wait for about 10 cars to pass before getting on," Myers instructed.

Myers jogged alongside the train, grabbed a pole, and pulled himself up. Matthews was impressed at the ease with which Myers hopped on. The 10th car approached and Matthews tried to do the same. He jogged and grabbed the railing, but didn't pull himself up. Matthews stumbled, nearly falling on his face. He held onto the railing and regained balance, continuing to jog. He jumped again, this time getting on. He looked to see where Myers was. Myers stood by the door of the third car, watching Matthews. Myers shook his head, and entered the car. Matthews pried open the door in front of him and looked around. He used a flashlight to check corners and around the large cardboard boxes. Knowing there were several dozen cars that needed to be checked, Matthews wasted no time. If he didn't see anything obvious, he walked out and climbed across to the next car. The cars were lined up as far as he could see. A couple of minutes passed when Myers caught up to him.

"How did you check your cars so fast?"

"Half of the cars were grain and fuel transports that didn't have doors to get inside. I'll check one car while you check the next, so on and so forth till we get to the end."

They continued searching one after another, with flashlights in their mouths leaving both hands available to open stubborn doors.

Half way through, Matthews asked, "You think they got off?"

"There's no place to go to. If they hopped on, they should still be here. We caught the train just in time."

The officers approached the second half of the train faster than they thought.

Sparky saw the parked police jeep pass by. He whimpered and looked for a place to hide. Tommy finally awoke to his whimpering.

"Hey, hey, boy. Come here. I missed you," Tommy said.

He felt somewhat revitalized.

"You hungry?"

Sparky whimpered.

Tommy got up to take a look outside.

"It's getting hot, again. I feel it. There's still no stores around. When can we eat?"

Tommy saw Sparky licking his tongue, sucking it in and out of his mouth from thirst. Sparky came to Tommy and licked his arm, hoping there would be beads of sweat; anything to wet his mouth with.

"Whatcha doing, boy?" Despite the hunger and thirst Tommy experienced, his concern shifted to Sparky. "I know; I gotta get you something to eat."

Tommy looked around the train for anything that he might be able to feed Sparky. Sparky stood by Tommy's scarred arm. Ever since the accident, the first place that would start sweating was the area around his scar. Sparky noticed the moisture on the scar and licked it. Tommy looked at the scar and remembered the day of the cliff. He remembered how he nearly fell to his death. Tommy remembered Sparky saving his life. Now, he wanted to return the favor. The quest to quench Sparky's thirst intensified. He realized how he could take care of Sparky, until they came upon a store. Tommy knew the train wasn't going to stop soon, so he reached into his pocket and pulled out the knife that belonged to the guy who injured Sparky. After the attack, Tommy picked it off the ground and kept it in his jean pocket to defend Sparky against anyone who ever tried to harm him again. This time, he was going to save Sparky from a different kind of harm. Seeing the knife, Sparky whimpered. The knife probably brought back memories from the attack at Carson's Garage.

"I got an idea, boy. You're gonna be ok."

Tommy pressed the knife against his scar. Sparky dove into him, knocking the knife away and sending Tommy crashing against the hard metal floor. Sparky helped Tommy up by shoving his muzzle under Tommy's armpit. Tommy stood up. Sparky licked his face, apologizing and letting him know everything was going to be ok.

"It's ok, boy. It's ok," Tommy petted his head.

Tommy bent over to pick up the knife when Sparky intercepted his arm and gently bit down.

"Stop it, boy. I'm trying to help you."

Sparky whimpered. Tommy pulled his arm out of Sparky's mouth. He lifted the knife from the floor. Sparky stood on his hind legs and placed his paws on Tommy's chest, looking him in the eyes and whimpering, pleading for Tommy not to do what he was about to.

"It's ok, boy. I'll take care of you."

Sparky barked. Tommy rubbed and patted his face. He turned aside to get Sparky off of himself and sat down.   Again, Tommy pressed the knife against his forearm.   Sparky barked aloud, startling Tommy and causing him to drop the knife.

"Sparky!" Tommy yelled.   "Please leave me alone so I can do this."

Sparky froze.   He looked down.   Tommy didn't know what caught Sparky's attention.

"Sparky.   Boy," he waved his hand in Sparky's face. Sparky didn't bat an eye.   Tommy noticed Sparky was staring at his arm.   Tommy looked down.   There was a little cut and blood on his arm.

"Wow, it worked.   Just a little bit more and I can feed you," Tommy cheered.   "Come and take a lick," Tommy lifted his arm.

Sparky continued to stare, but didn't approach.   He stopped whimpering.   He was confused.   Sparky felt déjà vu.   The feeling brought him back to the day of the cliff. Sparky shook his head, snapping himself out of the thought.   He walked into a corner, as far away from Tommy as possible, and sat, looking up into the corner. Tommy grabbed the knife.   He placed the knife on his forearm and pressed down.

"Ouch, this hurts."

Sparky turned around.   He didn't think Tommy was going to continue to hurt himself.   Tommy wasn't going to give up, and neither was Sparky.   Tommy noticed Sparky's attention turn to him.   He knew Sparky was going to try and stop him again.   He put the knife against his forearm.   Sparky ran at him.   Tommy pressed the knife firmly against his arm and cut down before Sparky made his way.   Sparky crashed into Tommy, sending him to the floor, and the knife smashing against the wall.

Sparky lifted the knife in his mouth and walked it to the opening of the door. He spit it out and watched it bounce on the walkway before falling off the train. Sparky felt relieved. He turned to comfort Tommy when he noticed Tommy holding his arm, squinting in pain. Sparky ran over and looked at his arm. It was bleeding profusely, and Tommy couldn't get it to stop. Sparky became alarmed. He ran around the cabin and found an old dirty rag, rushing it over to Tommy. Tommy placed it over the cut and cried in pain. Tears rolled down his dirty face. Sparky wouldn't stop whimpering.

The police were closing in. The rumbling of the train drowned out other noises.

Sparky heard noises from the neighboring car again. His ears perked up. There was a lot of noise and it was louder than the night before. Sparky poked his nostril out of the gap and sniffed, trying to pick up on what was going on. He ran back to Tommy in even more panic. He caught wind of the officers. The noise from the other car continued to escalate. Rapid whispers turned into panicky chatter. The door screeched open. Sparky felt like he was losing his mind.

"Stop," Officer Myers yelled out.

Sparky froze and fell silent. A dozen people, including two children, jumped out of the train car next to theirs. Hand bags and back packs tore open exposing its contents. Shirts, pants, and socks littered the tracks. Matthews turned to see what the ruckus was about. People were jumping off the train like it was on fire. They scurried in different directions. One lady shot off the ground after falling, ran to her child, lifted her by the arm, and dragged the little girl through the rough terrain.

"What the hell," Matthews mumbled.

He looked to Myers for instruction. Myers waved him down, telling him to get off the train. Matthews jumped off and waited to see what Myers would do.

"I'm gonna check this last car," Myers yelled out.

Matthews didn't know who to chase. Like a predator, he decided to go for the easy target, the mother and child who fell behind. Myers made his way to the last car. He was completely distracted by the fleeing people. Myers held onto the door handle, but didn't open it. He was overwhelmed at the sight of the fleeing mother and child running for their lives. Myers watched the desperate mother pulling her daughter's arm out of its socket in their attempt to get away from Matthews, who was closing in on them. Just as Myers pulled on the handle to open the door, he heard the woman yell for her life. Her high pitched scream sickened Myers. He turned to see what was happening. The lady slapped and kicked Matthews as she tried to pull away from his grip. He let go of the handle, and jumped off the train to assist Matthews. The lady's attempts became louder and more aggressive. Matthews grabbed her, turned her around, and hugged her tightly. He lowered her to the ground, sitting right behind her.

"Relax, please, just relax," Matthews said.

The little girl stood there, crying and watching her mother trying to wrestle herself away from the police officer. Snot ran down the girl's nose to her lips. She licked the mucus away from her lips. Everyone else who jumped off the train disappeared. There wasn't a soul in sight.

Tommy wasn't able to tie the rag around his arm. He became lightheaded and was barely able to keep the rag on the wound. Sparky whimpered. He didn't know what to do. Tommy's body tilted sideways. Sparky licked blood off Tommy's arm, and then licked his face. It was no use. Tommy fell on his side. His eyes were closing. A pool of blood formed around him, soaking his pants and the side of his shirt. Sparky couldn't take it anymore. The love of his life was about to die. The unbreakable bond was on the brink of shattering. Sparky mustered up all of the energy he had, and barked. Its echoes rattled the car walls. Myers turned to see what the noise was. Thinking it might have been a bump in the tracks causing a loud thump from the train, he ignored it and proceeded toward Matthews.

Sparky stuck his muzzle out of the car, and barked at the top of his lungs. He howled and cried like a wolf. Myers turned around.

"That's them!"

Matthews turned back to look at the train. The lady kept screaming. The child kept crying and wiping the snot from her face.

"Is that the dog?" Matthews asked.

"Yea. Matthews, let her go. We found them."

Matthews let the lady go. She grabbed her bag from the floor in one hand, yanked her daughter's hand with the other and ran off, disappearing as soon as the landscape permitted. Sparky pried the door open wide enough to shove his head through. The officers chased after the train. Sparky took in a deep breath and let out a thunderous bark. It sounded like a bomb, and created a shockwave that knocked Myers on his butt. Matthews, who was further behind, continued running after the train. Myers sat for a second, stunned, trying to grasp what just happened. He couldn't believe he was knocked back from the shockwave of a dog's bark. The thought sent chills up and down his spine. He didn't have time for contemplation, so he got up and continued the chase. They caught up to one of the cars a few sections behind. Matthews looked like an expert this time, getting on with ease. They drew out their guns and aimed it at Sparky, who pulled his head back inside, waiting for the officers to enter. The officers went from car to car until they reached the one Sparky and Tommy were in. Myers pointed his gun inside the opening, looking around in all directions. He looked inside and saw Tommy lain down.

"Keep your gun drawn on the dog," Myers ordered Matthews. Myers put his gun away and pulled the door open. They went inside. Sparky whimpered, walking to and fro near Tommy's body. He nudged Tommy and looked at the officers, hoping they'd help his best friend right away. Tommy's face was pressed down against the blood on the floor.

Myers radioed, "We need an ambulance to the cargo train, headed west toward Colorado Springs."

Matthews kept his distance from Sparky and his gun drawn. Myers tried to move in on Tommy to check his condition, but Sparky stood right next to him. His paws were soaked in Tommy's blood.

"Move aside, boy. Move aside, so I can check on your friend," Myers said.

Sparky moved a few feet away, but not far enough to give Myers comfort.

"A little bit more, boy. It's ok. I'm here to take care of your friend. I'm not gonna hurt him."

Sparky whimpered and walked backward to the end of the car. He sat and watched Myers.

"Dogs always impress me," Myers said. "He understood everything I said. But, I don't get why he would've done this."

"How's the boy?" Matthews asked.

"Not good. By the time we get to the stop –."

Sparky whimpered out loud. He wouldn't stop. He pounded his paws against the metal floor, shaking the car, and echoing booming sounds throughout. Myers and Matthews looked at each other. Matthews felt bad watching Sparky exhibit such sadness. He saw the worry in Sparky's eyes. He felt Sparky's pain, but didn't understand how he could, or why he would attack someone he loves so much.

"I feel bad for the dog," Matthews said, "But I don't understand this."

"Matthews, the dog didn't do this. It looks like the boy tried to commit suicide. He's got a gash across his arm from a knife or something sharp. And from the looks of the amount of blood he's lost, he sliced right through an artery."

Myers looked around for something to tie Tommy's wound with, but only found the soiled, wet rag. Myers got up, took off his shirt, removed his undershirt, and used it to wrap Tommy's arm. Matthews lowered his gun. His arm was tiring, and Sparky didn't feel like a threat.

"The bleeding stop?" Matthews asked.

"It slowed, but he's lost too much already."

Myers turned to Matthews.

"Keep the gun pointed, Matthews. Bad things happen when we let our guard down."

Matthews reluctantly pointed his gun back at Sparky.

"He ain't doing anything, just sitting in the corner, being sad."

"Just keep your gun pointed."

Sparky got tired of pounding against the floor. He lay down to rest and turned his head away from Tommy and the officers. Sparky didn't want to see his best friend in this condition any longer. Matthews walked toward Sparky. Sparky's ears perked up, but he wasn't alarmed.

"I'm going to sit beside you. Is that ok? Is that ok, boy?" Matthews asked.

Sparky whimpered and turned to face Matthews.

"That's a good boy."

"Matthews, what are you doing?"

"I'm ok. You handle the boy. I got the dog."

Matthews put the gun in his other hand so he could pet Sparky. Sparky turned away and whimpered. Matthews placed the gun on the floor. Sparky heard the gun settle against the floor. He turned back to Matthews, looked at the gun, and then looked to see how Tommy was doing. Matthews rubbed Sparky's head. Myers watched them.

He radioed again, "Get that ambulance here, fast. And get animal control here too."

The train came to a stop as soon as it entered Colorado Springs. Police cars lined both sides of the road closest to where the train stopped. Two ambulatory vehicles, a fire truck, and an animal control vehicle were on the side of the road.

The medics were about to board the train when a voice called out from behind, "Wait, wait. There's a dog inside, and we need to contain it first," an animal control officer said.

"Ok, hurry up. This boy's lying in a pool of blood and nearly dead."

The animal control officers got inside the car and saw Sparky.

"Oh, what the hell is that? Why didn't they tell us – we're gonna need –," he was at a loss for words."

Matthews was right beside Sparky with his arm around the dog.

"Guys," one of the medics called out. "We don't have this kind of time. Does he need to be put down?"

"Whoa, hold up," Matthews said. "No one needs to be put down for anything. You guys get in and take care of the kid, I'll handle the dog."

The medics went inside.

"Sorry, Officer. We didn't know anyone was here with the dog."

They checked his pulse.

"We got a faint one. Quick, let's get him outta here."

Sparky watched the medics. His feeling of sadness and helplessness worsened. There was nothing he could do to save Tommy's life this time. Sparky remembered lifting Tommy up from the cliff. He remembered the superb sense of satisfaction he felt, just before the taste of the blood took over. He was ecstatic about snatching the love of his life from the jaws of death. Sparky hoped he would get that same feeling today, at the hands of those who helped Tommy. He waited patiently for good news from the medics. The medics placed Tommy on a gurney and rushed him to the ambulance. Sparky got up to follow.

"Hey, boy. Listen, they're gonna take your friend to the hospital to make him better. You have to stay with me, ok?" Matthews instructed Sparky.

Sparky whimpered. He followed the medics with Matthews beside him.

"Slow down, boy. Slow down."

"Matthews, make sure you get this dog into the nearest animal control," Myers instructed as they passed by him.

"Come on, this way," Matthews told Sparky.

Sparky whimpered and caught the attention of the other emergency personnel. Conversations came to a stop as they stared in awe at the passing dog. Sparky wanted to follow Tommy, but didn't force Matthew's hand, which literally was placed on Sparky's back trying to guide and nudge him toward the animal control van. Sparky's cries intensified as Tommy was taken further and further from him. Tommy was finally placed in the back of the ambulance. Sparky ran away from Matthews into a clear opening. He jumped around and ran back and forth. He cried and whimpered. Several police officers drew their guns and kept aim at Sparky.

"Matthews, we gotta take the dog down," Myers said.

"No!" Matthews demanded. "We're not doing any such thing. We're taking him to animal control."

"Matthews," Myers moved in closer. "What do you think they're gonna do to him there? Neuter him and adopt him out?"

"Yea, I know, but we're going to do this with dignity. This is no ordinary dog, and he ain't about to hurt anyone. I want his last moments to be calm and relaxed."

"Calm and relaxed," Myers laughed. "Like the last moments of those he's killed? Just calm him down. Right now he looks like a wild bull. If we get the impression that he might hurt anyone, bullets will be flying his way. Be careful."

Matthews tried to calm Sparky down.

"Easy now. Just relax. They're gonna take him to fix him. They're gonna help him. Come on, boy. Let me take you to the shelter, where you'll be safe."

Sparky saw the ambulance drive off. He saw Officer Myers get into a patrol car with another officer, and follow the ambulance. Sparky whimpered. He knew things weren't going to be ok. Even if they heal Tommy, the police will take him to jail. Sparky didn't think he would ever see his best friend again. Tears wet the fur on his face. Matthew's felt his chest tightening as he watched the anguish Sparky was in. Sparky stopped jumping around. Matthews stood in his way, trying to direct him to the animal control van. Sparky went around him, watching Tommy get further and further away. His breathing deepened. Tears kept falling from his eyes. Matthews put a gentle hand on Sparky, trying to get him to the van. Sparky couldn't handle the distance anymore. His heart felt like a rubber band being pulled before snapping.

Sparky took off, blowing past Matthews, and after the ambulance. The power in his strides dug deep into the dry and hard ground. He looked like a horse in a race catching up to first place. All of the emergency personnel looked on. Not only have they never seen a dog that size, but the speed, which increased with each stride, astonished them. Everyone looked on like spectators in a sporting event. Sparky gained on the ambulance, shaking the ground behind him with each step. Sparky huffed, breathing in deep, knowing this was his last hope to reunite. He continued to close in on the ambulance. Suddenly, he felt a sharp poke in his back. He didn't stop. Tommy was getting closer. He felt another pinch on his rear. Sparky felt queasy. He continued running, but his running slowed and his legs wobbled. Sparky trembled before falling face first into the ground.

"Good shot," a voice called out.

One of the animal control workers pulled back a tranquilizer rifle and set it in the van. He jumped in the van and drove to retrieve Sparky. Sparky kept his eyes on the ambulance. His vision blurred. The ambulance turned a corner and was finally out of sight.

The driver sped toward the hospital. Tommy's gurney rocked from side to side. The shortcut to the hospital was littered with unrepaired and unpaved roads, making for a bumpy ride.

The animal control worker drove to Colorado Springs Animal Control with Sparky sound asleep in the back. Matthews squeezed himself in the front with the other animal control worker. Matthews grew anxious at the driver's slow and relaxed pace. He was afraid Sparky might wake up and cause chaos in the back.

"So, what's the story with the dog?" the driver asked Matthews.

Myers was anxious about Tommy's outcome. He needed to question Tommy to learn about what happened, where his father was, and Tommy's involvement in the murder of the postal worker. This would amount to the biggest murder case in the history of Selkirk, and Myers needed to get answers.

"When are we gonna get to the hospital?" Myers asked.

"Few more minutes, and we'll be there," the officer replied.

"Few more minutes, and that kid is dead. I need to find out what the hell happened."

"Yea, so I heard. You don't have the story?"

"Not much, no. Just that the dog is suspected for killing at least one person."

"Not much I really know or can discuss right now," Matthews replied.

"I understand." The animal control officer allowed silence to reign for a minute before asking another question. "I also understand, or heard, the dog's mauled more than one person to death."

Matthews looked at the driver and then looked straight ahead.

"Where did you hear that?"

"We hear everything that makes the news in the AC world."

"AC?"

"Animal Control."

"Oh. It's not confirmed," Matthews said.

He felt an odd sense of responsibility to defend Sparky until proven guilty.

"How many people?"

"Matthews," Myers radioed.

"Yea, Myers."

"We just arrived at the hospital. They're rushing the boy in. Make sure you put the dog down."

Matthews didn't reply. He went into thought.

"You got that? Put the dog down. He's not needed, and too much of a risk. We need the boy. If this dog does anything else, it's both our asses, and I mean it. We can't screw this up."

"Got it."

"Let me know when it's done. I'll keep you posted on the boy."

"Got it."

The animal control officer sensed Matthews's regretful tone.

"We put down animals all the time for simply biting someone, let alone killing people."

Matthews didn't respond. He felt alone, that no one understood him. He was still in thought.

"Don't take it hard or personal, it's just something that has to be done," the animal control officer explained.

"I got it. It's not like he's my dog. It's only a dog."

"Exactly."

They pulled up alongside a white long house that was turned into an animal clinic. The paint on the front siding was chipped. Like Carson's Garage, this clinic also sat atop a gravel parking lot. They rolled Sparky out on the gurney, across the bumpy lot, and into the clinic.

"This dog's gotta pay for another gurney. This one's destroyed," the AC officer laughed. "I'll get the tech. She'll be putting him down. Her name's Myra."

He left Mathews with Sparky in the lobby. Sparky's eyes opened. His vision was still hazy. He was calm and relaxed. Although he didn't know where he was, he knew Tommy wasn't beside him. Sparky's breathing deepened again. Sadness overcame him. He was alone and weak. He couldn't get himself off the table to run and find Tommy like he did before. There was no life without Tommy; no reason to live on if he couldn't be with him. Myra walked into the room and nearly fell back.

"Whoa. What the – ." She was taken aback by Sparky's size. "Is he out?"

"Looks like he just woke up, but still very weak," Matthews said.

"We need another tranq?"

"Not sure," Matthews responded.

He wanted Sparky to remain in a relaxed state for as long as possible while he thought of what to do next, as if he had any options. Matthews wished it didn't have to end like this. He wished the dog didn't kill anyone. He even thought about other ways the murders could have happened, without Sparky as the culprit. Sparky was too nice and lovable to kill people. It didn't make any sense to him. Matthews even entertained the thought of taking Sparky home until they could figure out what really happened. He knew he wouldn't be allowed to do so, so he'd have to hide him.

"Myers, shouldn't we wait to get the story before putting this dog to sleep?" Matthews radioed.

He waited for a response. Myra rolled Sparky back to the euthanasia room, and Matthews followed.

"Matthews, put the dog down."

"I'm just thinking, a dog like this, its size and power, he's not normal. Maybe we could experiment on him, you know? He's a freak of nature. Scientists could check his genes – we might find a cure or something."

"Matthews, put the dog down. That's an order."

Radio silence resumed.

"You've grown attached to the dog in the little time you had together, hey?" Myra asked.

"No, it's not that," Matthews tried to deny his feelings. "I don't wanna do anything premature. We can always kill him, but we can never bring him back."

"Umm, hmm. I heard emotion in your voice," Myra said.

At that moment an image outside the window, behind Matthews, caught her attention. She saw a thin gray dog standing in the front lot watching them. Myra was mesmerized and she didn't know why. There was nothing special about the dog; it was a regular, ordinary looking dog. She went to the cupboard where the euthanasia kit was placed, which was right beside the window. She opened the cupboard while keeping an eye on the dog outside. Myra opened the cupboard and pulled out a drawer. A tray fell to the floor, startling everyone in the room, including Sparky. He lifted his head. Matthews became concerned. Sparky appeared to have regained some of his strength. Myra lifted the tray, placed it back inside the cupboard, pulled out the needles, closed the cupboard door, looked outside and saw nothing but the van. She looked left and right, the dog wasn't there. Myra came back to Sparky. Sparky appeared alert.

"Officer?"

"Yes my girl?" Matthews responded.

"The dog. He's awake and – will he remain like this?"

Matthews rubbed Sparky's head. Sparky rested his head on the gurney. Life was not worth living anymore, not without Tommy, not without his best friend. The unbreakable bond was broken by the only thing they were both helpless to defend against, fate. Sparky knew why he was here, on the gurney and in this room. He knew Myra held the end of his life in her hands. Sparky closed his eyes, took a deep breath, and decided to spend his last moments thinking and dreaming about Tommy. It was the only thing that gave him comfort. Sparky remembered the first time he laid eyes on Tommy.

"My God, he's smiling," Myra said.

Sparky remembered the countless times they played hide-n-seek and tag. He remembered chasing Tommy around Carson's Garage. He remembered Tommy chasing him around the chicken coop and into the trees. Sparky remembered the heroic day at the cliff; how he wished they could return to the good ol' days. He remembered embracing Tommy after the long journey on foot to the garage. Sparky thought about the train ride, how much time they spent so close to each other. He remembered the sacrifice Tommy committed for him. The smile disappeared from Sparky's face. He remembered the knife, the cut, and the blood. He thought about the gurney and his best friend's life-less body being carried off. A final tear drop rolled out of Sparky's eye.

Myers watched the nurses and a doctor working rapidly around Tommy in partition room 14 of the emergency room.

"Code blue," a nurse called out. "Code blue!"

Two more doctors rushed over to Tommy's side. One held her hand against his jugular vein and wrist; the other placed a stethoscope over his chest. She moved the stethoscope all over Tommy's chest, searching for any sign of a heartbeat. They looked at each other. They shook their heads in the negative.

"Nothing. Record the time of death. Get him cleaned up, and keep him in a room until the next of kin arrives," the doctor said.

"Damn it," Myers said. "He's got no next of kin that'll be coming. We have to take him back to Selkirk when we're done here. Myers left the emergency room and got on the radio with Matthews.

"The boy didn't make it, Matthews."

If Sparky wasn't dead yet, Myers' words just killed him.

Matthews dropped his head and replied, "The dog is dead." A couple seconds of silence passed and Matthews asked, "Where in the hell is the father?"

"I don't know, but we gotta get back to town, find his parents, let them know about their son, and question them about what happened here."

"You know," Myra explained, "It's not that dogs are bad. It's their owners. Dogs pick up the energy, emotion, and behavior of their owners."

Matthews felt some comfort from Myra's words. It was in defense of Sparky.

Myra continued, "Most owners don't know how to train a dog, just like most people don't know how to parent a child. They're very similar. It's easy to adopt a dog or have a child."

She rubbed Sparky on his side while removing the needle from his hind leg.

"If you ask me, I would make it a requirement to attend a class on parenting or pet rearing before people could take their child home after birth, or before adopting a pet, especially a dog."

"You're smart, Myra. If you're not already, you'll make a good mother."

Myra blushed. "Thank you."

"We need more people like you," Matthews continued.

Myra felt uncomfortable with his praises, so she continued to talk, "I guess we technicians have to grow a cold heart to survive in this line of business. Like a doctor working in an emergency room, we have to talk about our patients as if they're objects, like machines that need to be fixed. If we don't, then we'll be a wreck every time we have to put down an animal. We'll wanna take them all home."

Myra picked up the needle. Sparky was sound asleep. Matthews stroked Sparky's neck. His tail jerked up and fell back down, startling Matthews and confirming to Myra what she's seen hundreds of times before.

"It's ok," Myra said. "He's all relaxed now. He won't feel any more pain."

Matthews walked out of the room. He saw the animal control driver locking drawers and turning out the lights while the other worker waited inside the van.

The driver called out, "Hey, Myra. Make sure to roll that big ass dog to the backroom. Cremation will be coming in the morning to pick him up."

Myra rolled Sparky to the backroom. She pulled a sheet over him, and passed her hand over his head before exiting from the back door. Matthews and the driver left through the front at the same time Myra exited through the back.

The driver looked up at the darkening sky. "The storm's comin'."

Matthews looked up, "The storm's already here, and it's gonna be a big one."

He looked straight ahead and noticed a gray dog sticking its head out from the bush on the side of the lot. Matthews felt déjà-vu, but he couldn't associate a memory with the feeling.

The driver took Matthews to the hospital, where Myers awaited him. They needed to locate the Carson's to find out what happened at Carson's Garage.

About the Author

I have many dreams, one is to have my work noticed by a movie producer, and turned into a blockbuster hit. I dream to be on the best seller's lists, and make millions in book sales. I hope my love and passion for story creation sets me into an early retirement, to dedicate full time on this lovely mind-escaping craft. I missed the opportunity to show dad my first publication. Not that I live with regret, as I believe everything happens, in its time, for a reason, but, it's one of those "I wish" thoughts that come to mind.

My journey starts with my sister, who encouraged us into writing assignments during our breaks from school. I didn't mind, as I loved writing and receiving praise for my penmanship. My cousin and brother, on the other hand… Writing became a hobby and instead of having my sister give me assignments, I decided to write short fictional stories. Horror was my niche.

In middle school, I fell in love with sports, particularly football. During junior year at Bayside High, carrying over to my senior year in River City, I joined the Journalism Team as a sports writer, combining two passions in one. Unlike most teens going into college, I knew what I wanted to be, a sports writer.

My older brother did his best to instill confidence in my shy self, telling me things like, "Your mind can make or break you," and other "Sky's the limit" stuff. Although it didn't make an immediate impact, its energy waves echoed throughout my limbs and veins to this day, hoping to inspire a sleeping author.

College was a success (as in earning a BA), the married life happened (not to mention it in passing as if it wasn't one of the best things that's happened to me), employment in the workforce began (not as a sports writer), and life went on.

In 2013, I attended a success seminar, invited by my employer, who may have seen potential in me that I wasn't aware of. I was one of three chosen, from over 100 others, to attend this life changing event. Les Brown stimulated my spirits, Joe Montana and Bill Cosby (guys I only thought I would see on TV) set me in awe, and smaller personalities with larger passions, such as James Smith, inspired me.

I believe 95% of the attendees went back to their regular life, not to demean or minimize their "regular" life, which might be very motivational and inspirational compared to mine, but for the second time in a row, I fell within a small, but important, percentile; I was changed by the seminar. Since then, my sister had a stroke, my father got sick and died, both of which took the winds out of my sails, and... Enough with the excuses, if I'm really going to have any hope of my dreams coming true, I need to prioritize it, and that's what I've done!

2019 has become the year of my first publication, and it's all because I've decided, "Enough with the excuses." That's why you're holding these pages in between your supportive hands. Thank you!

I've never seen any life transformation that didn't begin with the person in question finally getting tired of their own bullshit. – Elizabeth Gilbert

A Token of Gratitude

Thank you to my supporters, those who couldn't wait for my book (sorry it took nearly three years), those who purchased the book (and even more to those who purchased several copies), those who subscribed to my social media channels, those who shared my posts, my coworkers (past and present), my friends, relatives, and family. If I were to list your names, I'd have to write another novel; you know who you are. My wife, my biggest critic because she's my quality assurance, finally broke into tears after reading the latter chapters of Carson's Garage. Impressed by the story, she boosted the trajectory of my mission to new heights.

Thanks to Tony Robbins for helping me understand the psychology behind the limiting mind and how to overcome obstacles. Thanks to Les Brown and James Smith who awoke my dormant dream during the 2013 Success Seminar in Sacramento (and thank you Sacramento County for sending me to the event). Eric Thomas carried the mantle by continuing to encourage me with his "in your face" style videos. A few other motivational speakers deserve thanks as well, not to mention former NFL player, Ray Lewis. Will Smith, whom I consider the best actor of all time (not to distract from my message) is also atop the list as an inspirational leader. His clips on overcoming fear have been extremely empowering, and I try to utilize his advice on a daily basis. Sylvester Stallone is another actor whose motivational themes have impacted me since I was a child – Rocky 4 is the most motivational movie of all-time. The newest raw man on my radar, who's pushing me to confront my fears and challenges, has been David Goggins. His incredible transformation has added to the list of success stories that's helped me to keep striving to empower my mind; an empowered mind is useful anywhere, especially in my recent struggle with my dying father.

To that point, I must not neglect to mention spirituality; the only thing I can fall back on as a support when no one else can untangle the webs of mental chaos.

Last, but not least, is an individual who created the first spark. He was such an inspiration during my youth that I would strive, not just for myself, but for him; not to disappoint him. He was the talk of our neighborhood. Girls wanted to be around him, young men such as myself wanted to be like him, and his enviers wanted to challenge him. He believed in me when I didn't know what it meant to believe in oneself. He told me that I could be anything I wanted, if I strived for it. He pulled me out of a scary nightmarish high school, when the administrators said I had no choice but to go to the school I was zoned to, and enrolled me into Bayside. He told me to look up, or at least look straight ahead, because looking down brings about a sense of defeat and surrender. Then, life happened, and the man who was held in high-esteem seemed to be losing steam. I had his support to succeed, whereas, he had no one to look up to. His journey's been knocking the wind out of him for a long time, and the man who I thought could not be conquered occasionally speaks words of surrender. Then I recall the stories of people like Goggins, Thomas, Brown, and Stallone. Their stories are the prominent ones, and there are countless others who've come up from much greater difficulties to "succeed". Thank you, thank you loved ones, thank you friends, and thank you family. And if you're reading this, a big thanks goes out to you too.

I'm looking ahead, and I hope you continue to do the same too. Carson's Garage is just the beginning of greater works to come, if I'm destined to be around. Looking forward!

Embrace the suck! – Military proverb

Stay Connected

Like the book?   Consider leaving a review from the website you ordered from.   Let others know why they should read the book.

For updates, giveaways, events and book signings, add your email address to our support base at www.KdStorm.com.

Last, and definitely not least, don't forget to connect with the Storm on YouTube, Instagram, and Facebook.

Thanks again, and happy reading.

Upcoming Blockbuster Hits

Help me decide.

Go to KdStorm.com and submit your comments to help me decide where the Storm should go next.

<u>Pride</u> – Inspired by lions on animal shows, a pride of cats go on a quest to rule their neighborhood and show they are the kings of their jungle. Friendships are made, and foes are encountered. Bonds are rocked by waves of challenges to see if these furry critters can withstand the storm of being a pride.

<u>Mindless</u> – This is not just another mindless story of cannibalism created by the spread of a disease. Scientists discover new truths when mindless people succumb to cannibalism in their attempt to reclaim a life that was once theirs. Thoughtlessness leads to mindlessness, which leads to thoughtfulness in this new paradoxical world of the zombie.

The Closet – A sister and brother discover a set of stairs that lead to a world of magic and mystery from deep within their parents' closet. The young siblings cautiously follow paths and clues until they're sucked into a world that's awaited them. Initially, the world is filled with fun and laughter. However, they soon discover its dark side, and the siblings are urged by the residents to rectify the evil so they can be free at last.

Rain – The long awaited and anticipated book may not be far off from publication. A young couple takes a trip to an exotic destination full of food, fun, and culture, when one night the husband disappears. Determined to find him, Zaylee's confronted by locals who tell her she travelled alone. The young woman has to figure out whether she's lost her mind, or if there's a conspiracy surrounding his disappearance. What lengths will she go to in her quest for the truth?

The Magician – As Ann's favorite show from Carson's Garage indicated, The Magician is about a man from high-class society whose choices forced him and his family to live amongst the Outcasts. He falls for a girl from the High-Class, but the shame of being an Outcast makes it impossible for them to be together. The man soon becomes a prized magician for the tyrant king, redeeming himself and his family's honor. Fate finally brings them together, but not if the Mystery Man has anything to say, sent to rock the world of the High-Class.

Share your thoughts at www.KdStorm.com.

Carson's Garage was sponsored by:

Made in the USA
Lexington, KY
21 November 2019